# WORTH DYING FOR

# Also in Rita Herron's Slaughter Creek series

*Dying to Tell*
*Her Dying Breath*

# WORTH DYING FOR

## A SLAUGHTER CREEK NOVEL

## RITA HERRON

Montlake
Romance

Text copyright © 2014 Rita Herron
All rights reserved.

Published by Montlake Romance, Seattle

www.apub.com

Amazon, the Amazon logo, and Montlake Romance are trademarks of Amazon.com, Inc., or its affiliates.

ISBN-13: 9781477820056
ISBN-10: 1477820051

Cover design by theBookDesigners

Library of Congress Control Number: 2013954787

Printed in the United States of America

*To my fabulous editor, Lindsay Guzzardo, and my great agent, Jenny Bent, for giving me the idea for the beginning of the book!*

*And to my other fabulous editor, Maria Gomez, for liking the creepy factor!*

*May we plot many more murders together . . .*

# Prologue

———— o ————

The hand floated in the creek in the thin stream of light. A golden circle illuminated the blood seeping from the mutilated cartilage and skin.

It was beautiful, really, the fingers curling upward as if reaching for help.

Pathetic as well as beautiful.

A bitter laugh escaped him.

Or maybe those gnarled fingers that had once clawed to escape were now curled toward the sky, reaching for the hand of God or some angel to grab the hand and pull it up to heaven.

The hands of a woman were supposed to comfort a child. To gently stroke and ease a little one's pain. To be loving.

But that hand had never been loving.

And it certainly did not belong in heaven.

It had brutalized him and so many others.

Rightfully so, it lay in its own abyss of misery, separated from the body and mind of the person who'd used it in vicious ways. A bloody stump drifting aimlessly in Slaughter Creek, where the fish and bugs would gnaw away the remaining bits of skin until only the thin layers of jagged bone remained.

*An eye for an eye, tooth for tooth, hand for hand . . .*

The woman's vile face suddenly flashed in his mind. A wicked gleam had brightened the dull hues of her eyes as she prepared to strike.

That gleam had faded tonight.

Pure, sweet pleasure stole through him, rippling through the very air that he breathed as his body hummed to life.

She had deserved to die.

Finally.

*It is my time. I don't intend to waste it entertaining mindless, frivolous things. I have an agenda.*

This woman was only the beginning of those who were to receive their punishment.

*From them I will take back my sanity and my mind, and get my revenge.*

They would suffer.

*And then I can live.*

# Chapter One

———— o ————

Two teenagers found a severed hand floating in Slaughter Creek."

Special Agent Rafe Hood tightened his grip on his cell phone. At Special Agent Nick Blackwood's words, an image of another case where a woman's body had been left near water flashed in his mind, making his gut knot with dread.

That case hadn't ended well.

Rafe had nearly lost his job.

And his relationship with Special Agent Liz Lucas, the profiler on the case, had been permanently damaged.

Could this possibly be the same killer?

No. Different MO. That woman's neck had been slashed; her hands hadn't been amputated.

Besides, Rafe had shot the bastard, sending him over a ridge into the raging current below. There was no way he could have survived.

"Has the rest of the body been recovered?" Rafe asked.

"Not yet."

"I'm on my way," Rafe said as he jogged to his black SUV.

"Jake and I will meet you there."

Rafe hit disconnect to end the call, flipped on the engine, punched the address into his GPS, and sped from the parking lot of the TBI office. He'd just finished a debriefing with his chief where they'd hopefully tied up the case revolving around Arthur Blackwood—aka the Commander—and the inhuman experiments he and others had conducted on innocent children years ago at Slaughter Creek Sanitarium.

The latest arrest of Senator Stowe had come as a shock to everyone. Stowe had finally admitted he'd worked with Blackwood in spearheading the experimental CHIMES—Children in Mind Experiments—program, which had destroyed numerous lives.

Seven children had been used as guinea pigs, tortured, drugged, and given electroshock treatments to alter their personalities and minds, all in hopes of creating perfect soldiers for the United States. Instead of names, they were given numbers to make the project less personal and eliminate the human element.

Neither Nick nor his brother Jake—Blackwood's sons, the elder now the sheriff of Slaughter Creek, the younger an agent with the TBI—had known that Rafe had an underlying agenda: to find out whether the brothers knew about the project and their father's activities.

Rafe had cleared the two men and passed along that info to his superiors.

And now this severed hand—was it a random crime, or could it be related to the project?

The city landscape gave way to wilderness and the Tennessee mountains as Rafe drove toward Slaughter Creek. Thick forests populated only by wild animals stretched for miles. The winding switchbacks climbing the steep mountain ridges were scenic but dangerous; it would only take one wrong move for a car to careen over the edge into the ravine below.

Rafe lost track of time as anxiety needled him. Everyone at the bureau knew that Nick and Jake had been searching for the missing research subjects, but the original files were missing, complicating the investigation. Four of the subjects had been murdered to cover up the project, and one had become a trained killer before committing suicide on Blackwood's command. Amelia Nettleton, a local and Jake's sister-in-law, the subject known as Three, had developed multiple personalities, and was undergoing therapy to merge her alters.

The last subject they'd located, Seven, Jake and Nick's sister, had been dubbed the Slaughter Creek Strangler after she was found to have murdered several men, but now she was in prison under psychiatric care.

The subject called Six was missing, his real name unknown. Law enforcement believed Six and Seven had escaped a compound where they'd been held prisoner.

Seven had refused to reveal where Six was hiding out.

Rafe reached the turnoff for the deserted RV campsite along the creek where the severed hand had been discovered. As he wove through the pines and oaks lining the graveled road, late-night shadows flickered between the moonlit patches, creating an eerie glow. Ahead he spotted Nick's black sedan, Jake's sheriff's car, and a battered Jeep Wrangler. He assumed that the two other vehicles parked there belonged to the crime unit and the ME, although if they hadn't found a body, this might not qualify as a murder.

Yet.

Rafe swung his SUV between two trees and parked, then climbed out and strode toward the Blackwood brothers. Crime-scene tape had been strung around the area, and flashlights dotted the woods as searchers combed for the body.

A camera flashed as one of the techs photographed the scene. Two teens were near a boulder by the water. The taller one leaned against a pine tree, his face ashen. The stocky guy next to him tried to look tough, although the way he jiggled his leg betrayed his nerves.

"These are the boys who found the hand?" Rafe asked.

Nick gave a quick nod. "Bo and Roy Crowley. Said they were here for a campout and fishing. They're both pretty shook up."

Rafe studied them for a moment, wondering if they could possibly have put the hand there, seeking attention. Some teenagers played sick, twisted pranks. He also couldn't dismiss the idea of gang warfare. And God knows drugs could be a factor.

But the boys' eyes appeared clear. And he didn't see any tats or clothing that indicated gang membership.

"Where is it?" he asked.

Nick gestured to the ME with a grim look. "Dr. Bullock is examining it now."

Bullock peered over the rims of his glasses where he was stooped by the water's edge. "Hand belonged to a woman. My guess is she was mid-fifties. Bone cut straight through, probably by an ax."

Rafe grimaced, and the stocky boy leaned over the rock and threw up. His brother looked as if he might join him, but instead he dropped his head into his hands and gulped in deep breaths.

"Did you find the weapon?" Rafe asked.

Jake knelt to look at something on the ground while Nick answered Rafe. "No weapon. No body. But the crime unit will scour these woods and drag the creek until we find it."

"It's possible the person survived," Rafe said. "Have you contacted ERs and hospitals?"

Jake looked up at him. "Done. I also called to see if any mental patients had been released recently or escaped, but both were dead ends."

"Except for Six," Nick interjected.

Jake nodded. "Except for Six."

Rafe shifted. "We'll need to look for inmates who've been paroled as well."

Jake stood. "I'll get right on it."

Rafe nodded and then turned to the boys. "When did you guys get here?"

The thin one wiped clammy sweat from his forehead. "We camped down the creek last night, then hiked up here this afternoon. Went swimming for a while, roasted some hot dogs, then decided to fish." He shuddered, his eyes straying to the hand. "That's when we . . . found it."

Understanding dawned as the ME pulled a fishhook from the index finger. He had a feeling these kids wouldn't be fishing in the dark again.

"I'm going to give them a lift home." Jake's sympathetic gaze shot toward the kids.

Rafe raked a hand over the back of his neck. "Go ahead. I'll wait here with Nick and help search."

Maybe by morning they'd have the body. Then they could identify their victim. That identification might lead them to the killer.

Nick's cell phone buzzed, and he checked the display. Lips thinning into a straight line, he punched connect. "Special Agent Blackwood."

Leaves rustled in the wind. An animal howled somewhere from the forest. The creek water lapped at the shore.

Nick angled his body toward the creek and looked across the mountains, his shoulders going rigid.

"What the hell?" A pause. "You're fucking kidding me." Another tense second, then Nick spun back toward him and Jake. Rage glittered in his dark eyes.

"What's wrong?" Rafe asked.

"The Commander's escaped prison."

———————————— , ————————————

Liz Lucas jerked awake, gasping for breath. But she couldn't get the air into her lungs. She was trapped.

Back in that hellhole where she'd been kept for days.

She jumped from bed, throwing open the blinds to let the sunlight stream in. Heedless of the temperature outside, she opened the windows next.

She needed air as much as she needed light.

She'd been deprived of both once.

Never again.

Self-recriminations screamed through her head. Had she survived? Or was she just the broken shell of the woman she'd once been? A woman afraid of her own shadow?

Hearing sounds and voices in her sleep—and that grating sharpening of the man's knife as he prepared for his next kill?

That kill was supposed to be her.

Desperate to regain control—and her sanity—she leaned against the French doors in her bedroom, wishing she could open them and step outside without worrying about being attacked. Dawn was just cracking the sky, the moon still a sliver on the horizon as early morning shadows flickered above the trees.

Spanish moss hung like spiderwebs draping the ground, making the woods look even creepier.

But she didn't dare go out yet. What if *he* was out there? Ned Harlan, aka the Blade. What if he found her and returned to finish the job?

He's dead, she reminded herself. He had been for months. At least, according to the police report.

But his body had never been found.

Although Liz was a profiler and had studied behavioral analysis, she also dealt in facts. Without a body, she could never be quite sure that Harlan hadn't made it out of that river alive.

But it had been months since the attack. It was time for her to get over it.

Hating the paranoia clawing at her, she rushed to close the windows again, then brewed a pot of coffee and took a mug out to the glider on the screened-in porch that ran the length of her Williamsburg house, overlooking the river. A porch with a security alarm to keep intruders out.

Instead, it felt like a prison.

How many sleepless nights had she spent curled up like a terrified cat, watching the woods? Seeing imaginary shadows, stalkers and predators lurking in the dark, just waiting to snatch her and kill her?

God knows she'd considered selling and moving to another state. Every time she looked out at the water, she remembered the cabin where he'd kept her. The section of river where he'd taken her to slice her throat.

The same place where her mother had died.

Rafe had run up to her and saved her—but her captor had escaped.

And it had been too late to lock up Harlan and make him face the families of his victims.

Too late because Liz had made a mistake and gotten the profile wrong. Hadn't realized the man who'd killed her mother and several women had been working with a partner. A female.

Rafe had killed the accomplice and shot Harlan. But his body had never surfaced.

If he had survived, she would find him one day and make him pay.

Until then . . .

She had to take it one day at a time. Focus on the fact that she was alive.

Liz studied the photo of her mother in the locket she wore close to her heart to keep her near. The photo had been taken at Christmas. Wavy brown hair curled around her heart-shaped face, and she was smiling. That particular day, Liz had given her a pair of silver earrings she'd bought from a local art festival The earrings were supposed to be light catchers; they twinkled different colors as the sunlight bounced off the cut glass inside the base.

Her mother was wearing the earrings the day Harlan abducted her, but they'd never been recovered.

Liz balled her hands into fists. That phone call from the police had changed everything in Liz's life. At sixteen, instead of dating and shopping for a prom dress, she'd been grief-stricken and in shock. Instead of looking at college catalogs, she'd studied crime-scene photos of her mother's death and hounded the local police for answers.

Her grandmother had begged her to move on and let the case go. To enjoy her teenage years.

Then Gran had passed, and she'd been alone.

Graduation night, she decided to study police work. The courses in behavioral science and analysis interested her most.

She was obsessed with understanding why the man who'd killed her mother had been so brutal. Why he'd slashed her throat.

Why he'd taken her life when there had been no apparent reason to target her. He hadn't known her personally. She'd never wronged him in any way that the police could discover.

The need for those answers had become the driving force in Liz's life.

So she'd earned a degree, joined the TBI, and worked her way up to a position as a behavior analyst.

Meanwhile her mother's case had gone cold. But not in her mind.

Then a few months ago, Liz caught a break.

Guilt nagged at her for thinking of another woman's murder as a break, but the similarity in MOs had given her reason to have her mother's case reopened. Rafe had agreed to help her look into the murder.

Because they were already involved. Had slept together.

Then a woman disappeared. Another single mother.

The day after Liz's profile aired, the killer came after Liz, but not before killing the woman he'd abducted before her.

Liz had to live with that death.

She rubbed the puckered scar along her neck, a constant reminder that she wasn't the same woman she had been before the kidnapping. That even with all her training, she'd still been weak, had lost to him. That he'd marked her with his ugliness.

The fact that he'd stolen her confidence hurt more than anything.

He'd also ruined her reputation—or at least Rafe Hood's trust in her, trust that had meant so much to her, just as he had. But how could she ask Rafe to totally trust her again when she'd kept things from him?

She wouldn't allow Harlan to take anything else.

Her determination renewed, she returned to the kitchen and grabbed a breakfast bar while she watched the news, mentally outlining her day.

Yoga after the news to relax her. Then she'd hit the gym for fitness training. After a pounding workout, the shooting range.

She had to stay in shape in case Harlan rose from the dead.

And when—or if—her boss finally assigned her to a case, she needed to prove she could do the job.

"This is Brenda Banks reporting to you live from Slaughter Creek, where last night a woman's severed hand was found floating in the creek near Pine Grove RV Park. Sheriff Jake Blackwood along with Special Agent Nick Blackwood, who headed up the investigation into the Slaughter Creek Sanitarium project, are both at the scene, along with the medical examiner, Dr. Barry Bullock." Cameras panned to the wooded area, where she spotted Nick Blackwood in a heated phone conversation.

The camera focused on another man as Brenda approached him with her microphone.

Rafe Hood.

The world seemed to stop, life crashing in around Liz. Rafe looked even more handsome and intimidating than he had the last time she'd seen him, standing over her hospital bed.

He'd walked away because she'd failed.

Sunlight flickered off his dark, chiseled jaw. His thick black hair was too long, brushing his wide shoulders, which stretched against the confines of that white button-down shirt.

Lord God, she knew the muscles that lay beneath, and for the first time in months, her body hummed to life, aching with the need to touch him.

But that had been a mistake the first time.

One she wouldn't repeat.

Not that Rafe wanted her. He'd made that plain and clear the night he'd left her alone, traumatized and angry and . . . so in love with him she could barely draw breath.

Still, she craved his arms around her. To feel his lips on hers. To have him remind her that she was still desirable, even though the killer had scarred her inside and out.

And tainted her soul with the need for revenge.

In the background she saw Nick heading toward Brenda. Other crime techs combed the woods in search of evidence.

"Special Agent Rafe Hood of the TBI is here as well," Brenda continued, drawing Liz's attention back to the reporter. "Can you tell us what you know pertaining to this case?"

"Not much at this time," Rafe said in that gravelly voice. "I can verify that a severed hand was discovered in the river. It belonged to a white female, mid-fifties. As of now, we haven't located a body, but we're still searching. If anyone has any information regarding this crime, please contact the local police."

"You have search teams combing the creek for the body now?" Brenda asked.

Rafe nodded, but he looked distracted. His dark brown eyes were scanning the woods as if he expected the person who'd severed the hand to be watching.

Maybe he was, Liz thought. He could be anywhere, even right in front of them, and they might not know it. Some criminals liked to return to the scene and watch the police scurry around, chasing false clues.

Some even insinuated themselves into an investigation.

The police had to stay on their toes.

She'd learned the hard way—no one could be trusted.

He placed the jar on the shelf he'd built for his trophies.

Trophies—that was what the federal agents and profilers called the treasures men like him took.

The bloody stump and fingers were dirty and vile, the fingernails jagged and bitten to the quick, the skin pocked with early liver spots. An ugly hand.

And a reminder that that hand would never hurt anyone else.

A smile curved his mouth, and he massaged his cock, which had grown thick with excitement as he'd watched the life drain from the bitch.

The cops would recover the rest of the body soon. A pity that he hadn't had a meat grinder to dispose of it, so nothing else would be left behind except for this hand. The bad hand.

Really, he had no use for the rest of the woman's remains. Just the hand.

His medical training kicked in, his photographic memory flashing anatomical details. Twenty-seven bones comprised the skeleton of the wrist and hand. Three main nerves—the median, ulnar, and radial—innervated the hand. The bones—carpals, metacarpals, and phalanges. Five phalanges made up the fingers. The thumb was the most mobile.

More information about the wrist and the scaphoid, one of the bones in the first row of carpals, streamed through his mind as he studied the treasure in his jar.

It wasn't the anatomy that had enticed him to keep the hand. That hand spoke to him. Had punished him. Had slapped and beaten him and made him feel intense, excruciating pain.

It was only justice that she'd felt the same before she died.

Then again, leaving the body would give the police something to do. Things to investigate.

Then he could prove that he was smarter than them.

He was in charge of his own destiny. And he could be anyone he wanted to be. A chameleon.

Pure joy warmed his insides as he ran a finger over the jar holding his souvenir.

Her blood was on his hands now, and it tasted like wine.

Anticipation flooded him.

Soon it would be time for another drink.

# Chapter Two

———— o ————

As the news story continued, Liz massaged the ache in her leg. The break had healed, but sometimes it still throbbed when the winter chill set in.

"Special Agent Hood," Brenda Banks continued, "you assisted in the investigation into the recent Slaughter Creek Strangler case, which we now know was directly related to the CHIMES project. Do you think this crime is also related?"

Rafe shot the reporter an irritated look. "It's too early to tell at this point. Now, excuse me. I have work to do."

Special Agent Nick Blackwood reached Brenda, but he looked angry, worried. They spoke in hushed voices.

Something was wrong.

A second later Brenda straightened her jacket and pushed the microphone toward Nick, her professional demeanor intact. "Agent Blackwood, can you confirm that Arthur Blackwood, the man awaiting trial on multiple murder charges, and the man who oversaw the CHIMES Project—"

"My father."

Brenda cleared her throat. "Your father, yes." She likely wasn't used to such bluntness. "Can you confirm that he escaped from prison last night?"

Nick's eyes turned steely. "Yes, it's true. He killed three guards during the breakout and is considered armed and extremely dangerous. If you know anything about his disappearance, please call the FBI immediately."

Brenda's fingers seemed to tighten around the microphone. "Do you think his escape had anything to do with the severed hand found in the creek?"

Nick glared at Brenda with an intensity that made Liz shiver. Commander Blackwood had killed almost everyone related to the CHIMES project and had put hits out on those investigating it. He'd also tried to kill Brenda.

Meaning she was in danger now.

"As Agent Hood said earlier, it's too early to tell. Removing body parts has not been a part of the Commander's MO, though."

"But not all of his subjects have been accounted for yet," Brenda pushed.

"That's true."

"And the last case, in which the woman named Seven strangled and killed several men—she was not only Commander Blackwood's daughter but a victim of the experiment, correct?"

A muscle twitched in his jaw. "That's true also."

"So the killer could be another one of his subjects?" Brenda suggested.

"It's possible, but purely speculative at this point. This crime could be completely unrelated." Agent Blackwood exhaled. "However, we do believe that the Commander had an accomplice who aided in his escape. When that person is found, he or she will be prosecuted to the fullest extent of the law."

A commotion started in the background, and Brenda's cameraman panned across the area. A shout erupted from one of the crime-scene workers, several hundred feet from the spot where the hand had been found.

Brenda pivoted to watch the action. "Folks, stay tuned for more on this late-breaking story. We'll bring you details as they unfold."

"We have a body!" the crime tech yelled.

Nick and Rafe jogged toward the tech. Brenda and the cameraman hurried toward the scene, but Nick stepped in front of them to prevent the victim from being captured on camera.

Liz zeroed in on Rafe. Judging from his grim expression, the scene was bad.

She paced the room, agitated, the need to do something nagging at her. She grabbed her crochet hooks and started to work on a new blanket. Her therapist had suggested she find a hobby, something to occupy her hands and mind while she healed. She'd read about a charity that donated handmade blankets to hospitals for sick children. Fifty blankets later, and her hands had finally stopped trembling every time she remembered the past. But the news story haunted her, and she had the sudden urge to join the case.

To stop feeling sorry for herself.

The bottle of antianxiety pills she'd been prescribed mocked her from the table, and she tossed the crochet hooks into the basket. Making the blankets was rewarding in its own way, but she was a detective. She'd worked damn hard to make it at the bureau. To be a profiler at her age.

But going back to work meant facing the ugliness again, confronting cold-blooded killers like Harlan.

Her hand trembled, and she reached for the bottle of pills. But a voice echoed in her head. A voice that called her a coward.

Anger surged through her. She had good reason to be scared. She wasn't a coward.

Maybe she just didn't want to hunt down killers anymore.

She touched the scar again, then gritted her teeth. She could resign from the TBI, and no one would think badly of her. Agents burned out all the time.

But Liz was a fighter. She always had been. Always would be.

She had to go back. She'd show everyone that that bastard hadn't defeated her.

Liz reached for her cell phone.

It was time for her to come out of hiding.

———————— , ————————

Rafe grimaced at the sight of the woman's battered body. Her dress, a floral-printed orange housedress, was torn and ripped to shreds, hanging in wet patches around her pale arms and legs. Bruises covered her limbs—caused by the killer pre-mortem.

Rafe's eyes moved to her hands.

Or where they should have been.

The unidentified subject—unsub—had cut off both of them. Where was the other hand?

The leader of the crime team, Lieutenant Marc Maddison, who'd also worked the previous case with the Blackwood brothers, approached Rafe as one of the crime techs laid the woman's remains on the grassy embankment.

Leaves fluttered to the ground in the breeze as the crime team continued to search the bushes for more evidence, moving upstream.

Dr. Bullock knelt to examine the corpse. The crime techs' cameras flashed, capturing images of her injuries for analysis. Another CSI, a man named Perkins with thick ropelike scars on his arms, focused on the ground in the area where the body had been found. Brenda and her cameraman had been forbidden to take pictures and ordered to stay behind the crime-scene tape.

"Can you tell the cause of death?" Rafe asked.

Dr. Bullock used a magnifying lens to study the victim's wrists and the bloody stumps where the killer had inflicted his damage. "This small wound at the base of her neck indicates that the killer subdued her with a stun gun. She probably bled out from the amputations, but I won't know until I get her on the table. If there's water in her lungs, she might have been dumped in the creek alive."

Tension tightened every muscle in Rafe's body. Either way, the woman had suffered. "See if your guys can find the other hand," he said to Maddison.

Brian Castor, one of the CSIs, stooped down beside the ME to snap close-ups of the woman's injuries. He seemed especially intrigued by the bone and skin around the severed part of her arm.

"What do you think, Dr. Bullock? Was she beaten? Any sign of sexual assault?" Rafe asked.

Dr. Bullock raked dirt and leaves from the woman's lower extremities. "I don't see signs of sexual assault, but the water could have washed away fluids. I'll have to perform a more extensive exam when I get her to the morgue."

"How long do you think she's been dead?"

"Since last night. But again, this creek water is frigid. The temperature could have slowed down decomp."

"Let me know what you learn from the autopsy."

Heated voices rumbled from the top of the hill, and Rafe saw Nick arguing with Brenda Banks. Brenda had helped solve the Strangler case and exposed Nick and Jake's sister as the killer. She was also writing personal profiles on the subjects of the experiment.

Nick said something about the Commander, that he wanted Brenda out of the picture. Judging from the snippets he heard, Nick wanted Brenda to go to a safe house. But Brenda wanted the story.

Stubborn woman. She reminded him of Liz.

Dear God. Liz. If she saw this news report, it would resurrect memories. Nightmares of her past.

A past where he'd failed her.

His cell phone buzzed. His chief.

He punched connect. "Yeah?"

"Agent Hood, I just got a call. Agent Lucas is going to be working with you."

"What? No!" Hell, no.

"Yes," the chief said tersely. "We're running short on manpower. With Blackwood's prison escape, we need every agent we've got. Besides, Liz insists she's ready to come back to work."

Sweat beaded on Rafe's forehead. "She called and *asked* to work this case?"

"Yes."

"I don't want her here. She needs more time." He scraped a hand over his beard stubble. "You of all people should know that. You're the one who told me she had paranoid delusions, that she was on medication."

"Well, the doc has cleared her, and she's tapered off the meds," the chief said.

"She still could be fragile."

"If that's the case, don't go messing around with her."

The chief didn't have to tell Rafe that. He'd lost his focus last time because he'd let his emotions get in the way.

Still, memories of holding Liz in his arms, of their naked bodies gliding together as they made love, pummeled him.

Then an image of her—bloody, beaten and traumatized from her captivity, and her scream as Harlan slashed her neck . . .

"Tell her to let me handle this case," Rafe said. He hated the desperate pleading in his voice.

"I realize it's dangerous and that she's walking a fine line, but she's also driven like no agent I've ever known, and she's a damn good profiler," his chief said. "We need her, Hood."

The chief hung up, and Rafe cursed. He had screwed up by touching Liz the first time.

He wouldn't touch her again. And he sure as hell wouldn't allow himself to care for her.

Because a curse dogged him. Every time he cared about someone, they ended up dead.

Rafe used the new computer program the TBI had purchased to organize the photos of the crime scene that he'd displayed at the meeting.

The chief filed in, along with Lieutenant Maddison and Dr. Bullock. Their expressions reflected the same grimness he felt. CSIs Castor and Perkins also joined them. Castor spread out photos of the body, along with close-ups of the amputated portion of the victim's arms.

CSI Perkins fidgeted with his glasses; he seemed jittery, as if he was agitated or excited. Rafe wasn't sure which. It might have been his first case. Or maybe the thrill of detective work just excited him. It definitely took a certain kind of person to enjoy his field of work.

Everyone took a seat, chairs scraping as the men settled down. A second later the air shifted as Liz walked in. Nothing like a gorgeous woman to stir up the testosterone.

Rafe's heart instantly jumped. She was even more stunning than he remembered in his dreams. And man, did he dream about her.

Almost every damn night.

She was every man's wet dream. Silky blond hair, legs to die for, a mouth that tasted like honey and sweetness . . . one that had kissed him senseless and done wicked things to his body.

She was also smart and feisty and had survived some hard knocks in life without letting it sour her on every person she met. Had the cases destroyed her trust?

They damn well had his. Trust was not in his vocabulary.

Suddenly his gaze was drawn to that dark blue satin scarf around her neck, and his throat tightened. She'd worn it to hide the scar.

Not because she was vain.

Because it was a stark reminder of the fact that he'd screwed up, and she'd almost died because of it.

The chief introduced her to Dr. Bullock and Lieutenant Maddison. A second later, Rafe's gaze locked with hers.

Unspoken tension crackled between them. Rafe had the insane urge to touch her. To drag her from the room and lock her up so no man could ever hurt her again.

But he could do none of those things. They were colleagues, for fuck's sake.

So he cleared his throat and addressed the others. "Let's get started. I've organized photos of the crime scene." He flashed them on the screen, focusing his thoughts on the case instead of the woman who obviously still had the power to tie him up in knots.

This time the chief would be watching him every step of the way.

He couldn't show a flicker of personal interest in Liz, or his ass would be toast.

"We have identified the victim as fifty-five-year-old Ester Banning. Her prints were in the system from a DUI when she was twenty-two. She's from West Tennessee, and worked at a nursing home for years before disappearing a few months back." He paused for a breath. "She has no family. The paper trail for her went cold about eight months ago. We're currently tracking down her last known address."

"So you don't know where she's been or what she's been doing the last few months?" the chief asked.

"Not yet," Rafe said. But he would find out. Knowing everything about her would help them determine why she'd become a victim.

Liz's soft voice broke the silence. "What if the unsub abducted her months ago and has been holding her ever since?"

"A possibility," Rafe said. "Before we speculate further, though, let's hear from Dr. Bullock on COD."

Dr. Bullock stood by the display of photos. "Cause of death was exsanguination. She hemorrhaged as a result of the amputations of both hands." He gestured toward the close-up of the woman's arms. "The right hand was discovered in the water, but the crime techs dragged the creek, and the left hand was never recovered."

Liz waved her fingers. "Maybe he kept it as his trophy."

Rafe contemplated her comment. "That's also a possibility, although it could also have floated downstream and been scavenged by an animal."

Liz scribbled a note in her notepad.

Dr. Bullock pointed to a photo of the victim on a slab in the morgue. "There are no indications of sexual assault, and I found no foreign DNA or trace evidence on the victim. Of course the water could have washed away fluids and trace, but I didn't find bruising or physical evidence indicating intercourse. I did find something interesting, though."

A collective quiet fell over the room in anticipation of his statement.

Dr. Bullock gestured toward the woman's face in one of the photos. "Not only were this woman's hands removed, but the killer also used them as a weapon against her."

"What do you mean?" Maddison asked.

Dr. Bullock hit a button and enlarged the photo, giving them a detailed view of the woman's left cheek. Red fingerprints marked her pale skin. "I mean, our unsub used her own hand to beat her."

"He wanted her to suffer," Liz said. "Either she'd hurt him, or she reminded him of someone who did. The most common theory with serial killers is that they suffered terrible childhood abuse at the hands of a loved one, often the mother. But the abuser could have been someone else. A family member, neighbor, teacher, priest. Even a coworker." She paused, tapping her fingers on the table. "If this was his first kill, it could be very personal." That the woman had been conscious when the unsub severed her hands underlined the depth of his perversion.

Dr. Bullock scratched his head. "The victim also had particularly dry skin in patches, as if she used some kind of strong chemical on her hands."

"Like hospital soap?" Liz asked. "That would fit with her job at the nursing home."

Dr. Bullock twisted his mouth in thought. "Possibly. Or she could have been an obsessive hand washer. It's a form of OCD."

"Ironic that she kept her hands clean, yet they were the part the killer chose to remove," Liz commented. Rafe saw the wheels turning in her mind as she sorted through the information, silently analyzing the killer's thought processes.

That was what she did, and she was good at it. Unfortunately, inside the killer's mind was a treacherous place to live. The darkness could swallow her at times, pull her down.

Put her in danger.

Rafe folded his arms. "Agent Lucas and I will interview the people at the nursing home where the vic worked," he said. "Dr. Bullock, let me know if you find anything else." He angled his head toward Maddison.

"Same for you, Lieutenant Maddison. We need to nail this bastard before he hurts someone else."

---

Since the CHIMES scandal had broken, Slaughter Creek Sanitarium had been cleaning house. Almost everyone at the place, from the janitors to the director, was new.

Which made it easier to hide among them and slip in and out as he pleased.

He had a mission to do here, and nothing would stop him. He could manipulate records, files, names . . . hell, anything he wanted. And the police would only find out what he wanted them to know.

Changing names and identities was a way of life for him. A matter of survival.

He slipped into the basement room where the experiments had taken place. The Commander had hidden his files in a secret space, and none of the investigators had found it.

But he remembered it.

He listened to make sure no one was coming, then crossed the dark room to the corner, removing the bricks and the folder inside.

He thumbed through the file, relief seizing him when he located the page he needed. He dropped it into the metal waste-basket, lit a match, and tossed it in as well. The page caught imme-diately, flames curling the edges and quickly turning the thin paper into black ashes.

He watched the glow flicker, a stream of smoke filling the metal container, then slowly die.

The page was dust. History.

And just like that, the information was erased. No one, includ-ing the Commander, understood the bond they had all formed.

That they would do anything to protect each other.

# Chapter Three

———— ◦ ————

Nick's heart pounded as he met with the warden at the maximum-security prison where his father had been incarcerated. For time's sake, he and Jake had split up. Jake was interrogating their sister, Seven, in hopes she'd finally confess where the sixth subject was hiding out.

He could be their latest killer.

Nick's job was to find out more about the prison escape, in case it threw light on the Commander's plans.

"How the hell did this happen?" Nick asked.

The warden rubbed at his head, his face agitated. "We're conducting an internal investigation now."

"You think one of your own helped him?"

The warden sank into his chair with a muttered curse and turned to address Chet Roper, one of the head guards. "What do you think, Roper?"

"I don't think so," Roper said. "But who knows? Anything's possible."

"I want you personally to look into it," the warden said. "Put out some feelers."

"Yes, sir." Roper left the office as if he was on a mission.

Nick studied the warden. "You trust him?"

"He's one of our best," the warden said. "Former military. As tough as they come."

"Do you have any clue what happened?"

"Not yet. But I will. We had your father under surveillance every minute of every damn day. All his conversations were recorded. His visits, which were restricted to you, your brother, Brenda Banks, and other police who questioned him, were also taped."

"What other police?" Nick asked.

The warden checked his records. "Two detectives tried to persuade him to give up the other victims of the experiment and his accomplice in overseeing the project. You can look at their notes yourself. They got nowhere."

Nick nodded. He would have been notified if they had.

The warden drummed his fingers on the desk. "There were also two CIA agents. Each of them had clearance."

He'd already spoken to them. A dead end. "What about a cell mate?"

The warden shook his head. "We kept him isolated. No cell mate. He even took his meals in his cell."

Yet somehow his father had orchestrated an escape.

"What about my sister?" He hated calling her Seven instead of using her real name. But Seven was the name his father had given her, and the only one she'd ever known.

He would remedy that when he saw her. He'd tell her what his mother had called her.

"No contact at all."

Nick frowned.

"That said," the warden continued, "the inmates in here are intelligent, manipulative, and manage to get contraband no matter what measures we take. Hell, they can make a shank out of anything."

Nick knew good and well how prison life worked. Gang wars, rape, beatings, weapons, phones, narcotics . . .

Some snuck drugs in through body cavities. Women filled balloons with dope and stuffed them in their bras. One sick fuck had even sewn a weapon inside a dead cat and left the cat by the exercise yard for a convicted child molester to find.

"I want the Commander's mail sent to our TBI analyst. If someone's using a code and we crack it, it might lead us to whoever helped him."

The warden murmured agreement. "I'll keep you abreast of our investigation. As of now, the entire prison is on twenty-four-hour lockdown."

Nick shook his hand and thanked him, although he didn't hold out much hope that they'd find his father's accomplice. For all they knew, some psycho woman who'd sent him a marriage proposal had snuck him a weapon through another visitor. His father might literally be getting himself some ass while he and Jake were chasing their tails looking for him.

---

Liz forced herself not to react to Rafe as she climbed in the passenger side of his SUV to drive to the nursing home. But his scent invaded her nostrils, making her dizzy with memories and the need to be closer to him.

God help her. She could not do this again. Couldn't allow herself to fall under his spell.

"You know I don't want you working this case," Rafe said, cutting into her thoughts.

So much for him feeling something for her.

No, he *did* feel something. Disdain.

Liz squared her shoulders. "I'm a good agent, Rafe. Just because—"

His brow shot up. "Because you and I messed up last time."

Yes, they had. They'd jumped into bed when they should have been following a lead, and a woman had died because of it. "We won't make the same mistake," she said. "*I* won't make the same mistake."

His jaw tightened as he looked back at the road. "Neither will I."

Her stomach fluttered at his gruff tone. She knew what he meant—that he wouldn't sleep with her again. Rafe had never loved her, but he had climbed into her bed because it was convenient.

Not because he wanted a long-term relationship with her.

She had to remember that.

They lapsed into a strained silence as he wound around the mountain. Winter was setting in, the temperature freezing, a sea of dead leaves blanketing the ground. More fluttered down in the wind, the gray clouds adding a dismal cast to the sky.

The nursing home was on the same side of the mountain as the sanitarium, although the two facilities were run separately. The building was weathered and aged, paint peeling off the cinder-block walls. The flower beds were patchy, overrun with weeds, the windows needed cleaning, and the garden area to the left needed serious landscaping.

As Liz stared out the window, her mind turned to the case. She was still contemplating the fact that the woman's second hand hadn't been recovered. The killer could have performed the amputations to keep police from identifying her—or to get rid of trace evidence in case she'd fought him and had skin cells or DNA under her fingernails. That was the logical explanation.

But other possibilities entered Liz's mind, ones far more gruesome. If the unsub had taken the hand as a trophy, it could be part of his signature.

Of course she needed more details to put together a profile. If the latter was true, they were dealing with a psychopath.

Which meant the man might have killed before.

And he would kill again.

Rafe parked in one of the guest spaces, next to an older Chrysler. A few other cars, probably belonging to the staff or visitors, were scattered around the lot.

They headed to the entrance in silence, their earlier conversation lingering in the air, creating more tension. Inside, Liz scanned the reception area. A few potted plants added a little color to the drab interior. The walls were painted white, but the paint had faded and yellowed, and cheap, outdated landscapes hung askew over threadbare plaid couches that needed to be tossed.

The receptionist sat behind a counter and window in front of them. The sounds of food carts, machines, and footsteps rumbled. A gray-haired man rolled his wheelchair toward a side door, an elderly woman walking beside him. She rested her hand on the man's shoulder affectionately, and Liz's heart swelled. They must have been married a long time. Now the man needed care that his wife couldn't give him. How sad.

Still, they were lucky. Very few people found a love like that. She had lost hope for it herself.

Rafe stepped up to the counter and smiled at the plump middle-aged woman with curly hair. He introduced them, and they both flashed credentials.

"What can we do for you?" the receptionist asked.

"Ma'am, we found the body of a woman named Ester Banning in Slaughter Creek. This nursing home was the last place listed on her work history."

The receptionist's eyes widened. "Ester is dead?" Her voice rose a notch.

"Yes. So you knew her?"

She nodded, a frown pulling at her brows.

"How long did she work here?" Rafe asked.

"A couple years, but"—she leaned closer—"the patients complained about her."

Rafe narrowed his eyes. "What were the nature of the complaints?"

"Some patients said she was mean to them," the receptionist continued. "But I'm not supposed to talk about it."

"Did she ever actually hit anyone?" Rafe asked.

She chewed her bottom lip for a second, as if debating how much to reveal. "A couple of folks. Regina in Eleven A and Myra in Three B. But nothing was ever substantiated."

Rafe made a low sound in his throat. "We'd like to talk to those patients, please."

The receptionist fidgeted. "I'm afraid that's not possible. We lost Regina last month."

"What happened?" Liz asked.

"Heart failure."

"Did the hospital perform an autopsy?"

She shook her head. "There wasn't any need. She had an enlarged heart."

"What about Myra?"

"I'm afraid she won't be much help," the receptionist said. "Poor woman had a stroke six months ago. She's paralyzed on one side, hasn't said a word since."

"Was Ester still working here at the time?" Liz asked.

She nodded. "Yeah, but the director fired her afterward. Said too many people complaining would draw unwanted attention to the nursing home."

Of course it would, Liz thought.

"What about these two ladies' families?" Rafe asked.

"Well, Regina had a son. He was upset and threatened to sue the facility."

"What happened?" Liz asked.

"His mama died, and he dropped the case." The receptionist fidgeted again. "To tell you the truth, I think the hospital might have given him some kind of settlement."

"What about Myra's family?" Rafe asked.

"Her husband passed on two years ago. She has a daughter and son. They visit every now and then, but not regularly."

Rafe removed his phone from the clip on his belt. "Get their contact information and addresses for me, please."

RITA HERRON

"Sure. I'll need to talk to our director though," she said. "She'll have to sign off on releasing the paperwork."

Liz shifted as the receptionist phoned the director. Maybe this was as simple as a man wanting revenge against an abusive caretaker, not a serial killer.

She had a bad feeling, though, that her first instincts were right. Call it women's intuition, gut instinct, or maybe just the fact that she'd worked too many cases and seen too much darkness.

An image of Ester Banning's severed hands flashed in her mind, and worry gnawed at her. The cruel, calculating violence of the crime suggested the man was a psychopath. Which meant he had enjoyed the kill.

And he would do it again if they didn't stop him.

# Chapter Four

———— o ————

"I want to see Myra," Liz told the nurse.

The woman made a low sound in her throat. "I told you, she had a stroke. She hasn't said anything in months."

"Please," Liz said. "Just for a minute."

The woman huffed, then gestured down the hall. "Room Three B. But don't upset her."

Liz offered her a smile, hoping she wasn't wasting their time. But she had to try to communicate with Myra. She headed down the hall, well aware that Rafe followed close behind.

The strong odor of alcohol and body waste permeated the air as they passed two rooms, a testament to the sad conditions inside the nursing home. When they reached Myra's room, Liz knocked softly on the door, then gently eased it open.

She poked her head in and saw a frail white-haired woman lying in bed, her eyes closed, her freckled arthritic hands folded across her stomach. She was snoring softly and actually looked peaceful.

"Maybe we should come back," Rafe suggested.

"No, we're here. We might as well talk to her before we leave."

Liz walked over to the window and opened the curtains, letting light spill in through the window. Myra wheezed a breath, then opened her eyes. She looked disoriented for a moment, blinking rapidly as if to figure out where she was.

Sympathy for her welled in Liz's chest.

Myra looked small in the bed, vulnerable. Had Ester hurt her?

"Myra, my name is Liz Lucas," Liz said as she walked over to stand beside the bed. "And this is my partner, Special Agent Rafe Hood."

Myra's eyes darted sideways as if she understood. Remembering that she was paralyzed, Liz motioned for Rafe to move over beside her. When Myra spotted him, her eyes widened in acknowledgment, suggesting that Myra might be able to communicate after all.

"We understand that you had a stroke, and that it's difficult for you to speak, but we need to talk to you about a nurse who used to work here named Ester Banning."

Myra's breath rasped out, once, twice, three times, as if she was on the verge of a panic attack. Sympathy filled Liz. How horrible to be trapped in a body that wouldn't work.

"We're not here to upset you, Myra." Liz placed a hand over the woman's thin, gnarled one to comfort her. "We want to help. We've been told that Ester wasn't nice to her patients. That complaints were made against her for mistreating the patients."

Anguish, distrust, and fear darkened Myra's eyes, the sheets rustling as she struggled to move and failed.

"Don't worry, Myra," Rafe said in a gruff voice. "Ester is dead. She can't hurt anyone anymore."

Liz angled her phone so Myra could see the picture of Ester she'd pulled from the DMV records. "This is Ester, the woman who hurt you, isn't it?"

Myra blinked rapidly, her lips parting as if she was trying to speak, but no sound came out.

"Did she hurt you?"

More rapid eye blinking, and the woman began to wheeze again, a low sob escaping her. Then her body began to jerk, her eyes rolled back in her head, and a strangled sound emerged from her throat.

"She's seizing," Liz said. "Call for help!"

Rafe stepped into the hallway for a doctor while Liz tried to soothe Myra. Seconds later a nurse and female doctor rushed in.

"What happened?" the nurse bellowed.

"We were just talking to her," Rafe said.

The doctor pulled a hypodermic from the pocket of her lab jacket, jammed the needle in the vial of medicine, tapped it, and injected Myra.

She glared at Liz and Rafe. "You two need to leave. Now."

"I'm sorry," Liz said. "But we're working a murder case and Myra knew the victim."

Myra slowly relaxed as the medication seeped into her system. The doctor gestured to the door. "Out in the hall."

They stepped outside the door, and the doctor turned to them, hands on her hips. "I'm Myra's primary care physician. How could Myra possibly help you with your investigation?"

Liz showed her Ester's driver's license picture. "Because the victim was Ester Banning, and we have reason to believe she mistreated Myra and other patients here. Did you know her?"

"Yes." The doctor's voice cracked. "What happened to her?"

Liz nodded. "She was murdered."

The doctor gasped.

"According to our research, this is the last place she worked."

The doctor massaged her temple. "She was fired shortly after I was hired. In fact—" She broke off, hesitating.

"In fact what?"

She folded her arms across her chest. "She was fired because of me. I caught her slapping a patient, then found her shoving pills down Myra's throat." Emotions flared in her eyes. "That woman caused Myra's heart to go into distress, which triggered a stroke."

Liz's stomach lurched. If Ester had caused Myra's condition, someone in Myra's family might have good reason to hate her.

And a valid reason to want her dead.

———————————— , ————————————

His lips curling in disgust, he stared at the picture of Ester Banning on the front page of the *Slaughter Creek Gazette*.

The story didn't reveal any important details. There was no mention of suspects either. Did the police know that Ester had helped Commander Arthur Blackwood with the CHIMES project? That she was a soldier for his evil? She'd obeyed his every command with no questions asked. Punished the children without a shred of remorse in those cold she-devil eyes.

Just as they all had.

Her picture was deceptive, though. In it, she looked normal. Like a victim.

Ester Banning had been no victim.

He closed his eyes, remembering the way she'd looked at the end. Her stringy matted brown hair had grayed and was gritty from the creek water. Bruises darkened the skin beneath her eyes, and there were cuts on her face. And those eyes . . . they'd been black with evil.

She looked battered and ugly.

She *was* ugly, inside and out.

Nurses were supposed to be tenderhearted. Caring. Gentle. Loving.

Ester had never been loving.

He rubbed a finger along the number carved behind his ear.

Yes, Ester was one of the most coldhearted people he'd ever met. And she had deserved to die. Just as all the worker bees in the Commander's army did.

Soon they would be picked off, just like flies.

Dead. Crushed. Their blood splattered across the town, running like a river of crimson through Slaughter Creek.

He stared at the master list. Who would be next?

———————— , ————————

A half hour later, Liz and Rafe left the nursing home. Three different employees had confirmed the doctor's story about Ester. All said they'd noticed her being cruel to a patient and were relieved when she'd been fired.

They stopped at a small coffee shop to phone Myra's children. They also needed to speak to the other patient's son. The fact that he'd filed a lawsuit but dropped it after his mother's death was suspicious.

Rafe ordered them coffee and punched in Myra's daughter's number.

When she answered on the third ring, he put her on speakerphone.

"Hello, Evans residence."

"Ann?" Liz said.

"Yes, who is this?"

Liz explained the reason for their call. "We saw your mother and spoke with her doctor."

"You talked to my mother?" Ann's voice rose a decibel. "What happened? Is she okay?"

Liz inhaled. "She grew anxious when we showed her Ester's photograph," she said. "But we assured her that Ester can't hurt her anymore."

"My mother's suffered enough," Ann said. "Leave her alone."

"We didn't mean to upset her, Ann." Liz hesitated, softening her voice. "Did you have any contact with Ester after she was fired?"

Ann heaved a weary breath. "No. And if you think me or my brother had something to do with her death, you're wrong.

We discussed filing a lawsuit, but the head of the nursing home assured us that Ester would never work there or anywhere in nursing care again."

"Did they give you a settlement?" Liz asked.

A tense heartbeat passed. "Yes. But I want to clarify something. We only took the money to help pay for Mother's care. And if there's any money left after Mother passes, we've designated it to go into a trust fund for our children."

"Of course." Liz jotted down some notes. "Have you spoken to your brother lately?"

"He's in Hong Kong on business. He's been there for a month, and won't be back for another three weeks."

"Thank you," Liz said. "We appreciate your help."

Ann released a weary breath. "I would like to say that I hope you find Ester's killer," Ann said. "Even though I'm not sorry she's gone. She was a horrible woman who caused my mother's stroke."

Liz couldn't blame Ann for her animosity, but she didn't think she'd killed Ester.

Because the doctor was right. Whoever had severed Ester's hands was a psychopath. And Ann sounded . . . normal.

Bitter but normal.

Maybe Regina's son could give them some answers.

---

Nick and Brenda joined Jake, Sadie, and Amelia at Jake's house. Thankfully, Gigi, the woman who'd half raised Jake and was now his daughter Ayla's caretaker, had carried Ayla to the park, giving the adults an opportunity to talk.

Nick and Jake wanted their families and loved ones unharmed. Sadie agreed to the safe house automatically. She was as protective of Ayla, Gigi, and her sister Amelia as Nick was of Brenda.

Both of them were worried that the Commander's escape would cause Amelia to relapse in her recovery.

Sadie gripped her twin sister's hand.

"The Commander escaped?" Amelia asked in a shaky voice.

Sadie nodded. "I'm sorry, Amelia."

Amelia's face paled. Nick hated to put her through this ordeal. She'd been diagnosed with DID, dissociative identity disorder, as a result of the abusive experiments she'd undergone and the drugs she'd been given as a child. But she'd made great strides in therapy and merging her alters.

Jake cleared his throat. "Amelia and Sadie—you two, Ayla, and Gigi are going to a safe house until my father is caught."

Amelia lurched up and began to pace, her fingers tapping a rhythm on her forearm. "I can't be locked up. It'll be like I'm a prisoner in that hospital again."

Jake shot Nick a concerned look.

"You won't be locked up," Nick assured her. "I made arrangements for you to stay in a nice log cabin on the river. Think of it as a vacation for you and Sadie."

"A vacation with security," Jake added. "Please, Amelia—it'll be easier for Nick and me to do our jobs if we don't have to worry about you."

Sadie curved an arm around Amelia. "He's right, sis. Besides, we can take canvases and paint. The mountains in the winter are so beautiful."

Amelia chewed her bottom lip, her voice low. "I suppose."

Sadie's tone gained enthusiasm. "A cabin on the river sounds inspirational, too. If it snows, we can go sledding with Ayla and build a snowman."

"I'll go with you to help you get situated," Jake said.

Amelia paused, the tapping continuing on her arm. Nick noticed a cut mark that hadn't been there before. Cutting hadn't been a characteristic of any of her alters.

Unless she'd developed a new one that nobody knew about yet . . .

# Chapter Five

———— o ————

He stared into the woman's cold, listless eyes, excited to have his next victim.

Whoever said looks could kill was right.

Hers had destroyed him as a child.

Now it was his turn to destroy her.

He laid her body out on the floor of the sanctuary he'd created for himself, the plastic beneath her crinkling as her limbs fell limply by her sides.

He paced, ticking off the information in his head as if a computer had been turned on, spewing out details.

There were three layers to the eye: the outer layer, the sclera, in which the cornea formed a bulge at the front of the eye; the middle layer, the choroid, which formed the iris toward the front; and the inner layer, the retina, which contained nerve cells that processed visual information and sent it to the brain.

That was the part he found most interesting. The retina had millions of sensitive nerve cells that converted light into nerve impulses.

So did her brain tell her eyes that she liked watching children be tormented, or was something about her nerve impulses warped?

Eyes were supposed to be precious gifts, enabling us to enjoy the beauty of the world.

But hers held nothing but ugliness. Evil.

Now those eyes stared, wide open, terror and shock etched into the brown irises, the whites bulging as if they might explode as she struggled to escape.

She had never expected him to find her. To seek revenge. She thought she'd obliterated his free will and the fight inside him, that she could control him with those devilish laser looks.

Not anymore.

He removed the scalpel from his pocket and held the shiny blade above the pale skin of her cheek, smiling as the steel glistened beneath the light. Cutting her up would be just like dissecting an animal.

She kicked harder, yanking at the heavy chains holding her down. The metal rattled, music to his ears, as panic distorted her stark features.

"What is the old adage about the eyes?" he murmured as he pressed the scalpel to her cheekbone.

She screamed, a shrill animal noise that echoed in the empty building, boomeranging over and over. They were so far from anyone that he didn't bother to try and stop her cries.

No one could hear her.

"Yes, yes, I know what it is," he said, his voice singsong. "'The eyes are the window to the soul.'"

She shook her head back and forth violently as if she'd suddenly guessed his intentions.

Really, she had odd features. The cheekbones were set too far apart. Her face was asymmetrical, one eyelid drooping lower than the other. A dark mole dotted the corner of her lip, a melanoma probably.

Odd that with her training, she hadn't bothered with treatment.

"Oh, and there's the other—'Beauty is in the eye of the beholder.'" His bitter laugh echoed off the concrete walls. "But there's nothing beautiful about you."

A tear seeped from her eye and trickled down her cheek, then another. His brain told him that this was simply nature's way of cleansing the eye; this woman had no real emotions.

His pulse pounding with lust for the kill, he pierced the skin below her left eye. The chains clanked with her protests. A drop of blood seeped from the scalpel point, whetting his appetite for more.

He leaned close to her ear, watching her terror as he whispered, "But you have no soul, do you?"

Slowly he raised the scalpel and jabbed it into her eye socket. She screamed, flailing and crying, the wretched sounds reverberating around him.

Soon she would realize that crying and screaming wouldn't help. And it sure as fuck wouldn't stop him.

Because he'd been called to rid the world of the ugliness, just as a preacher was called to give a sermon and save lost souls.

In a way, he was saving souls too. Saving others from the abuse this woman inflicted.

And he was just getting started.

---

Rafe wove through traffic, veering off on a desolate-looking road that seemed to lead to nowhere.

He and Liz lapsed into silence as they covered the miles. Dry grass and land stretched far across the countryside, an occasional house or roadside stand popping up. A gas station with a sign reading BOILED PEANUTS sat at the crossroads, a produce stand on the opposite side. Run-down chicken houses sat on a hill near a chimney marking where a house once stood.

Liz considered the profile of the killer. She needed more information first.

"Regina's son J. R. lives out here?" Liz asked.

Rafe nodded.

"I wonder what he does for a living."

"I suppose we'll find out." Rafe cut her a sideways look. "Liz, you didn't have to come back for this. You know I could have handled the case."

"True, but I need to work. I sure as heck don't intend to let what happened destroy me." Memories of Rafe looking at her with lust made her body tingle for his touch. They'd been attracted to each other from the start, but they'd tried to keep their relationship professional.

Rafe had big hands, strong hands. The things he could do with them made her crazy with desire.

She wanted to feel those hands on her again. Because his touch made her pain dissipate.

*Do. Not. Go. There.*

It had hurt too badly when he'd walked away to even consider getting close to him again.

And she had her secrets.

Besides, his look didn't hold desire now. More like disdain.

He turned onto a dirt road bearing a hand-painted sign that read HOG HOLLER, the SUV bouncing over gravel and ruts. The area was flat, the land parched and deserted, winter taking its toll. Why anyone would choose to live out here, she didn't know.

They veered around a curve, and then she spotted a small clapboard house on a hill. Beside it, several pigpens housed dozens of animals.

Mud splattered a long cement building that Liz assumed was the slaughterhouse.

An ax hung on the wall outside, stained in blood.

If Regina's son slaughtered animals for a living, he obviously had a strong stomach, and the sight of blood didn't disturb him.

Would he cut off a woman's hands to get revenge against her for hurting his mother?

———————— , ————————

Rafe scanned the property, his mind assimilating to the fact that Regina's son, J. R. Truitt, raised and slaughtered animals for a living. He also lived off the grid, miles from anywhere, meaning he could easily have brought Ester out here and killed her, and no one would have heard her scream for help.

Rafe parked, wiping perspiration from his forehead, the stench of the pig houses assaulting him as he climbed out. He blew out a breath to stifle the smell, then glanced at Liz, who coughed as she slid from the passenger side.

"You can stay in the car if you want," Rafe offered.

Her gaze shot to his.

Understanding dawned. She still didn't have closure over Harlan, and she thought she could make up for that lost feeling by locking up this killer.

Jesus. He understood the drive, the compulsion to solve a crime and bring justice.

He'd hoped to give that to her with her mother's killer.

But he'd failed. He'd missed something on the case—Harlan's real motive. Why he'd come after Liz's mother in the first place.

Why he'd stopped killing for years, then started again.

"I'm not going to fall apart on this case, Rafe. You can trust me."

That wasn't the problem. He didn't trust himself around her. And he sure as hell didn't want her anywhere near this latest psycho. "I do, but you also suffered a terrible trauma only a few months ago. Everyone needs time to recover."

Liz squeezed his hand. "Stop treating me with kid gloves. I survived. I've had therapy and time to heal."

"Have you?" he asked softly. "Healed, I mean?"

Pain darkened her eyes. "Rafe . . . please . . ."

Emotions crowded his throat. "I can't help but worry about you."

"I appreciate your concern," Liz said, struggling to keep her voice from quivering. "But I need to work, Rafe. I need to find this guy."

He was well aware of her devotion to her job, but he didn't necessarily like it. His gaze shot to the scarf around her neck. Images of her bloody body and weakened state, her throat slashed.

The front door of the house screeched open, jarring Rafe from his thoughts, and he swung around. A heavyset man with a shaved head, wearing overalls stood on the rickety porch, aiming a shotgun at them. Tattoos snaked up and down both arms, and his left hand was scarred badly, as if he'd been in an accident.

Or perhaps one of his hogs had mauled him.

He also seemed sweaty and out of breath, as if he'd been running, or he'd just gotten home.

"What the hell you doing on my property?" he bellowed.

"Mr. Truitt," Liz said, throwing up a hand to calm him. "I'm Special Agent Liz Lucas, and this is Special Agent Rafe Hood, with the TBI. We just want to talk."

Truitt kept the gun trained on them. "You're a fed?"

"Actually, the TBI is state." Rafe gestured to the gun. "Now, like I said, put down the gun."

"It's about your mother," Liz said.

"My mother is dead," he snarled.

"That's why we're here."

Rafe's hand itched to put Liz back into the car. To protect her. He stepped forward, half blocking her in case the man took a pot shot. "We talked to the staff at the nursing home where your mother stayed and heard that a nurse named Ester Banning mistreated your mother."

He shifted, lowering the shotgun to his side. "Yeah. But that was a long time ago."

"Not so long that you've forgotten what she did," Liz said softly.

"So?" he asked.

"Ester Banning's body was found in Slaughter Creek."

Truitt's lip curled up. "That bitch is dead?"

"Yes."

Truitt grunted. "I thought she was too mean to die." He rubbed a hand over his pocket.

Rafe stiffened, then stepped to the right, again trying to block Liz.

Instead of another weapon, though, Truitt pulled a cigarette and lighter from his pocket, propped the shotgun against the front of the house, and lit up.

"Haven't you seen the news?" Liz asked.

"Naw, TV's broke. And I don't get the paper out here."

Rafe cleared his throat. "We're trying to find out more about the Banning woman. If we can retrace her steps, find out where she went after she left the nursing home, it might lead us to her killer."

Eyes narrowed, Truitt took a long drag on his cigarette. Rafe stepped onto the porch, still worried about how the man might react when he realized they were treating him as a person of interest in Ester's murder.

Hoping to relax him, Liz paused to pet the mangy dog sprawled on the tattered plaid sofa on the porch, next to an old washing machine. Muddy work boots were tossed beside it. A broom, toolbox, and dust-coated dog bowl sat next to the door.

"I don't know where she went, and frankly I don't care." Truitt tapped ashes onto the porch floor.

"Mr. Truitt," Liz said, "we understand that you filed a lawsuit against Ester."

"Hell, yeah, I did. You would have too, if you'd seen bruises on your mama like I did. Bad bruises and bedsores." He cursed beneath his breath and blew smoke into the air. "But then Mama died, and the lawyer said the hospital fired Ester, so I figured wasn't no point in spending money to go to court."

"The hospital probably didn't want publicity," Rafe said. "We heard they gave another patient's family a deal to settle out of court."

Liz raised an eyebrow. "Did they cut you a deal, Mr. Truitt?"

Truitt's lips curled into a snarl again. "Do I look like I'm floatin' in money?"

"So that's a no?" Rafe asked.

Truitt shrugged. "A small settlement, not enough to amount to anything."

Rafe slanted him a cold look. "That probably pissed you off, didn't it? First Ester abuses your mother, then you try to sue, she dies, and the hospital insults you by barely giving you anything for your suffering."

"You wanted to get back at Ester, didn't you?" Liz said quietly.

Truitt reached for his gun. "I hated the woman, all right. But I didn't kill her. Now get off my property."

Rafe put one hand on the shotgun to keep Truitt from retrieving it. "Here's what I think. You run a slaughterhouse. It was probably nothing to you to lob off Ester's hands."

Truitt muttered a curse word, but Rafe didn't back down. "Leave the shotgun on the porch. You're going with us to answer a few more questions."

"I didn't do nothing," Truitt muttered

"Where were you last night?" Liz asked.

The big guy shrugged "Here."

Liz folded her arms. "Anyone with you?"

"My hogs."

"Unfortunately they can't alibi you." Rafe pointed to the bloody ax leaning against the concrete building, deciding that since they weren't getting anywhere, he'd play bad cop. "If we check that ax, we'll find Ester's blood on it, won't we?"

"Screw you," Truitt growled.

Liz cleared her throat, taking Rafe's lead to play good cop. "If you're innocent like you say, then we'll clear you, and you won't have to see us again."

Truitt glared at her. "All right, take the damn ax. That old bitch's blood ain't on it."

---

Liz phoned the chief to request a warrant for Truitt's farm. "We have motive and opportunity, and he has no alibi for the night of the murder."

"You think he did it?"

Liz glanced at the concrete slaughterhouse with revulsion. "I don't know. But the guy is . . . off. And he certainly was belligerent when we confronted him. Pulled a shotgun on us. And there's a bloodstained ax by the slaughterhouse."

"Could have been used on his hogs," the chief said.

"I know, but it could also be the murder weapon, so we have to process it."

"All right, I'll get the warrant. Lieutenant Maddison will bring it with him when his team comes out."

Liz studied Truitt. Last time she'd made a crucial mistake and missed the part about Harlan's partner.

Rafe stood beside the car where Truitt sat in the backseat, handcuffed. "Did you get the warrant?"

"The CSI team is bringing it." Liz yanked on gloves, removed the shells from the shotgun, and stowed Truitt's shotgun in the back of Rafe's SUV. "I'll wait here for the crime team if you want to drive him to the sheriff's office."

Rafe's dark eyes turned stony. "No way. I won't leave you alone in this godforsaken place."

"Then I'll drive Truitt to the station."

"Hell, no," Rafe said. "He weighs nearly three hundred pounds. He could crush you in a second."

Liz forced her voice to stay calm, though she was seething inside. "Rafe, you can't treat me like I'm not capable. If you don't respect me at work, no one else will."

His breath hissed out. "Dammit, Liz. It's not that I don't trust you. But you're small, and I don't want a repeat of last time's disaster."

Liz's heart stuttered at the self-recrimination in his voice. The last few months, she'd been too consumed by her own tumultuous feelings to realize that Rafe felt guilty.

"It wasn't your fault that he got me," she said. "We both just . . ."

"Screwed up," he said. "Because we let emotions interfere with our jobs."

Because they'd slept together.

"We won't repeat that mistake," she said.

"You're damn right we won't." He glanced at her scarf, a reminder that he saw her as weak. Scarred.

Not beautiful, as he once had.

That hurt, and made her even more angry.

Dammit, she shouldn't care how Rafe looked at her. Hadn't her therapist assured her that she was still attractive? That if a man really cared about her, he wouldn't even notice the scar?

But he saw it.

Still, like a fool, she wanted to touch him, tell him she didn't blame him. But touching him would only make her want more.

Too many nights she'd dreamed about working with him during the day, then having his arms around her, his big body next to her, keeping her warm and safe at night.

She couldn't reveal her weakness, or he'd sure as hell push to have her relieved of the job. And truthfully, she didn't think she could stand it if he rejected her.

A siren wailed in the distance. Liz stepped away from Rafe and went to meet the crime team as Jake's deputy roared up in a squad car to escort Truitt to the jail.

Hopefully when they searched the place, they'd find Ester's missing hand.

Unless Truitt had fed it to the hogs to get rid of the evidence.

# Chapter Six

———— o ————

Liz was grateful to search the house instead of the slaughter-house. Advances in the industry had made pig slaughtering and processing more humane, but judging from the house and setup, she doubted Truitt was that progressive.

The crime team took a walk through for obvious evidence before starting a thorough search.

Perkins adjusted his ball cap. "I'm going to work the slaugh-terhouse."

"I'll take the house," Castor agreed.

Liz watched Perkins head out across the yard to the brick building. He must have a strong stomach. He didn't even seem fazed by the stench, or the prospect of finding body parts.

She surveyed the house. Truitt obviously had an aversion to cleaning. Dust and grime coated every surface. Gun and farming magazines littered a scarred oak table, along with a stack of papers that looked like receipts from places where he sold his meat. A game show blared on an ancient TV in the background. The house smelled musty, as if something had rotted inside.

A body?

But there wasn't one evident.

She walked through the small five-room house, sizing up the interior to give herself a better idea of Truitt's character. The kitchen was cluttered, dried food crusted on the counter, the sink full of dishes that looked as if they hadn't been washed in weeks. A box of takeout fried chicken sat on the table.

Searching the cabinets next, she found an assortment of canned goods, garage-sale dishes, and battered pots and pans. Castor lifted a jar of pickled pig's feet from the counter.

Revulsion hit Liz, but an odd smile creased Castor's mouth. "Looks like he likes to keep some for himself." Castor opened the refrigerator and gestured toward the stacks of packages wrapped in butcher paper. "I'll check these out."

Relieved to let him take that job, she moved to the bedroom, noting a faded bedspread on an iron bed with the footboard sawed off.

The closet was tiny and held work boots, a pile of dirty clothes on the floor, flannel shirts, and more overalls.

She scrounged through the dresser drawers, which held only ratty underwear and socks. Anxious to finish, she checked under the bed and found a wooden box with a lock.

Her nerves tingled.

She removed a tool from her pocket and picked the lock. If they found Ester's missing hand, they'd have everything they needed to close the case.

But inside there were no body parts, just dozens of pictures of Truitt and his mother. Pictures of him as a kid on camping trips with her and a man Liz assumed was his father. Another one of Truitt fishing when he was a teenager.

Odd—why would he keep pictures in a locked box?

She studied a more recent shot. Mrs. Truitt had white hair and age-speckled skin, and wore a bed jacket as she lay propped on a stack of pillows.

Liz flipped it over and noted the date: just a few weeks before Mrs. Truitt's death.

An envelope below the photographs caught her eye, and she removed the papers inside with a frown. It was the settlement offer from the hospital.

They had given him a lousy ten thousand dollars.

Ten thousand was all the value they'd put on his mother's life?

Had that insulting settlement made Truitt angry enough to kill Ester?

She dug deeper and found another photo. A photo of Ester, taken from a distance.

Ester was entering a building called HomeBound. Liz quickly googled it on her phone and learned it was a home health care business.

She checked the date. The picture was taken after the settlement, which stipulated that Ester's license had been revoked and that she could no longer practice nursing in Tennessee.

Maybe Truitt had discovered that Ester had defied the contract and landed another job. Maybe that had triggered him to take matters into his own hands and kill her.

---

Rafe's phone buzzed just as he made his way back to his SUV to meet Liz. "Hood speaking."

"Rafe, it's Maddison. We found Ester Banning's last known address."

"Text it to me, and Liz and I will check it out. By the way, Truitt's on his way to the sheriff's office."

He disconnected just as Liz walked up. "Did you find anything in the house?"

"The hospital settlement papers Truitt signed. According to them, Ester's nursing license was revoked. But Truitt must have followed her. There was a picture of her entering a health care organization called HomeBound dated after the settlement."

Rafe chewed over that information. "Truitt definitely had motive and opportunity."

"He certainly did." Liz sighed. "Did you find anything in that building?"

"A lot of blood, but no human body parts." Rafe opened the door and slid into his SUV. "We'll have to wait and see if the lab analysis verifies that some of the blood is human. I have the address for Ester's home. Let's drive over and take a look."

Liz slid into the passenger seat. "I have to admit I'm glad to leave this place."

"Me, too. It takes a strong stomach to work in a slaughter-house."

Liz buckled her seat belt as he pulled down the drive. "People's occupational choice reveals a lot about their past and their personality."

Just as his choice to hunt down killers did.

He'd grown up in foster care, bouncing around from house to house, never quite belonging or feeling wanted.

Seeing kids smaller than him being picked on and abused had roused his anger, and he hadn't always channeled it in productive ways, landing himself in trouble more often than not. His smart mouth hadn't helped, and he'd locked horns with his foster fathers, especially the ones who took their frustration and rage out on innocent kids.

When one of his foster sisters died at the hands of the family the two of them had been placed with, he'd lost it.

He ratted out the couple who'd locked the girl in a closet, beaten her, and rarely fed her, instead using the money they got for taking care of her to buy booze and cigarettes. The system had let her down badly.

He'd realized then what he wanted to do with his life. He had to make a difference; he had to stand up for those weaker than him.

Just like little Benny at the Boys' Club needed someone to stand up for him now.

Rafe couldn't get that kid out of his mind. Benny reminded him of himself at that age. Scared. Alone. Small for his age, but tough. Benny never cried. It was almost as if he saw it as a weakness.

Hell, he understood that. Caring meant letting people in your heart. And losing them hurt. Better not to hope for a family or a real life.

Put up a wall and pretend you didn't need anyone.

The boy needed a home. Rafe just hoped the social worker found one for him soon.

In spite of the temperature drop, Liz powered her window down as if she needed fresh air to wash away the smell of that farm, and Rafe did the same. Wind whistled through the trees, beating the SUV and tossing pine needles across the road and onto the windshield.

Liz propped her elbow against the door edge and leaned her head against her hand. "You've been busy working other cases these last few months?"

Rafe tensed. "A couple." But that didn't mean he hadn't still been hunting for Harlan.

"I wanted to call," he said by way of an apology.

"I didn't expect you to," she said quietly.

Her comment made him feel even more like a heel. "It's not because I—"

"Don't." Liz waved a hand to ward off his explanation. "You don't have to say anything. We both got caught up in the case, the adrenaline high, the . . . tension. Once the case ended, I knew it was over."

Because her expectations for men were so low? Or because she thought so little of him?

Hell, if she only knew how many times he'd driven by her place, parked, almost knocked on her door.

How many times he'd punched her number and hung up before she answered. He'd wanted to tell her they could see where their relationship might take them.

He'd never felt like that about a woman before, and it scared the hell out of him.

But he'd restrained himself; he knew Liz needed time to heal from the trauma of the case and Harlan's attack on her. She was vulnerable, and he would have been a bastard to take advantage of that vulnerability. So he'd given her time. Space.

And reaffirmed his resolve to keep his emotions and heart out of work.

Because caring for someone meant putting her in danger.

They lapsed into silence until they reached a run-down apartment complex that had been built for low-income families. Battered toys were scattered around, an old pickup and Chevy were parked in the grass beside the unit where Ester had supposedly lived, and weeds choked the patches of grass between the ground-floor units.

He glanced around for security cameras but didn't see any. A streetlight burned at the end of the lot, but the one in front of Ester's place had been broken.

Rafe parked, and Liz jumped out as soon as he cut the engine. Together they walked up the cracked sidewalk, a stiff breeze stirring the leaves and sending trash across the yard.

Mud stained the concrete building, and the shutters desperately needed paint. Liz knocked on the door, and Rafe scanned the area for signs of life.

When no one answered, Liz knocked again, tapping her foot as she waited. Rafe stepped to the side and peered through one of the front windows. Broken blinds allowed him to glimpse inside.

Worn furniture filled a tiny den cluttered with books, DVDs, and yellowed newspapers. But there was no movement inside.

Rafe jiggled the door, and it screeched open. A musty odor mingled with the smell of stale beer and damp carpet.

Rafe used his flashlight to illuminate a path, and they picked their way through the cluttered den.

It looked as if there had been a struggle in the bedroom. The bedside lamp had been overturned and lay shattered on the floor. The bedding was torn and smeared with blood. The blinds were broken and hung askew, as if Ester had grabbed at them to save herself from a fall.

More blood stained the carpet, which was scuffed as if a body had been dragged across the room.

"Looks like Ester Banning was abducted from the house."

Liz phoned Maddison. "Yes, we're at Ester Banning's apartment. Send a team to process the place."

Rafe began to snap pictures and search the bedroom for evidence.

Liz ended the call, removed latex gloves from her pocket, and yanked them on. "I'll check the bathroom."

Leaning over to examine the bed, Rafe plucked a hair from the corner of the faded spread and bagged it to send to the lab. The door to the closet was ajar, mud marring the floor.

Calling Lieutenant Maddison again, Rafe asked him to collect the pig farmer's shoes, especially those with mud on them, and to take samples of the soil outside his house and by the slaughterhouse for comparison.

If the samples matched, they could nail Truitt, close the case, and give the dead woman justice. Not that she deserved it, from what he'd learned about her, but at least it would indicate that this was an isolated case.

That they weren't dealing with a serial killer.

---

The voices whispered inside Amelia Nettleton's head again as she looked out over Slaughter Creek. The voices of the alters.

Skid's. Viola's. Then Bessie's.

Sweet little Bessie, the scared little kid who'd turned to the alters for help. Viola, the hussy who liked sex and men. Skid, the violent teenager full of rage.

She'd managed to stifle those voices, but a new alter was fighting to take control.

Rachel, a religious zealot, had started talking to her. Rachel called Amelia a whore for seeking comfort in a man's arms.

*Because he's the wrong man.*

He was part of the project.

Six.

*Ting. Ting. Ting.* The wind chimes tinkled.

She hadn't known that when she'd met him in the park a few weeks ago, though. She was deep in therapy, working hard to merge her multiple personalities, and she'd been painting a scene from her mind—one where she'd been strapped to a table and the Commander was standing over her.

When she'd glanced up, Six was standing in the shadows, watching her. She'd been terrified at first, afraid he was working for Arthur Blackwood.

But he'd told her how beautiful her painting was. How real. How much depth it had.

Then she realized he was familiar, that she knew him.

She admitted that her painting felt real because she'd lived that scene. Then she shared her story, that she'd spent time at Slaughter Creek Sanitarium. That she was purging her hatred on canvas for the man who'd stolen half her life so she could finally be free of him.

He smiled and assured her that he understood.

Something about him had drawn her to his side. To his bed.

Of course he'd felt familiar and understood—he'd been there with her. They'd shared a childhood that most people couldn't imagine, much less understand.

She shivered, wrapping her arms around herself as she searched the woods. Images of the Commander flashed behind every tree. His evil eyes glaring at her. His icy, hard voice ordering her to kill herself.

Sadie had saved her that night.

Amelia owed it to her twin now to be strong. But what if *he* came back for her?

Her phone buzzed, and she skimmed the text.

*Meet me at midnight.*

Amelia began to tremble. What was she going to do?

At first the sex with Six had been exciting. Exhilarating. He'd made her feel special. Wanted. Desirable.

Until his dark side had emerged. A dark side that she'd also been drawn to. Or at least Viola had. Viola had a penchant for rough, violent sex.

Knowing Six's dark side, she'd wondered if he'd killed the woman in the newspaper, Ester Banning.

If so, she had to tell Sadie and Jake . . .

But how could she betray Six? He'd suffered too much already, just as they all had.

She rubbed her arms to ward off a chill. She'd meet him and find out.

But another voice reverberated inside her head, one she didn't recognize, whispering a warning that meeting him was dangerous.

That if he'd murdered Ester, he might turn his rage on her at some point.

She'd worked too hard to survive to die now.

# Chapter Seven

———— o ————

Liz searched Ester's desk drawer while Rafe walked next door to begin canvassing the neighborhood, in case any of the residents had known Ester or had seen the killer.

In the drawer, Liz found past-due receipts for rent, power, and phone bills, along with a checkbook that indicated Ester had been overdrawn. She looked for an address book, computer, or cell phone, without any luck. When she picked up the handset for the house phone, there was no dial tone. The phone company had probably discontinued service.

Beneath a bag of rubber bands and a box of paper clips, she found a business card with the logo for the health care company HomeBound–the same company she'd seen in Truitt's picture—printed in bold letters at the top.

Liz stuffed the card into her pocket. She'd pay them a visit.

A fake leather purse lay on the floor next to a wooden chair in the kitchen. She rummaged through it: lip gloss, Kleenex, a wallet with a driver's license. There were no credit cards and only a few pennies in cash. Keys to the apartment were inside, but no car keys.

She dug deeper and found a phone number scribbled on a piece of paper. Curious, she punched in the number.

"Hayes State Prison," a voice answered.

Suspicions rose in her mind—that was the prison where the Commander had been incarcerated.

———————— , ————————

Rafe directed the crime team to rope off Ester's house and search for forensic evidence.

The two units next to Ester's were empty, but lights were on in the third. A young woman in her twenties answered when he knocked on the door, two toddlers hanging on to her leg.

He identified himself and explained about the investigation. "Did you know Ester Banning?"

The woman ushered the kids behind her as if to protect them. "I spoke to her in passing a couple of times, but we weren't friends."

"What did you think of her?"

She stooped down, told the kids to go into the den and play, and waited until they'd run off before answering him. "She didn't like children," she said. "One day the boys were playing outside and tossed a plastic ball into the yard in front of her place. She went ballistic. I thought she was going to hit little Barry."

The more he heard, the less Rafe liked Ester. "Did she have any visitors? A man maybe?"

The woman shook her head. "I never saw anyone over there. I don't think she had many friends. She was . . . she seemed bitter about something. Angry all the time. I couldn't believe she was actually a nurse."

Rafe frowned. "How about last night? Did you see anyone there?"

"I'm afraid not. My husband was out of town, so the kids and I stayed at my sister's." She gestured toward her apartment. "This is just temporary, you know, till my husband finds work again."

Rafe handed her a business card. "Call me if you think of anything else. And, ma'am, please be careful."

Her eyes widened as if it had never occurred to her that she might be in danger. "You think whoever killed her might come back here? Is he targeting residents in the complex?"

"No, the murder was personal. But a dangerous prisoner has escaped the state pen and hasn't been recovered."

She chewed on her lip, with a wary expression, then shut the door, and he heard the lock turning. He walked to the next unit and knocked, and an elderly man answered. Once again Rafe explained the reason for his visit.

"Did you know Ester Banning?"

"That's that woman they found at the creek?"

Rafe nodded. "It appears she was abducted from her apartment."

"Jesus, what is this world coming to?" The man rubbed his comb-over with a shaky hand.

"Did you know her?"

"I saw her coming and going, but she didn't speak. I thought that was odd, being she was a nurse. I sure as hell wouldn't want her tending to me if I was sick."

His comment confirmed everything else Rafe had heard. He thanked the man and canvassed the rest of the units, but no one else was home.

When he made it back to Ester's, Liz met him outside. "Did you find anything?" she asked.

"Nothing new. Apparently Ester wasn't very friendly, disliked children, and wasn't the compassionate kind."

Liz flashed a business card at him. "Then why did HomeBound hire her?"

---

An hour later Liz and Rafe entered the office for HomeBound, identified themselves, and explained the reason for their visit.

The director of the center, a man in his early thirties with thick black hair, a goatee, and wire-rimmed glasses introduced himself as Charles Samson. He seemed young to be in the position of director.

"Mr. Samson, how long have you worked at HomeBound?"

"A few weeks." He gestured for them to take a seat in his office. "I took over when the former director retired because of health concerns."

Liz showed him Ester's photograph and the business card she'd found at Ester's. "Did you hire her?"

The young man studied the picture for a moment. "She applied a couple of weeks ago. We were checking her references, but when I called to follow up, she didn't return my call."

"So you didn't give her an assignment?"

"No, we were still checking her references. Why?"

"She was murdered."

Mr. Samson's jaw dropped. "When? How did it happen?"

"That's what we're trying to determine," Liz said. "You met her in person?"

Mr. Samson nodded. "She said she'd moved to the area and needed work. We're always trying to fill spots for patients in need."

"How about her references?"

He clicked a few keys on his computer, then looked up at her. A scowl slanted his mouth. "Hmm . . . my assistant made a note that she called both references, but there was no one at the facilities by the name she gave."

"She didn't expect you to check her references?" Liz asked.

Samson's brows furrowed. "Actually, the references were over ten years old, so no surprise that the people she listed no longer worked there. We planned to follow up and see if she had more current addresses for them." He stood, then buttoned his jacket. "I'm afraid I can't tell you anything else about her. I hope you find the person who killed her."

They thanked him and headed to the car. "That was a dead end," said Liz.

A heartbeat passed. "Let's talk to Truitt. Maybe he's ready to spill his guts."

Liz hoped he was right. Still, she had more questions, so she phoned the prison and asked the head of security about the call Ester had made to the prison. It took him a moment to find the recording.

"What did she want?" Liz asked.

"To see if Commander Blackwood was allowed visitors. Of course she was told no."

"Did she say why she wanted to see him?"

"No. She just hung up when she discovered that his visitors were restricted."

Damn. With Ester dead and Blackwood missing, they might never know why she wanted to see him.

But Liz would bet her job that it had something to do with the project. And it might have something to do with the reason she was killed.

———————— , ————————

Rafe drove toward the Slaughter Creek jail, contemplating their conversation with Samson. When they entered, the deputy greeted them with a grimace.

"That pig farmer bellowed the whole way here."

"What did he say?" Rafe asked.

The deputy shrugged. "About how unfair it was that we brought him in. He kept yelling that the Banning bitch deserved to die."

From what he'd heard so far, Rafe couldn't argue. But he didn't believe in letting people take the law into their own hands.

Except . . . he wanted to do that to the sadistic man who'd hurt Liz.

"We'll question him now." Rafe and Liz stepped through the doors leading to the back while the deputy moved Truitt from his cell into the interrogation room. Liz paced the room, her body jittery.

"It's scary to think that HomeBound was about to send Ester out to tend to another patient. Makes you wonder about the health care industry."

"There are good people and bad in every business," Rafe said.

The door opened, and the deputy escorted a handcuffed Truitt inside. His jowls were red with anger, his scowl menacing. "You got no right to hold me!" he yelled.

"Sit down," said Rafe.

Liz situated herself in a chair across from him. "All you have to do is answer some questions. Help us clear things up."

Rafe propped his hands on the table and leaned forward, hoping to intimidate Truitt as he slumped into the chair. "Tell us what happened. When did you decide to kill Ester? Was it after the lawsuit?" Rafe laid the settlement agreement they'd confiscated from Truitt's house on the table.

"You had to be insulted when they gave you that pitiful offer," Liz said. "As if ten thousand is enough to pay for your mother's life."

Truitt's eyes flickered with rage. "You had no right to look through my stuff."

"We had every right," Liz said. "Ester Banning mistreated your mother. You hated her and had a motive to kill her."

"That don't mean I did it!" Truitt stood and slammed his fists on the table. His handcuffs jangled in the silence that followed.

Rafe raised an eyebrow. "You obviously have a violent streak."

Sweat trickled down Truitt's jaw.

"If a caretaker, especially a nurse who I trusted, hurt someone in my family, I'd want to get back at her," Rafe continued.

Truitt's eyes darted to the door, but a second later he must have realized that escaping was impossible, and he dropped back into the chair. "All right, I admit I hated the mean bitch. And I'm not sorry she's gone. But I didn't kill her." He gestured toward his fingers, which he spread out on the table. "My hands are clean of that."

Rafe noted the dirt under the man's nails. "Then you won't mind if I scrape beneath your nails to make sure there's no human tissue or blood there."

A vein pulsed in Truitt's forehead. "Go ahead. If that's what it takes to clear me, have at it."

---

Liz rolled her shoulders to alleviate the tension thrumming through her. Night had fallen, her headlights slicing across the asphalt as she drove along the winding road toward her house.

Her ears popped as she climbed the mountain, and she swallowed, slowing as a deer raced from the woods across the road. She'd driven these mountains forever, but still on nights like tonight, when images of death and violence filled her head, shadowy ghosts floated between the trees, and the cries of the dead floated around her.

Hoping to calm her nerves with her favorite acoustics, she flipped on the radio, scanning through until she found the Coffee House station. Another car zoomed up on her tail, and she checked her rearview mirror.

His headlights were so bright that the glare was blinding her. She flipped the mirror up to diffuse the light, blinking to clear her vision. But the car jolted forward, then sped up beside her, skimming her side, jolting her toward the embankment.

She gripped the steering wheel, slowing to let him pass. The road twisted sharply right, and she swerved just in time to avoid plunging into the ravine as the other car raced on. She squinted to read the license plate, but the sedan had already disappeared into the darkness like a bullet.

Her breath puffed out as she righted her vehicle and accelerated. She wanted to catch the other car, but another curve caught her off guard, and she skimmed the guardrail. Reminding herself that it wasn't worth dying to catch the creep, who was probably drunk, she forced herself to slow as she pulled back into her lane.

By the time she'd reached her house, her muscles felt as strained as her nerves. She parked, then looked through the windshield, and thought she saw the silhouette of a man.

Ned Harlan was standing in the shadows behind a moonlit live oak.

Could it be . . .

All these days and nights she'd imagined him coming back for her. Whispering her name in the dark.

Slitting her throat until the blood drained from her.

Her therapist had convinced her she was delusional, suffering from PTSD.

But this didn't look like a damn illusion to her.

She pulled her weapon and got out of the car. She would kill him this time.

But when she inched closer, the image faded.

God . . . she blinked to regain her focus.

She scanned left and right. Trees rustled. Gray clouds moved, covering the moon, making it even darker. A bobcat wailed from somewhere in the mountains.

After the attack, she'd seen Harlan everywhere. On the street. In the coffee shop. In the woods behind her house.

In the street when she'd gone shopping.

Her therapist assured her that her reaction was normal, that victims often felt as if their attackers had returned to stalk them.

That Ned Harlan was dead.

Her hand shook as she held her weapon at the ready, making her way up the sidewalk to her front door. Leaves rustled in the wind, and the sound of her own erratic breathing filled her ears.

Had she imagined Harlan's face watching her?

She fumbled with her key, but finally managed to unlock the door. She'd left a light on in the den—she always left a light on—but it was off now. A tremor ran through her as she reached for the light switch.

Then the faint scent of a man's aftershave hit her. A musky odor.

Harlan's scent. Dear God, *was* he alive?

Or was she imagining things again?

# Chapter Eight

———— o ————

Rafe didn't want to make the drive back to his cabin. He wanted to be close in case Liz needed him.

Why he felt that way, he didn't know. Hell, it had been months since he'd seen her. Since the night she was rushed to the ER.

But this case stirred up old anxieties and memories. Memories of that night.

And the nights in bed with Liz, the best nights he'd ever had.

He rented a room at the Slaughter Creek Inn, then walked across the street to the diner for a late dinner. The place was virtually empty, although when he entered he heard two old-timers talking about Ester Banning's murder.

A middle-aged waitress brought him a plate of country-fried steak, mashed potatoes, gravy, and biscuits. He thanked her, then dug in, but his phone buzzed halfway through.

"Rafe, it's Nick. Any progress on the murder?"

"Too early to say. We brought a man in for questioning—a pig farmer whose mother was abused by Banning. He admits to hating her, had motive and opportunity, but we didn't get a confession. I thought sitting in jail overnight might change his mind." Rafe sipped his sweet tea. They could hold him for twenty-four hours, but then they'd have to charge him or let the bastard go. "How about news on the Commander?"

"Nothing definitive there either. We questioned Seven, but she's not talking. And so far we haven't found a connection between the Banning woman and my father. She wasn't on the visitor log, and none of the inmates near Blackwood's cell remembered hearing him talk about her. We'll keep looking."

"So how did he escape?"

"Took a homemade dose of some concoction to make him sick enough to go to the infirmary. Stabbed a guard there, then stole his uniform and weapon. All the authorities have been notified at the airports, bus stations, train stations, and ports."

They suspected the Commander had connections that ran deep and wide, though. He'd been involved with the CIA. Hell, the government could have helped him escape to keep him from disclosing information about the project. Not that Blackwood had talked. But since Senator Stowe's arrest, no one was safe.

Everyone was a suspect.

———————— · ————————

Liz inhaled deeply as she entered her house, reminding herself that she was a professional agent. She was trained. Smart.

And she'd learned her lesson.

Sure, Harlan had gotten the jump on her once, but he'd caught her off guard because his accomplice had approached her, pretending to be a woman in trouble, one of Harlan's victims fleeing the cabin where Liz had tracked him. Liz's protective instincts toward females had kicked in, overriding her sense that something was off, that she was walking into a trap.

She'd never let down her guard again.

Holding her gun at the ready, she started to call for backup. But she was taking antianxiety medication, and if Rafe found that out, she'd look unstable.

She quickly scanned the den and kitchen, an open room with a bay window overlooking the woods and river.

She eased open the pantry. Everything seemed in place. No one inside.

One look at the corner chair where she kept her crocheting, and something about the way the supplies were arranged struck her as odd—had she left the yellow blanket on top, or the purple one?

*God, you are crazy, Liz. An intruder certainly wouldn't bother with your craft supplies.*

But paranoia still seized her, defying common sense. Her hands shook and her vision blurred as images of the dark place where Harlan had held her resurfaced. There was no air, she couldn't breathe . . .

She counted to ten to calm herself. She could not relapse now. Could not give in to those damned panic attacks.

Inching her way down the hall, she glanced in the bathroom, then her office, finding them empty as well.

Tension knotted her muscles as she eased her way to the master suite. But the room looked intact. Her bedding was in place, the windows closed, her vanity just as scattered with jewelry and makeup as she'd left it.

Her vanity was in complete disarray. She kept telling herself she'd organize it, but she never seemed to find the time.

Her therapist had actually applauded her for being able to let go in that one area of her life.

Liz must have fooled her, if she thought Liz was in control. Just the hint of an intruder had brought it all back.

She summoned her courage, determined to prove she was on solid ground.

If one day on the job made her come unglued to the point of imagining Harlan again, she'd never convince Rafe she was stable enough to work with him.

She inhaled several deep breaths, struggling to separate reality from delusions. But the lines were blurred . . . she still smelled him in her house. Garlic . . . the faint scent of garlic clung in the air. Garlic . . .

He'd chop it up and put it in the food he gave his victims, food to make them sick. So sick they'd be weak and couldn't fight him . . .

Yes, chop, chop, he'd told her as he'd sharpened his knife. Chop, chop, he'd cut the vegetables and smash the garlic.

Chop, chop, he'd slice her neck . . .

She shuddered, nausea burgeoning. He had been here, hadn't he?

Or was that smell only in her head as well?

---

The wind chimes tinkled as Amelia slipped outside her condo to meet her lover. *Ting. Ting. Ting.* They were music to her ears. Playing a beautiful melody that the wind and nature created on its own.

Now she knew her infatuation with them had come from the experiment.

But she refused to give them up. They were both a good and a bad reminder of the past, and she chose to focus on the positive.

Still, her mind raced with dos and don'ts. Sadie had urged her to pack so they could leave for the safe house in the morning.

The thought of being confined reminded her of her days at the sanitarium. Sadie assured her they'd take canvases and paints. Painting was the one time she felt safe.

Sane.

But would she ever be?

Jake insisted she and Sadie both needed protection from Arthur Blackwood. And so did Ayla. Jake's five-year-old was the Commander's only grandchild. What if he tried to kidnap her?

Amelia would die herself to protect that precious child.

She wove through the garden, missing the summer flowers but enjoying the hardy ones that, thanks to several of the residents' gardening skills, bloomed year-round.

The moon painted a path through the foliage as the sound of frogs and crickets echoed in the air.

A breeze made goose bumps scatter on her arms, and she considered turning around and running back to her place. If she hid from Six, she'd never have to know if he'd been bad.

Never have to ask him if the experiment had turned him into a killer.

The sound of leaves rustling made her pause, and she clenched her teeth, battling the voice in her head. Rachel whispered that she was a whore, that she should repent and run from this man.

That sex was dirty and wrong.

She shut out the voice.

Amelia reached the creek, where the air was filled with the sound of the water rippling over the jagged rocks. But suddenly she sensed someone else there.

A shadow moved from an oak tree. Then his hands were on her. "I've missed you."

His breath bathed her neck, and then his lips trailed kisses down her throat. Amelia's knees buckled. In spite of her fears, she had missed him, too.

But if he'd murdered that woman, she had to break it off. She had to tell Sadie and Jake . . .

"Did you miss me, Amelia?"

In spite of her common sense, erotic sensations heated her blood, and she turned in his arms. They had known each other since they were children. Had suffered together under the Commander's thumb.

He couldn't be the man who'd cut off that woman's hands.

His fingers skated down her arms, and then he peeled away her blouse. Cool air brushed her nipples as he stripped her lacy bra and placed his lips on her tender skin.

Amelia moaned. She'd been alone so long, had struggled with the voices in her head.

Had nearly died at the hands of Blackwood.

She refused to let him take everything away.

Six knew the truth about her, and he still wanted her. Still found her desirable.

What other man would?

She was broken. Damaged.

She clung to him now, desperately needing that love.

He closed his lips around one nipple and tugged it into his mouth. She gripped his arms, holding on to him as he pushed her down to the ground.

Their clothes flew off, and he entered her with a deep, hard thrust. She closed her eyes and savored the feeling of his thickness inside her as he built a frantic rhythm, naked skin gliding against skin, sweat mingling, their breaths rasping out as her orgasm claimed her, and he tipped over the edge with her.

They lay curled on the ground together for several minutes, but reality broke through the euphoric haze surrounding Amelia. "Did you know that the Commander escaped?"

Six stilled in her arms and looked at her with a coldness that she'd never seen before. "We are what we are because of him," he said finally.

Fear seized Amelia, as she recalled the image of Ester Banning's dead face, and she pushed away. "I have to go."

He grabbed her arm. "Why are you running from me, Amelia?"

"I'm not running," Amelia said, her voice cracking. "But Sadie and her husband, Jake—he's the sheriff, you know—want us to go to a safe house until the Commander's caught."

"Yes, the Commander might come after us," Six said. "Do what your sister says. I don't want him to ever hurt you again."

Tension thrummed through Amelia. "What about you? He might target you, too."

"Don't worry about me," Six said, an evil glint in his eyes. "I'm not that terrified kid anymore. If he tracks me down, I'll cut off his damn head. Killing him is the only way we'll ever be free."

A shudder coursed through Amelia, and she quickly dressed, then ran back toward her condo and locked herself inside.

Inside, she picked up her paints and began to purge her emotions. An image of the Commander found its way onto her canvas, only this time his head had been cut off.

And Six was standing over him, smiling at the blood soaking the man's chest.

# Chapter Nine

———— o ————

S he couldn't breathe.

*He jabbed the tip of the knife into her throat, and she tried to scream, but the sound came out as a gurgle, and she felt blood trickle down her neck.*

*Sorrow wrenched her chest.*

*He was going to kill her, and no one would know what he'd done. She'd never finish the case. Get justice for her mother.*

*Get married and have a family.*

*Her mother's voice whispered for her to fight, and she grabbed at his hand, trying to yank it away. But he was stronger than her, and he pressed his knee into her chest and held her down . . .*

*Suddenly Rafe's voice broke into the night. Rafe was here . . . Rafe would save her. They'd take Harlan to jail, and she'd have justice for her mother.*

Liz jerked awake, panting for breath as she rubbed the scar on her neck. Sunlight streamed through the window. She pushed the covers aside and stood, surveying her bedroom.

Harlan wasn't inside. She'd had another nightmare.

She was safe, and he was gone.

But when she glanced in the mirror, that confounded jagged line on her neck mocked her. Trembling, she reached for her pills on the nightstand and tossed one down, inhaling deeply to fight the panic.

God . . . she had to get a grip . . .

Determined to get back to work, she jumped in the shower. The hot water helped to alleviate the tension in her muscles, and she shampooed her hair and rinsed it. Harlan's scent still clung to her as if he'd actually touched her again.

Hoping to elicit a confession from Truitt today, she dried off and dressed, then pulled her hair back at the nape of her neck. She added a scarf to camouflage her scar. But as she grabbed her phone, her calendar reminded her of the date.

Her mother's birthday.

Grief welled inside her. But as she stepped into the den for her purse and keys, she froze. Chilly morning air assaulted her—cool air blowing through the open French doors to the screened porch.

Doors that had been locked last night.

Or had she been so upset she'd forgotten? Sometimes the antianxiety meds clouded her mind.

Her training urged her to call for backup, but if she cried wolf every time she saw a shadow, she'd surely get pulled from the case.

Perspiration beaded on her neck as she hurriedly checked the house. There was no one inside, but the same aftershave she'd smelled the night before lingered in the air.

No, he was not back. This case was simply triggering her paranoia.

When she was first released from the hospital after the attack, she'd suffered terrible nightmares. A few times she'd even walked in her sleep—or, rather, run outside, wandering mindlessly, terrified, trying to flee her demons.

Sometimes she'd woken in the woods or her car. Her therapist said she was suffering from PTSD, that sleepwalking was her way of trying to escape.

Irritated with herself, she locked the door, then walked outside to her car. She scanned the edges of her property for Harlan, but didn't see him, so she opened the car door.

Her breath caught in her throat. A bouquet of white roses lay in the passenger seat. White roses just like the ones she placed on her mother's grave every year on her birthday.

She'd planned to pick up some today and take them by the cemetery.

But she hadn't bought them last night.

Her chest constricted at the message scribbled in red on the card.

"Till we meet again."

---

Rafe sipped his coffee while he checked the police databases for information on Truitt.

Although the man had no priors, complaints had been filed against him for inhumane treatment of his pigs. He made a decent living with his pork business, but in the last few years bad publicity from animal activists and competition from more progressive pig farmers had cut into his profits.

So he needed that settlement.

Rafe drummed his fingers on his desk and then called the crime lab. "Any word on the forensics from Ester Banning's house?"

"Blood was the Banning woman's," Lieutenant Maddison said. "Truitt's prints were not in the house."

"So he wore gloves. What's new?"

"The mud on Truitt's shoes came from his farm, but it didn't match the dirt we found in Banning's house either."

Damn. "Any sign of the missing hand?"

"No. We also found more human blood at Truitt's, and will compare it to Truitt's when we get a sample."

"How about the stun guns? Did any of them match the size of the marking on Banning?"

"Afraid not."

Rafe chewed over the facts. Did they have the wrong man? "He could have ditched the stun gun he used, or buried it somewhere."

"True. Oh, but there's something interesting," Maddison said. "We did find a grave on his property."

"What?" Rafe's pulse jumped. "Why the hell didn't you tell me that up front?"

"Because we haven't identified the body yet."

"What *can* you tell me?"

"It was a female."

———————— ∕ ————————

Liz's hand trembled as she debated whether to take the flowers to the crime lab. If Harlan had left them to torment her, he would have worn gloves.

He *always* wore gloves.

Hate for the man who'd stolen so much from her mushroomed. If he was alive, she'd find him, and this time she'd make certain he was dead.

Determination renewed, she decided she had to play it by the book; she would take them in. She glanced around her property again, half expecting to see him watching her, but he was clever.

If he was alive, she'd see him only when he wanted her to.

Survival instincts kicked in. She wouldn't let him win by falling apart.

Tamping down her fear, she drove to the florist and purchased her own white roses, then stopped by the cemetery. Wind tossed dry leaves across the graves, fake flowers bending and swaying beneath the force. Gravel crunched beneath her shoes. She glanced at the church next to the cemetery, willing some peace into her soul, and then hurried to her mother's grave.

For a moment, she simply sat, taking in several deep breaths to calm herself, a technique her therapist had taught her.

As her nerves calmed and her hands stopped shaking, she removed the dead flowers from the vase at the head of her mother's tombstone and arranged the white roses in it instead.

The activity brought a sense of peace. Memories of her childhood resurfaced. When she was a little girl, Liz used to crawl onto the bed and watch her mother brush her waist-length hair, then braid it. She'd insist her mother help her fix her own hair the same way.

Her mother's warm smile lit up the room at breakfast, and she had the voice of an angel. A refrain of "Stand by Your Man" played in Liz's ears, making her smile. Her mother could have made it in Nashville as a country singer.

But instead of pursuing fame, she'd devoted her life to social work, helping lost children find homes and raising money for needy children, especially orphans. Liz had spent dozens of holidays helping her decorate children's wards at hospitals for parties and handing out gifts at Christmas in various orphanages.

Guilt swamped Liz. The morning before her mother disappeared, they'd argued. Her mother wanted Liz to help her at a charity that day, but Liz insisted she had more important plans.

Sneaking off to make out with her boyfriend.

That argument was the last conversation the two of them had before she died. Her mother had known that Liz loved her, hadn't she?

Tears streamed down her cheeks. "I'm so sorry, Mom. If I had it to do over, I'd go with you. I'd spend every minute I could with you." If she'd been with her mother, she might have been able to save her from Harlan.

Liz touched her throat, swallowing hard as emotions pummeled her.

The sensation that someone was watching her swept over her, and she turned and scanned the graveyard.

"Where are you, you bastard? If you want me, come and get me."

But only the sound of the wind rustling the trees and her voice drifted back.

A second later, an engine rumbled. Liz jumped up and ran across the graveyard toward the church. A dark sedan squealed from the parking lot and swerved onto the road. She strained to see the driver, but the windows were tinted.

Furious, she hurried to her car—but went cold when she saw the passenger's seat.

It was empty.

The flowers—her proof—were gone.

She jumped into her car to chase the sedan. Her tires squealed as she peeled from the parking lot, speeding away and veering onto a side road ahead.

Liz pressed the accelerator, gaining speed. By the time she made it to the turn, though, the dark sedan had disappeared. She slammed the steering wheel with her hand in frustration then swung onto the road.

Suddenly the sedan shot out from behind a tree, racing straight toward her.

Liz swerved to avoid hitting it head on. Tires screeched, gears grinding as she braked, but she lost the fight for control. Her car careened to the right and dove nose first into the ditch.

---

"I need to talk to you, Truitt."

Truitt sat up with his knees spread, his elbows braced on top of them. He'd been pulling his hair, and the mangy ends looked scraggly and damp with sweat. "What now?"

Rafe leaned against the bars. "Tell me about the body on your property. The *female* body buried by the house."

"Ah, shit." Truitt dragged out the last word as if it had three syllables.

Rafe crossed his arms. "Who is she, Truitt? Did you practice on her before you killed Ester Banning?"

Truitt stomped toward Rafe, then pressed his face against the cell bars. "Listen to me, I ain't killed nobody. That body belongs to my mama."

Rafe tensed. "Your mother?"

"Yes." Truitt's beard bristled as he rubbed his hand across his chin. "And before you go asking, that's what she wanted, to be buried at home."

"It's illegal to bury someone on your property," Rafe pointed out.

"Mama said that farm was home, and she wanted to stay there forever."

"Do you have any proof that those were her wishes? Maybe you just decided to save yourself some money on a funeral service and tombstone."

"It's not like that," Truitt snarled. "Mama told her preacher her last wishes. You can ask him."

"I intend to," Rafe said. "Just as I intend to verify that that body does belong to your mother, not another victim you've chopped up."

He strode from the room and then paced outside the sheriff's office, worry knotting his gut. If Truitt hadn't killed the Banning woman, the unsub was still on the loose.

Or he could have a partner.

He phoned Liz. Her phone rang once, twice, three times. Finally she answered, her breathing choppy.

"Liz, where are you?"

"I'm sorry, Rafe, I'll be there soon. I had a little accident. The tow truck is here, pulling my car from the ditch."

His pulse skipped a beat. "Are you hurt?"

"No . . . no, I'm fine," Liz said, although her voice wobbled slightly.

"What happened?" he asked again.

"I saw a sedan leaving the graveyard and thought the driver

was stalking me, so I chased after it. The sedan turned onto a side road, and I followed, but then he shot out from behind a tree and drove straight toward me."

Rafe clenched his jaw. "Did you see the driver?"

"No, the windows were too dark."

"What happened then?"

"After I crashed, he raced away." She sighed deeply. "But there's something else, Rafe. Last night I thought I saw Harlan outside my house when I got home."

Rafe's blood ran cold. "Where?"

"In the woods. But then he disappeared."

Rafe remembered the chief's comment about the FBI psychologist's report. That Liz suffered from paranoid delusions to the point of sleepwalking at night. That she saw Harlan lurking in every corner and bush. That she'd taken antianxiety medication.

Was Liz suffering from paranoia again as a result of PTSD?

Or was Harlan back, stalking her?

---

Sixteen-year-old Tommy Regan pulled his girlfriend along through the woods toward Slaughter Creek. "Come on, I stashed a six-pack by the canoe."

"I can't believe I'm skipping school to do this," Carina Porter said with a giggle. "My mother would kill me."

"What she doesn't know won't hurt her," Tommy said. "Besides, everyone skips now and then."

Tall weeds clawed at Carina's legs, the scent of damp moss filling the air. She spotted the canoe ahead, wedged on the bank, and her heart went pitter-patter.

She was in love with Tommy. Had been for six months. Today was the day she'd decided to go all the way. What if she did something wrong?

It was her first time. Would Tommy laugh?

He jumped over a tree stump, and she followed. He gestured toward his T-shirt. "You wanna swim first, or row downstream? There's a little nook where we can get out and party."

She wasn't ready to undress. Not yet. "No way I'm getting in the water. It's thirty-five degrees outside. It's probably freezing in the river."

Tommy grinned. "You're probably right." He leaned close to her and nuzzled her neck. "But I'm hot for you."

Carina laughed. He sounded like some slick guy from a movie.

But even if it was cheesy, she liked that he was trying to be romantic. Not like some of the jerks at school who made crude remarks about her boobs and wanting to get in her panties. At least he'd taken her on a real date. Twice to the movies. He'd even paid for their burgers after the football game, and he didn't make a lot of money at the Burger Barn.

Tommy climbed into the canoe, held out his hand and helped her inside. True to his word, he had a six-pack of Miller Lite waiting and a picnic basket filled with goodies. She peeked inside the basket. Cheese and crackers, chips and dip, chocolate . . .

Her heart squeezed with love for him.

She settled across from him with a lovesick smile, and he began rowing, his face lit up by the morning sunlight. Winter air brushed her face as they rowed, and she smiled at the birds flitting above the treetops.

The current picked them up and carried them downstream swiftly. Within minutes, Tommy was rowing to the edge of the creek, where he climbed out and dragged the boat onto the bank.

The sound of birds screeching made her look to the right. A group of vultures was swarming in circles, some dipping down to the embankment.

One bird pecked at something on the ground, then its wings fluttered as it raised its beak.

A scream of horror locked in Carina's throat.
"Oh, God, Tommy, look . . ."
A woman's dead body lay in the tangled weeds.
A woman whose eyes were missing.

# Chapter Ten

———— o ————

Nerves climbed Rafe's neck. He'd hoped Harlan was dead, but if he wasn't, Liz was in terrible danger.

He also had to consider the fact that the investigation into Banning's death might have driven this latest unsub to come after her. "I'll come and pick you up."

"That's not necessary," Liz said. "The tow truck can drop me off at a rental car place."

"No," Rafe said, making a snap decision. Liz needed a bodyguard, and he intended to take the job. "Tell me where you are, and I'll be right there."

Liz sighed in defeat as if she realized it was futile to argue with him, then gave him directions. Rafe rushed to his SUV and drove along the winding mountain road, irritation mounting when he saw Liz's car being towed from the ditch. The front was completely crushed, the driver's door dented, the paint scratched off along one side.

He pulled over to the shoulder of the road and parked, then hurried toward her, visually assessing her for injuries. She was talking to the tow truck driver when he approached her. "Are you sure you're okay, Liz?"

"I'm fine. My ribs are just sore from the air bag."

He tilted her head back to examine her eyes. "You didn't hit your head?"

"No, I told you I'm fine." Impatience tinged her voice as she pulled away and spoke to the driver. "Thanks for coming so quickly."

The driver handed her a business card. "We can give you an estimate on repairs and drop off a loaner for you to drive while yours is getting fixed."

"That would be great." Liz stuffed the card into her purse, and they watched the driver haul her vehicle away.

Rafe raked a hand through his hair. "Liz, are you sure you don't need to go to the ER?"

"I'm positive." Liz's gaze met his. "I'm more irritated than I am hurt. If I could have driven out of that ditch, I would have chased down that asshole."

"Did you get his license number?"

"No," Liz said, frustrated. "It happened too fast."

"You say he intentionally drove toward you?"

"Yes."

Anger heated Rafe's blood. On the heels of Liz thinking she'd seen Harlan at her house, the incident seemed suspicious.

Liz climbed in the passenger side of his SUV, and he drove toward her house.

"Where are you going?" she asked. "I thought we needed to be at the sheriff's office."

"That can wait. I want to check out your house."

"Why? I told you I already did that."

Rafe itched to stroke her hand, to erase the worry from her face. But he was a realist, and until he knew who had tried to hurt her, he had to chase every lead as if it was viable. "Just humor me."

They wound around the mountain, and within minutes he was parking at her house. Liz got out, scanning the property, looking for any signs of danger.

He trailed behind her, his weapon drawn—just in case they were walking into an ambush.

———————— , ————————

Liz hated to admit that she was shaken by the accident, but she was. And those damn flowers were messing with her mind.

Rafe pulled his gun and shouldered his way past her, entering her house first. Clutching her purse so she could remove her weapon if she needed it, she followed him inside.

Together they combed through each room, but the house was empty. For a millisecond he paused, his gaze drawn to the corner where she kept the basket of knitted blankets, but Liz quickly diverted his attention, pulling the basket lid closed to hide the contents.

Rafe had no idea how dark her world had gotten after the attack.

He never would.

If he asked about her crocheting, she'd lie. Baring her soul about her hobby—her *therapy*—would be too painful.

And Rafe could use it against her to keep her off the job.

Her job was all she had left.

"Does it look like anything's been disturbed?" Rafe asked.

Liz shook her head. "No, but this morning when I got up, the inside door to the porch was open. I locked it before I went to bed."

Rafe stepped onto the back porch and studied the woods. Crickets chirped, twigs snapped, and squirrels scrounged for acorns on the leaf-covered ground.

Despite the natural beauty, it would be easy for someone to sneak through the trees, come on the property, and break in.

"Rafe?"

"You locked your car last night?"

"Yes."

"Was it locked when you went outside this morning?"

Liz thought back. It had been locked, hadn't it? Or had she just opened the door? She'd been freaked out, expecting someone to jump her . . .

"I think so."

Rafe frowned. "You don't remember?"

Liz twisted her hands together. "I . . . I was busy looking around. I told you I was spooked because I thought I saw Harlan last night when I got home."

"Maybe you imagined seeing him. After the attack, you had spells where you saw things, imagined Harlan on every street corner."

"Of course I did," Liz said. "I was traumatized."

Rafe cradled her hands in his. "So maybe this case is triggering the same reaction. You have PTSD. You took antianxiety medication, didn't you?"

The truth dawned on Liz with sickening clarity. "How did you know that? Did you read my file?"

Regret darkened his eyes. "No, Liz. But the chief received a report from the doctor. He had to verify that you were stable enough to return to work."

They thought she was unstable? Hurt welled inside Liz, and she backed away from Rafe. "So you and the chief discussed my mental state?"

Rafe reached for her again, but she shoved his hands away from her. "Liz, it's not like we were gossiping in a bar. We both care about you. He thought I needed to know what happened in case the stress got to you."

"In case I broke," she snapped.

"Look, if the situation were reversed, the chief would have had the same conversation with you about me."

Liz saw her medication on the counter and shifted so Rafe wouldn't see the bottle. "So now you have me under a microscope, watching my every move, just waiting for me to fall apart or make a mistake."

"It's not like that, Liz." Rafe's voice cracked. "After all, I was there. I know how much you suffered. What he did to you."

Not everything. She didn't know if she'd ever share it all . . .

"Don't remind me." A coldness swept over Liz, an intense need to survive no matter what. She'd managed to be tough when she was held captive. Even during the beatings.

She could do it now.

Still, she felt raw, exposed. If she thought she saw Harlan again, she'd keep it to herself until she caught him. She wouldn't let Rafe see her as weak.

———————————

Rafe contemplated how much he'd screwed things up with Liz as he returned Jake's call. Dammit to hell, he should have handled things better. Should have been more tactful and never admitted he and the chief had discussed Liz's mental state.

If he were in her shoes, he'd be pissed as hell, too.

The phone rang for the third time, and Jake finally answered. "Sheriff Blackwood."

"It's Hood. What's going on?"

"Some kids skipped school to go canoeing on Slaughter Creek and stumbled on a body."

Rafe pinched the bridge of his nose, a headache threatening. "Are you there now?"

"Just arrived. Kids are pretty freaked out. I called the parents, and they're on their way. My deputy's at the jail with Truitt."

"Who's the vic?"

"A female, no ID yet. It's bad though, Rafe."

Rafe closed his eyes. "How bad? Were the woman's hands missing?"

A long pause fraught with tension followed.

"Jake?"

"No. Her eyes."

Rafe's chest constricted. "Jesus. You think it's the same perp?"

"I'll let you decide. I'm texting you the address now."

"I'm on my way."

Rafe ended the call, then rushed to find Liz.

———————— , ————————

Liz had to get her head in the case. In the mind of this killer.

A dark place to be when the perp was dissecting and collecting body parts.

Rafe parked on the edge of the road behind Jake's police car and grabbed his kit from the back. A Jeep Wrangler sat beneath some trees, a bumper sticker for the local high school on the back. The Jeep obviously belonged to the teens who found the body.

Together Liz and Rafe hiked through the woods until they reached the embankment where the girl and her boyfriend sat huddled together on a rock, clinging to each other. The girl had been crying and was leaning into the young man. He had his arm around her, offering comfort, but his features were strained with shock as well.

Jake stood between the body and the teens, his phone pressed to his ear.

Liz stopped beside the couple and knelt to speak to them while Rafe strode toward Jake. "You two found the body?" she asked quietly.

They both nodded, and the girl looked up at her with tear-stained eyes. "It's so horrible. The vultures were on her. . . ."

The boy hugged her to his side.

The girl sniffled. "My mom's going to kill me for cutting school."

Liz smiled softly. "I'm sure your mother will just be glad that you're okay."

"No, I'll be grounded for life," she sobbed.

Liz squeezed her arm. "Maybe, but she'll also be relieved that you aren't hurt." She turned to address the boy. "Tell me what happened."

He squared his shoulders in a show of bravado. She was sure that act was for the girl. In truth, he looked as if he might hurl any second.

He gestured toward the canoe on the bank. "We came out here to be alone."

"Did you see anyone else around the area?"

He shook his head. "Carina saw vultures diving toward the ground. That's when we spotted the woman."

"How about where you put the boat in? Anyone there? A car, maybe?"

They both shook their heads.

"Did you hear anything? Voices in the woods? A boat or car motor?"

The girl swiped at her tears. "No."

"The place was deserted," he said.

Liz pushed her card into the boy's hand. "If either of you think of anything else, please let us know."

The boy looked up, shading his eyes with his hand. "You're going to catch whoever did that to her, aren't you?"

Liz offered him an encouraging look. "Yes, we'll catch him."

Of course, the police had told her the same thing when her mother was murdered. But her case had gone cold until Liz re-opened it.

She wouldn't let this one go cold. She'd get justice for these women.

# Chapter Eleven

———— o ————

Rafe grimaced as he studied the scene. Leaving the woman's body in the weeds by the creek for the vultures to feast on was consistent with the last murder.

But if they were dealing with the same killer, why the eyes this time, instead of the hands?

In light of the fact that Liz thought she'd seen Harlan the night before, he had to consider the possibility that he had resurfaced and changed his MO. Instead of slashing his victim's throats, he'd decided to sever body parts.

But that was a drastic change.

He glanced at Liz, and saw her rub her fingers across her temple in thought. She was thinking the same thing.

Except for Liz's mother and Liz, who'd been abducted in a desperate attempt to cover his crimes and save himself from apprehension, all of Harlan's victims had been young single mothers, all DHS cases.

But Ester Banning was not a young woman. She was in her early fifties. The woman on the ground looked about the same age. The victimology didn't match the pattern of Harlan's targets.

Leaves rustled, and Dr. Bullock appeared, glasses slipping down his nose as he picked his way through the weeds. A tall, lanky man with dark curly hair, bright blue eyes, and a nervous tic in his jaw followed on his heels. Dr. Bullock introduced him as a bone specialist.

Liz joined them, her gaze raking over the victim's tattered clothing and mangled face. Blood had trickled down her cheeks, her face looked gaunt and muddy, and the vultures had pecked at her eye sockets, face, and arms.

"My God," Liz murmured. "Poor woman."

"What do you think?" Rafe asked.

Dr. Bullock knelt beside the victim and touched her skin, then conducted a liver temp test. "Hard to tell time of death till I get her on the table. Clothes are wet, so I'd say she was dumped in the creek like Ester Banning and washed up on the bank with the current." Dr. Bullock touched the ground and then gestured toward the creek. "A storm threatened last night, making the current stronger. Soil is damp, too."

Liz used her hand as a sun shield as she pivoted to look downstream. "There's an old dirt road that leads to a campground on the west side of the river. He could have put a boat in from there."

Rafe gestured toward the teens. "What are you going to do about them?"

"They already called their parents," Jake answered. "They should be here soon."

Dr. Bullock examined the ends of the woman's fingernails, then took scrapings. "Nails are jagged, indicating she put up a fight. Maybe we'll get some DNA."

"Any ID on her?" Liz asked.

"I didn't find any," Jake said. "No wallet or purse anywhere nearby."

"How about her eyes?"

Jake winced. "Found one of them. Other one is missing."

Liz released a weary breath. "Another trophy."

———————— , ————————

When Lieutenant Maddison arrived, he hurried over to Rafe. "We found something interesting on the Banning woman."

"What?" Rafe asked.

"A drop of blood that didn't belong to the victim."

Liz stepped closer. "It was from the killer?"

"That's the logical explanation."

"So you have DNA?" Jake asked.

"That's the strange part," Lieutenant Maddison said.

Liz cleared her throat. "What do you mean? It is human blood, isn't it?"

"Yes, but there's an odd marker that indicates that the person may have had genetic altering. If you find a suspect, this could make identification easier."

Rafe curled his hands into fists. "Damn. It also suggests that our unsub could have been part of the Commander's experiment."

"What if Banning worked with him? She called the prison to see if he could have visitors," Liz said.

"That's a possibility," Rafe said. "I still think Truitt is connected. He might even be working with an accomplice."

Dr. Bullock pushed his glasses up on his nose. "I detect a faint scent of some kind of strong soap on her hands."

"Like hospital soap?" Liz suggested.

Dr. Bullock nodded. "Yes. And maybe bleach. Which would fit if she worked in the medical field."

"Or the killer could have tried to wash away evidence," Rafe said.

"If the unsub knew both women, there's our connection," Liz said. "Let's check the HomeBound office and see if Samson recognizes this victim."

"Good thinking," Rafe said.

Liz frowned. "Considering that our unsub likes to collect body parts, what if he actually has some medical training himself?"

"I suppose that's possible." Rafe folded his arms. "But look at the crude way he extracted the woman's eyes. If he was trained in the medical field and had any skill, his cutting would have been more meticulous, wouldn't it? Smoother, not jagged."

"In theory, yes." Liz pointed to the torn skin and cartilage. "But our killer is not rational. These cuts are full of emotion. Rage."

"He's trying to throw us off?" Rafe suggested.

"That's also possible," Liz said. "Either way, I have a bad feeling he's not done yet."

---

He strolled the halls of Slaughter Creek Sanitarium, noting how little the mental facility had changed. The chipped paint and dank rancid odors reminded him of his childhood.

Painful memories had embedded themselves so deeply into his psyche that they'd become part of him. A familiar part that he didn't know how to live without.

Pain. Pleasure.

A fine line between the two.

The sound of a crying patient down the hall made him think of CHIMES. The others he'd been locked away with had been his friends, his brothers and sisters.

Yet most of them were dead now. Dead because the Commander was covering his tracks.

At least two others had turned into killers. Giogardi. Seven.

Ah, Seven. So beautiful.

But she was also the Commander's daughter.

Yet none of them had known it at the time. And the ruthless bastard had not spared her because of it.

He'd wanted to make them strong. Fearless.

Putty in his hands.

And then there was Amelia. Vulnerable, confused Amelia.

He had lusted after her from the time he'd been old enough to know the meaning of lust. He closed his eyes and felt her tender touch on his skin. Felt her lips touching his.

Felt her body opening up to him. His thick cock sliding into her. Pumping hard, thrusting over and over until they came.

A medicine cart clanged against a wall, and footsteps pounded the floor. Loud voices and shouts erupted from the end of the hall leading toward the lockdown unit, which held the most dangerous patients.

Seven had been there before they'd moved her to the psychiatric unit in the prison. Word was that she was being transferred back to the sanitarium.

That a special new doctor was coming in to treat her, to see if they could reverse the damage done to her mind.

Was there a way to reverse it?

And if so, could it erase the twisted thoughts in his own head?

A middle-aged nurse with a scowl on her face raced toward the area where the alarms were pealing. She reminded him of Ester Banning and the others who'd tortured him and Amelia.

If she wasn't careful, she'd end up dead, too.

# Chapter Twelve

———— o ————

Rafe and Liz left Lieutenant Maddison and his team to finish processing the area where the victim had been found. As with Ester Banning, the woman had been murdered someplace else and her body dumped into the creek.

If they found the original crime scene, they might learn more about their killer. But that was difficult to do at the moment, with so little to go on.

*The killer had an altered genetic structure.*

They needed a DNA sample from Truitt for comparison.

That was a lead, Rafe reminded himself, as he and Liz drove toward HomeBound.

Twenty minutes later they entered the office. A friendly red-headed receptionist greeted them. "We need to speak to Mr. Samson."

"Just a minute." She pressed an intercom and announced their arrival.

"I'll be with them in a second," Samson said.

"How long have you worked here?" Rafe asked the young woman.

She picked at the end of a fake nail. "I just started last week."

Liz flashed a photo of the latest victim that she'd taken with her camera. Although she had close-up shots of the woman's mangled face and eyes, she'd taken this shot with the woman's eyes closed to camouflage her injuries. "Do you recognize this lady?"

The redhead gasped. "Oh, my God, is she dead?"

"Yes—do you know her?" Rafe asked.

The receptionist shook her head. "No. Who is she?"

"That's what we're trying to determine," Liz answered. "Her body was found earlier, and we need to identify her."

"Did you know Ester Banning?" Rafe asked.

Eyes wide, she shook her head again. "No, but I saw her picture on the news."

Rafe studied her face. "We think the two deaths may be related."

"What's going on?" Samson asked from the doorway leading back to his office.

Rafe explained about finding another victim, and Liz showed him the picture. "Do you recognize her?"

"No—should I?"

"We thought she might have worked for you."

Rafe reminded himself that they had to keep the MO and other details of the crimes quiet, to weed out the crazies who inevitably called in false leads and information.

"She didn't work for HomeBound," Mr. Samson said. "It's unfortunate that the Banning woman was associated with us. When I came on board, I made it a point to carefully check applicants' references. I understand the dangers of the health care business, and want to provide quality care for our patients."

"Except that you hired Ester Banning," Liz said softly.

Samson's brown eyes flickered with irritation. "I told you we were still checking her references."

"Actually I did discover something," the receptionist said meekly. "When I called Dr. Lowens, a psychiatrist who was one of Ester Banning's references, I found out that he died ten years ago. According to the nurse I spoke with, Ester Banning never worked for him. In fact, the nurse I talked to worked with the doc back then, and remembered Ester because she was so volatile. She was one of his patients."

———————— · ————————

Nick Blackwood studied Seven from across the table at the prison. Her feet and hands were cuffed. Cut marks reddened her wrists and arms. A guard stood at the door for Nick's protection.

His sister was a cold-blooded killer.

She had murdered several men, repeatedly strangling them, then reviving them only to kill them again. She did this because their father, the Commander, had done the same to her as part of his training to make her stronger.

"Hello, Nick."

Her dark eyes were so much like his and Jake's that it still tore him up inside to think about how much she'd suffered.

"How are you doing in here?" he asked.

She shrugged, her dark hair falling like a curtain around her face. "Shrinks are having a heyday dissecting my mind." Laughter erupted from her, shrill and bitter. "They say they're going to move me back to the sanitarium, that some hotshot doctor from Europe is flying in because he wants to save me."

Nick arched a brow. "How do you feel about that?"

Seven traced her finger along a scar on her wrist, making him wonder how she'd gotten it. "You think I'm worth saving, Nick? After all, Daddy Dearest didn't even give me a name, just a number."

Nick swallowed hard. "Maybe he didn't name you, but our mother called you Gemma before you were born."

"Gemma?" Emotions spread across Seven's face, making her look vulnerable, so young and impossibly hurt that compassion filled Nick.

He nodded. "I was too young to remember Mother being pregnant, but Jake remembered. He said she called you Gemma because you were her first daughter, a precious gem."

Nick could have sworn he saw tears flicker in his sister's eyes— eyes that were usually either blank or black with an ugly rage.

"I really have a name," she said softly, almost reverently.

"Yes, and our mother wanted you."

She looked down at the table again as if the dark memories were flooding in. "The Commander said my mother died in childbirth."

"He wanted you to feel guilty. But he murdered her, then took you and told everyone you were dead."

A tense heartbeat passed. Nick had no idea what else to say, but even though she'd sadistically killed several men, she deserved the truth. "You got a raw deal being the Commander's daughter, being put in that experiment. But there's some good in you somewhere."

A cynical laugh. "You and Jake got all the goodness, brother dear. Me . . . I'm just like our old man."

"No, you're not," Nick said. "You were a victim. But from now on you're Gemma, and you can be anything you want to be."

She cut her eyes downward toward the handcuffs, then seemed to focus on a crude carving another prisoner had scratched into the table. "What fool thinks putting me back in that psycho ward where he hurt me can possibly make me better?"

Nick had no answer for that. "Have you heard from the Commander?"

She shook her head, but an odd look glinted in her eyes. Unfortunately he didn't understand his sister, didn't know her well enough to predict her behavior.

He only knew she couldn't be trusted.

"No. But I'm sure he has plans."

"What plans?"

"Who knows? He wasn't in a sharing mood the last time I saw him."

"But you have an idea," Nick said calmly.

Seven pivoted, crossed her legs, and looked him straight in the eyes. "I think he answers to someone else. Someone who wanted him out of jail to keep him from divulging who really headed that project."

"It wasn't Senator Stowe?" Her twisted look made him wonder if she *could* be saved. "Who else was involved?"

She pressed a finger over her lips as if mimicking turning a key, indicating that she'd locked the secret in the vault.

"Did you know Ester Banning?" he asked, hoping to throw her off balance by changing the subject.

A flicker of surprise on her face suggested she hadn't expected the question. "Why? Is she dead?"

Nick gave a clipped nod. "What do you know about her murder?"

She gestured toward her handcuffs again. "How would I know anything?"

"Because Ester Banning was a nurse. We're trying to find out if she worked with the CHIMES project."

"I don't want to talk about the project."

Nick leaned forward, switching tactics. "You and Six were held at that compound and tortured there, weren't you?"

She flicked her nails, studying the broken ends, but didn't respond.

He placed his hands over hers. "Gemma, please tell me. Where is Six now?"

She stared at their joined hands as if his gesture made her uncomfortable. "I have no idea."

Nick gritted his teeth. "Will you give me a description of him?"

Her mouth twitched. "Why? So you can hunt him down like some damn dog and kill him?"

"So I can stop him from murdering anyone else."

She stood, gesturing to the guard that their visit was over. But before she left the room, she turned back to him. "Come back when you want to find the bad guys. Six is not one of them."

She left without another word, leaving Nick to wonder if she meant that Six hadn't murdered anyone.

Or simply that, if he had, his victims had deserved it.

———————————— , ————————————

Liz punched in the number for the psychiatrist's office where Ester Banning had been seen as Rafe drove toward Amelia's. Rafe had phoned Jake and instructed him to take a DNA sample from Truitt to send to the lab.

Unfortunately Jake said he'd been forced to release Truitt or charge him with murder, and they didn't have a strong enough case yet to go to trial. But he was still at the top of their suspect list. Rafe insisted they put surveillance on Truitt, so Jake agreed to assign his deputy to the job. He also insisted the deputy collect that sample to analyze.

According to the receptionist at the psychiatrist's office, another doctor had taken over the practice. Maybe that doctor would know something.

A woman answered, and Liz explained about the investigation. "I need information about Ester Banning and the reason she saw Dr. Lowens."

"Ma'am, that's confidential."

"Let me speak to the doctor, please."

The woman sighed as if annoyed. "You'll have to wait a minute."

That minute turned into five, but finally a male voice answered.

Liz explained about Ester's murder and her need for information to help solve it. "We have one man in custody," she said. "I can get a subpoena for her records, but you can save us both some time."

"All right, let me pull her file." It was several minutes before he returned. "Hmm," he mumbled.

"What?" Liz asked, growing impatient.

"Ester came to see Dr. Lowens because of feelings she had over the adoption."

"Adoption?"

"That's what it says here." He recited the date. "According to Dr. Lowens's notes, Ester thought it was for the best."

"Why did she feel that way?"

"She was vague, but said she was in a bad situation, and felt her family might be in danger."

"Did she say what she was afraid of?"

"No. She was supposed to come back for more sessions, but she never did."

"Do you know what happened to the baby?"

"It doesn't say. But she told Dr. Lowens that she used a local adoption agency."

"Thank you."

Liz drummed her fingers as she ended the call. She relayed what she'd found to Rafe.

"Let me call a friend of mine who works in Social Services. Maybe she can pull some strings, research Ester, and find out what happened to that baby."

Liz made the call, explaining to her friend what she needed. Sienna promised to get back to her as soon as possible. Hopefully they'd get a lead soon and stop this maniac before he butchered anyone else.

They'd reached the complex where Amelia lived. Rafe pulled in and parked, and they walked up the sidewalk together.

Jake greeted them at the door. "Come on in. Sadie's with Amelia. Our nanny Gigi already took Ayla to the cabin."

Liz studied the canvases in the studio adjacent to the living room. She'd heard that Amelia was an artist, and knew Sadie used art therapy to help children cope with trauma, and that Amelia's psychiatrist did the same.

A dark, macabre painting of a cage enclosing a young girl made Liz shiver. Red streaked another canvas like a river of blood, against a black background. Yet another depicted several outlines of a figure, each turned in a different direction, as if the painting showed different sides of the same person.

Did that one capture Amelia's alters?

At the foot of the silhouette lay a shadowy black outline of a body on the floor. It looked like a police drawing at a crime scene; Liz wondered if it portrayed the death of one of Amelia's personalities.

Jake made the introductions, and Liz offered Amelia a smile. "Thanks for agreeing to talk to us."

Amelia looked so much like Sadie that it was startling, except that Amelia seemed wary and slightly thinner, her sharp eyes darting around as if she didn't know who she could trust.

Sadie offered them coffee, but Liz declined, and so did Rafe. For a moment, her gaze was drawn to Sadie's belly. The small baby bump brought a knot to Liz's throat.

"How far along are you?" she asked softly.

Sadie rubbed her stomach. "About four months."

"Do you know what you're having yet?"

Sadie smiled. "No. Jake and I decided to wait and be surprised."

"Congratulations." All the more reason Jake would want Sadie in protective custody. She was pregnant with the Commander's second grandchild.

Perched on the edge of the club chair, Amelia wrung her hands. Sadie covered them with her own. "Relax, sis."

Amelia bit her lip. "I don't know how I can help."

"Then you understand the reason we came?" Rafe asked.

Amelia nodded. "I know the Commander broke out of jail, and that two women have been murdered. You think he killed them?"

"We think one of his subjects did."

"We're just speculating now, but we think it was Six, the subject we haven't located," Liz filled in. "Do you remember him?"

Amelia bounced up and down on the seat, agitated. "Six? Why do you think he killed the women?"

Liz glanced at Rafe, both of them aware that Amelia had avoided answering the question. "The first woman who was murdered was named Ester Banning." Liz flipped her phone around to show Amelia Ester's picture. "Did you know her?"

Amelia's eyes widened, but she shook her head. "I . . . I'm not sure. She . . . looks familiar."

"She was a nurse," Liz said. "We're looking into the theory that she might have been involved in the experiments, or that the killer might have been her son."

Amelia's face paled. "I don't know anything about that."

"Maybe one of your alters met her," Sadie suggested.

Amelia nodded. "That's possible. Skid always used to come out when I got scared or one of the staff was abusing me."

Sadie rubbed circles along Amelia's back to calm her growing agitation. "I know this is painful for you, sis, but do you know anything about Six? Did he have a family?"

"No," Amelia said. "They told him his parents died."

Liz and Rafe exchanged looks. "They could have lied to him," Liz pointed out. "After all, they lied to you and the others."

"That's true, Amelia," Jake said. "The Commander made us all think that our sister, Seven, was dead. And that he was dead as well."

"When was the last time you saw Six?" Liz asked.

Amelia stood, her movements jerky. "I told you, I don't know anything."

Rafe showed her a photograph of Truitt. "Do you recognize this man?"

Amelia quickly looked away. "No. I don't think so."

"Look at the picture again," Liz insisted. "It's important, Amelia. Is this man Six?"

A mask seemed to fall over Amelia's face, as if she might be disappearing within herself. "No."

Tension stretched between them for a long second. Was Amelia lying to protect Six?

Liz flashed the second victim's photograph. "How about this woman? Do you recognize her?"

Amelia rose, her arms crossed, her fingers tapping along her arms. "I can't do this anymore. I just can't." Her voice broke, and she dropped her arms and ran from the room. The back door slammed, indicating she'd run outside. Sadie chased after her, leaving Liz, Rafe, and Jake alone with unanswered questions.

Rafe's phone buzzed with the ME's number. "Agent Hood."

"We ID'd the second victim."

"That was fast."

"Apparently she served in the military. Her name is Beaulah Hodge," Bullock said. "She was fifty-one. Never married. Joined the marines when she was eighteen and became a nurse."

"So she was a nurse just like Ester." Had Amelia lied about not recognizing her?

Bullock mumbled agreement. "The similarity could be significant."

"It could be." Rafe pulled at his chin. "Anything else?"

"Still working on the autopsy. Will let you know if something else comes up."

Rafe hung up and relayed the conversation to Liz. "Let's stop by the sanitarium and have a chat with the senator. Maybe his stay there has prompted him to talk."

———————— , ————————

He studied the message board for the followers of the Commander. Had the police discovered the site yet? Did they know that supporters of the Commander posted daily, bragging about the experiments he'd conducted, raving that he was an innovative genius whose mind had simply been too advanced for his time?

Others sent hate messages calling him cruel and inhumane.

In truth, he was both.

Where was he now? Had the CIA secretly helped him escape so they could hide him again?

Maybe he was already working on another project.

His head spinning like truck wheels churning for solid ground in a mud pit, he drove to the sanitarium where it had all started. He needed to remind himself of the horrors that had happened to keep him on track.

He slipped inside, soaking up the acrid smells of urine, sweat, and sickness, easing through the halls and locked doorways with the security card he'd stolen.

His next target had stayed hidden in the shadows of the investigation into the CHIMES project, slyly wielding her own brand of torment with that vile tongue of hers.

His fingers curled around the end of the scalpel he'd used on his last victim when he took her eyes.

This one killed people with her vicious words—words that had robbed him of his manhood and inflicted pain on Amelia and the others. It was time to end her reign of terror.

She wasn't here now, though. She'd moved on, while the rest of them were stuck forever in this horror, like rats on a wheel inside their cage.

Soon he would free himself—and exact revenge for the others.

# Chapter Thirteen

———— o ————

Rafe turned up the long, winding road that led through the mountains to the sanitarium. The mental hospital looked like a giant mausoleum or some Gothic castle out of a horror movie—a place where people were hanged, shadowy ghostly figures floated in windows, and screams filled the night.

Instead of helping its patients, the hospital had been a bed of horrors for Amelia Nettleton and several other children. Liz had seen photographs of the basement where the experiments began. No child should have been subjected to that cruelty.

Therapy helped, but nobody really ever forgot that kind of trauma.

When the senator had a breakdown in prison, the judge had ordered him committed to the sanitarium for treatment. Liz had expected them to close the place down after all the bad publicity, but apparently not. She'd heard that they'd brought in a new director, though, and the hospital was under close scrutiny.

Rafe parked in front, and they walked up the sidewalk to the entrance. A foreboding overwhelmed Liz, but she straightened her spine.

They identified themselves to the receptionist at the welcome station. "We need to see Senator Stowe," Rafe explained.

"Hmm, let me check with his doctor." The receptionist punched an intercom and paged the doctor.

Five minutes later a woman in a white coat appeared, introduced herself, and shook their hands, then led them to an office with dark wood furniture.

"We need to talk to the senator," said Rafe.

"You're aware he had a breakdown when he was arrested?"

"Yes. But he's been in therapy, correct?"

The doctor drummed her fingernails on the desk. "Yes, but he's still extremely depressed."

Liz had no sympathy for the politician. "This is important. We think he may have information that could help us solve the murders of two women. He may also know where Arthur Blackwood was going when he escaped from prison."

The doctor rubbed a spot behind her ear. "All right. But I'm warning you that he's not stable. He hasn't handled being confined well."

"Neither did those poor kids he hurt in that project," Liz shot back.

The woman slanted her a scathing look. "I'm well aware of what he did. I'm just telling you the facts. It's my job to protect my patient's rights."

"Even if it risks the murder of another woman?"

The doctor glared at Liz. "Point taken. But if you get him agitated, I'll have to ask you to leave." She stood, adjusted her lab coat, and gestured for them to follow her down a long hallway that echoed with lonely cries and the sound of metal carts clanging.

Seconds later they crossed through two sets of double doors, both requiring key cards to enter. "This is where we keep potentially dangerous patients and those on suicide watch," the doctor commented.

Keys jangled in her hand as she lifted them from her belt and unlocked the door. Liz sucked in a sharp breath at the sense of desolation in the room. Senator Stowe sat in a vinyl chair in the corner, apparently staring out the window, his back to them. His body was slumped forward as if he was asleep or heavily sedated.

What kind of narcotics were they giving him?

Liz eased forward toward the senator, but Rafe held up a warning hand, then circled in front of the man. When he looked up at her and the doctor, his face was grim.

"He's not going to tell us anything," Rafe said. "The senator's dead."

———————————— , ————————————

Rafe pressed two fingers to the senator's wrist to check for a pulse, following the routine although he knew he wouldn't find one. "He's still warm."

Liz and the doctor both rushed forward, the doctor's face turning ashen when she saw the bullet hole in the middle of the senator's forehead. "Oh, my God. I knew he was depressed, but I never thought he'd kill himself."

Liz gestured toward his fingers. "No gun, gunshot residue, or blood on his hands."

"It looks like a professional hit." Rafe pulled his weapon. "Call Security and lock down the hospital. Now."

Liz removed her gun from her purse and raced toward the door.

"Don't let anyone inside the room," Rafe told the doctor as he followed Liz into the hall. They jogged down the corridor until they reached a T, and he gestured for her to go left while he went right.

He inched down the hall, searching hospital rooms and storage closets, but didn't find the shooter. An alarm shrieked.

Employees scurried about, checking on patients, while Security rushed to guard exits.

One of the nurses in the hall froze at the sight of Rafe's gun. "What's going on?"

Rafe flashed his badge. "Senator Stowe was murdered in his room. The shooter may still be in the sanitarium. Have you seen anything suspicious?"

She shook her head. "No one but doctors and orderlies."

Rafe passed the nurses' station, checking more rooms and closets. When he reached the elevator, he noticed that the stairwell door was open. An orderly stumbled out, looking shaken as he rubbed at his arm. "Damn, that guy was in a hurry."

"You saw someone in the stairwell?" Rafe asked.

"Yeah. Some doctor about knocked me over running down the steps."

Rafe charged into the stairwell, taking the steps two at a time. Below him, footsteps pounded. Rafe whirled around a corner and picked up his pace, holding his gun at the ready.

If this was the Commander or one of his peons, Rafe had to stop him. A door slammed shut below, and he jumped down three steps, sprinting to the bottom floor.

There, the door from the stairwell to the hospital was standing open, and a guard lay on the floor, blood on his forehead. Rafe knelt and checked his pulse.

He was alive.

Shouting for a nurse, he glanced at the visitor's desk in the entryway and noticed two employees near it. Another alarm blared, and he looked to the left and saw an emergency exit door shutting.

It had to be the shooter escaping.

Adrenaline kicked in as he ran down the hall and pushed open the door. Outside, the sun was waning, dark storm clouds rolling in. The sky was gray, the air foggy.

A figure was running toward the side parking lot near the woods. Rafe sprinted in pursuit, then jumped behind the edge of the building just in time as the man turned and fired at him.

A second bullet flew toward him, nearly skimming his arm. He gripped his gun, took a deep breath, and glanced around the corner. The shooter was nowhere in sight.

The sound of an engine cut into the air, and a dark sedan peeled from the parking lot. Fuck. Rafe's SUV was on the opposite side.

He sprinted toward the sedan, firing at it, but the distance was too great. Yanking his phone from his belt clip, Rafe called the sheriff's office.

"Shots were just fired by a man escaping Slaughter Creek Sanitarium in a black sedan, tinted windows. No, I didn't get the license plate."

The deputy told him he'd call it in to local officers, and Rafe hung up and punched Liz's number to fill her in. She agreed to meet him in the senator's room.

By the time he spoke to Security inside and assured them that the shooter was gone, Lieutenant Maddison and his team had arrived.

"It looks like Blackwood either came back himself or sent someone else to make sure the senator didn't talk," Rafe said.

Liz tucked a strand of hair behind her ear, her brows furrowed. "What was he afraid the senator would tell us?"

Rafe's gaze met hers. "The name of the real person behind the project."

---

Rafe grimaced at the sight of the media rushing toward the hospital entrance.

Brenda Banks was a damn good journalist, and Nick Blackwood's fiancée. Despite what she did for a living, Rafe actually liked her. She was tough and tenacious, and had helped to bring down the Commander.

But Rafe wasn't yet ready to reveal to the public that he hadn't solved the case. Everyone was now calling the killer the Dissector. The people of Slaughter Creek would want answers.

Answers he didn't have.

And now Senator Stowe had been murdered.

Liz beat him to the steps to meet Brenda, but he jogged over for backup.

"We just received word that Senator Stowe is dead," Brenda said. Her cameraman raised his camera to capture live footage, and Brenda tilted her microphone toward Rafe.

"How did you hear that?" Rafe asked.

Brenda glared at him. "I have my sources. So it is true."

Rafe sighed. Might as well give her something, so she wouldn't bother the other agents, but he'd keep a lid on the details. "Yes, I can confirm that the senator is dead. At this point, however, I can't divulge any of the details."

"It's been reported that he was on suicide watch. Did he take his own life?"

Rafe shot her a warning look. "Again, I can't discuss the details until we've investigated and the medical examiner has performed an autopsy."

"But you saw someone suspicious leaving the senator's hospital room?" Brenda pressed.

How the hell had she heard that? Or was she just guessing?

"I can't address that at this point." Technically he hadn't seen anyone. Another party had.

Brenda pursed her lips and angled the mic toward Liz, obviously hoping female camaraderie would improve her chances of a scoop. "Special Agent Lucas, you're a profiler, aren't you?"

Liz was a pro. She knew how to play the game. "Yes," she said cautiously.

"Do you believe the senator's death was related to Commander Blackwell's escape from prison?"

Rafe bit his tongue. The answer to that question was obvious.

"As Agent Hood stated, we are just beginning our investigation."

"What about the other two murders in Slaughter Creek? Is Slaughter Creek dealing with another serial killer?"

The lines around Liz's mouth tightened, an indication that she was gauging her response. "I can't confirm that the two cases are related at this point. However, we are looking into several persons of interest, and there are indications that the murders could be personally driven."

"You mean committed by different perpetrators?"

"That's not what I said, although that's also possible. If there is another serial killer, he is extremely dangerous. Whoever killed these women has a personal agenda and a very sadistic side. Both victims so far have been middle-aged, so it's possible that he perceives them as mother figures." She omitted the other common factor, that they were both nurses. "We believe he's transferring his anger and rage toward his own mother or another figure who hurt him. I would caution all women in the area to be on guard until we know more."

"The last serial killer case in Slaughter Creek revolved around the CHIMES experiments. All of the CHIMES subjects have been accounted for except one. Do you think that person could be responsible for these women's deaths?"

"This interview is over." Rafe took Liz's arm and pulled her away toward his SUV.

"You didn't have to jump in, Rafe," Liz said. "I had the interview under control."

"I don't want you in the limelight."

Liz's gaze flew to his, realization dawning. "Because you think it'll draw Harlan back to me."

"If he's alive, it will. If he's not, we have another ruthless killer out there."

By the time they left, Liz's muscles were trembling with exhaustion, and her nerves were stretched paper-thin.

Rafe had a valid point—but maybe it wouldn't be a bad thing for Harlan to see her in public and realize that she was working again. That he hadn't completely destroyed her.

She'd rather have him come after her and give them a chance to catch him than be stalked and tormented for months, looking over her shoulder, wondering and worrying when he might appear.

And Rafe was right. This latest unsub might come after her, as well. He could come after Rafe, too, but Rafe hadn't mentioned that.

She'd thought she'd toughened up by now, but after seeing the senator's blood and brain matter splattered on the windowpane, all she could think about was a hot bath to cleanse the scent of death from her skin.

"I may go talk to Truitt again," Rafe said as he pulled up in front of her house.

She considered going with him, but it had been a long day, and Rafe could handle it alone, so she headed to her front door.

Just as the tow truck driver had promised, the owner of the garage had sent out a car for her to drive. A Ford Focus. She'd have to call him and thank him for the loaner.

Her phone jangled, and she fumbled with her keys on the porch. "Agent Lucas."

"Liz, it's Sienna. I lucked out and found the name of two different children who were adopted around the time frame you mentioned."

"What are their names?"

"A baby named Brian was born in Slaughter Creek General Hospital and given up for adoption when he was three months old. A family named Castor adopted him. That same month a four-year-old child named J. R. was adopted by a family named Truitt."

So Truitt was still a viable suspect. He could be Six, or he could be working with a partner.

The other name niggled at her. Where had she heard the name Castor?

Thunder rumbled, and she hurried to her door, jammed the key into the lock, and rushed inside.

The truth about the name hit her as she set her bag down. Castor was one of the crime techs. Dear God, with his experience, he could easily commit murder and cover up a crime.

And he had been working the investigation from the start.

"Thanks. That's a big help."

She crossed the room to the lamp and flipped the switch, but it didn't come on.

She tried again, but the room stayed dark. Her heartbeat quickened as a chill hit her spine.

She turned the knob faster. *Click click click.*

Someone grabbed her from behind. Liz screamed, focusing all her energy on defensive moves. She kicked backward with her elbow and leg to dislodge the man's hands.

But the sharp sting of a knifepoint at her throat made her pause. If she moved an inch, her attacker would slit her throat.

# Chapter Fourteen

———— o ————

W ho are you and what do you want?" Liz asked.
The man loosened his grip slightly, his breath brushing her neck. But he didn't speak. Instead the shiny glint of his weapon flickered in front of her eyes.

She swung her arm up and slammed her elbow into his chest, then kicked backward, connecting with his knee. He grunted in pain and reached for her again, but she whirled on him and sent a left kick to his midsection.

He staggered, then dashed out the door. It was so dark in the foyer she couldn't see, but she was sure he'd been wearing a mask.

Grabbing her gun from her purse, she ran outside after the man, but he'd disappeared. She checked the area, but didn't see any cars racing away. None at the security gate either.

He must have escaped on foot through the woods around back.

She raced around the corner, searching left and right. Leaves rustled with the wind, a dog barked somewhere nearby, and the sound of a trash can lid banged.

Then she thought she spotted someone running through the woods.

Sweat beaded on her skin as she darted across the back lawn and into the thicket. Rational thought warned her that chasing a predator in the dark was stupid.

She needed a flashlight. Needed backup.

What if this was a setup?

Her brain ordered her to go back inside and call Rafe, but adrenaline and anger made her charge ahead.

Thunder rumbled, and a scattering of raindrops began, making the area look even foggier. The air was frigid, the wind whirling, the rain turning to hail.

Twigs snapped beneath her feet as she inched deeper into the woods. She scanned in all directions, but only shadows flickered between the tree branches, though she thought she saw eyes peering at her through the dark.

An animal howled from the mountains. Then the sound of deep breathing . . . or was she imagining it?

She spun around, terrified Harlan was behind her, but there was nobody in sight. Something moved to the right. As she peered through the trees, a deer shot out, racing for safety.

Her chest heaved with relief, and she scanned the woods again. A noise sounded behind her. A pinging sound. Hail? Or something else?

A car? Voices?

Her instincts roared to life, and she headed back toward the building. When she reached the front, she saw only an older couple climbing into their Mercedes. Relief flooded through her, but still she slowed as she approached her front door.

Dammit. She'd been stupid and left it ajar.

Her attacker could have circled back and now be inside.

Liz eased her front door open, the hinges squeaking slightly. She quickly scanned the entryway, peering left and right, but the foyer appeared empty. She padded softly inside, her gun drawn as she checked the living area and kitchen. Everything seemed to be in place.

Slowly she moved to the bedrooms, her eyes and ears straining for trouble. A tree limb scraped the windowpane in her bedroom, but no one was inside.

Nerves still on edge, she checked the bathroom, grateful to find it and her closet empty. She glanced at the top of her dresser as she walked back through the bedroom. The framed picture of her mother that always sat on the dresser was lying facedown.

She held her breath as she reached to pick it up, her heart pounding. The glass was shattered, and her mother's photograph was gone.

Mind racing, she dropped the frame, ran back to the living room and reached for the phone to call Rafe.

———————— , ————————

Rafe put the visit with Truitt on hold when he received Liz's call. He raced to her house, his heart hammering.

He instinctively threw up his hands in surrender when Liz opened the door, her weapon pointed at him. "Liz, it's me. Put down the gun."

It took a second for her to register that it was Rafe on her doorstep, not her attacker. Relief softened her face when she did, and she dropped her hand, letting the gun hang at her side.

The shiny metal of the scalpel on the floor caught Rafe's eye, and his gaze flew to her throat. The scar was still there, a drop of blood seeping from below it.

"Liz?"

"I'm okay," she said, her breath vibrating with tension.

Hell, she was alive, but the fact that Liz was shaking told him she was far from okay. After he'd cleared the house, he returned to wipe the drop of blood away from her throat, fury building inside him.

He couldn't help himself. He dragged her into his arms. His chest ached with the effort it took him to slow his own breathing. "God, Liz."

She fell against him, her fingers clutching his shirt.

Rafe closed his eyes, inhaling the sweet scent of her body wash, comforted that she was alive. "I won't let anyone hurt you, Liz. Not ever again."

"Rafe . . ."

"Shh, I promise," he said softly. He'd die keeping that promise.

Liz clung to him, her mouth parting slightly. She looked so small and vulnerable, yet he knew she was tough as nails.

She protected others, but never asked anything for herself.

Temptation tore at him, the tender look in her eyes reminding him that once he'd held her in his arms and made love to her. That he'd never forgotten how she felt.

Or how beautiful she looked lying naked in his arms.

Heat flickered across her face, her breathy sigh of hunger so familiar that his body reacted, hardened, yearned for her.

Slowly she lifted one hand and pressed it against his cheek.

Unable to resist, he lowered his head and claimed her mouth with his.

———————— , ————————

Liz sank into Rafe's arms and parted her lips in invitation. She'd dreamed about kissing him again for months, craved being in his arms ever since he'd walked away from her, leaving her to pull herself together after the attack. She'd been broken then.

Maybe she still was.

But he was the glue that held her together.

His big, strong arms enveloped her, cradling her so close that she felt his thick length press against her belly. Instant need suffused her, racing hotly through her blood.

She threaded her fingers into his hair and deepened the kiss, savoring the sensual way he teased her with his tongue. She tasted his hunger in his hot kiss, heard raw need in his moan, felt the intensity of his desire in the way he stroked her back.

He whispered her name against her neck as he trailed kisses down her throat. She ran her hands over his chest, aching to touch his bare skin. His breath grew hot against her neck as he kissed her tenderly.

The memory of her scar broke the spell. Liz tensed.

"Don't," he murmured. "You're beautiful."

His husky words sent a tremor of longing through her, and instead of pulling away, she clung to him, dragging him closer. She rubbed her foot up and down his calf, moving against him in silent invitation.

He slipped the top button of her blouse free, then another button, until he parted the fabric and his lips seared the sensitive area between her breasts.

She wanted more.

Heat sizzled between them as he nipped lower, then covered one breast with his hand, molding her and touching her until she sighed, begging for more.

"Liz," Rafe whispered. "We should stop."

She didn't want him to stop. "Why?"

"I don't know," he murmured as he dipped his head to tug her nipple into his mouth. "I can't remember."

"Neither can I," she whispered. "That feels good."

He suckled her deeper, one hand sliding down to tease her between her thighs. She groaned his name, her body humming with desire. Desperate to be even closer to him, she pulled at his buttons, sliding his shirt open so she could slip her hands inside. She whispered his name, her fingers trailing through the soft mat of dark hair on his torso.

Memories of the two of them making love, lying naked, their bodies entwined, for hours, teased at her mind. She wanted to do that again.

Now.

She shoved at his shirt, tearing it off, and he removed hers, then unfastened her bra. Skin glided against skin as he gently eased her down onto the sofa. Lips met again, tongues thrusting as the heat intensified between them.

Rafe kneed her legs apart, yanking at her jeans until he had them off. Liz wound her legs around him, welcoming his weight on top of her as he kissed her again. His erection stroked her heat to a frenzy, an orgasm building as he lowered his head and slipped two fingers inside her panties. Emitting a low moan, he rubbed her clit with his thumb while his mouth sought her breasts again. He tugged a nipple into his mouth, teasing her with his tongue, then sucking while his fingers worked magic on her damp center. She thrust her hips up, pulling at his belt to free him, begging for more, wanting his thick length inside her.

He laved her other breast, then dropped erotic kisses down her belly and between her thighs. Her body quivered with sensations as he slid her panties down her thighs and threw them to the floor. His damp tongue found her clit, and he tortured her with his mouth.

She moaned and reached for his arms, desperate to feel him on top of her, inside her, but he pushed her legs farther apart and drove her mindless with his tongue until her orgasm teetered on the surface.

"Rafe?"

"Just enjoy," he whispered against her skin.

"I want you."

He lifted her hips higher off the sofa and plunged his tongue inside her. The mere touch of his lips on her clit again sent her over the edge. Colors blinded her as she quivered in his arms and cried out his name.

---

*Sticks and stones can break your bones, but words can never harm you.*

Whoever made up that stupid saying had never met Ruth Rodgers. Ruth Rodgers had a viper's mouth. A tongue that made children bleed from the inside out.

She had gotten away with her viciousness for too long.

He had to stop her.

But first he wanted to see Amelia again. *Needed* to see her.

Wanted to hold her. To remember what it felt like to have someone to love him.

He peeked inside her condo, but the place was dark. Completely dark. She wasn't home.

Fuck. Fuck. Fuck.

Enraged, he punched her number into the burner phone he'd picked up at the convenience store. The phone rang and rang, but she didn't answer.

Her voice mail clicked on, and he started to leave a message. But goddammit, her sister was married to a fucking cop. What if they listened to Amelia's messages?

He couldn't leave a trail.

He punched disconnect, furious. Where was Amelia? Had she left him?

No . . . she couldn't have. He needed her.

He jiggled the back door and then slipped around her condo to her bedroom window and picked the lock. Maybe she'd just gone out for a while.

She'd be back. She wouldn't desert him like everyone else. They had meant too much to each other over the years for her to do that. He'd met the alters long before she even knew they existed.

Soon she'd return and let him fuck her. She'd beg him to give her pleasure.

Because she needed him just as desperately as he needed her.

He crawled into her bed and pulled up the covers, inhaling her sweet scent and imagining that she was lying naked with him. Kissing him, climbing on top of him.

Moonlight slivered through the blinds, casting lines across a canvas against the wall.

The outline of a man. Dark features. Sharp angles. Evil, dead eyes.

It was *him.*

What did the painting mean?

That she was in love with him? That when he finished punishing the ones who'd hurt him, he and Amelia could finally be together?

His hand eased between the covers, and he began to stroke his thick cock, the blood churning and making it harder. Making it throb until he felt erotic sensations splinter through him, felt the first spurts of his cum dripping down his thigh.

Yes, when the mission ended, he and Amelia would have a life together. Free of the experiment. Free of their tormentors.

Free of the Commander.

Amelia would look at him as her hero.

And no one would ever tear them apart again.

# Chapter Fifteen

———— o ————

Rafe's body craved more with Liz, but her phone buzzed, and he froze. He desperately wanted to tell her not to answer it. To close her eyes and stay in bed with him forever.

But the call might be about the case. Or if Harlan was back, he might taunt her on the phone. He'd done it before he'd kidnapped her. Called and left sick, breathy messages. Whispered nasty things he wanted to do to her.

Challenged her to find him before he took her.

Her phone buzzed again.

Liz made a frustrated sound, not of pleasure this time. "I guess I should answer that. Maybe we've got good news or a lead."

His body throbbed for release, but the case and her safety were more important, so he handed her the phone.

"Hello. Agent Lucas."

Rafe frowned as she sat up, tugging the sheet over herself. "Yes. What?" A pause, and she rubbed at her forehead. "Who is this?"

A second later, she growled in frustration and slammed her phone down onto the bed.

Rafe's pulse hammered. "Who was that?"

"I don't know," Liz said. "A man. He said that our second victim, Beaulah Hodge, used to work at Slaughter Creek Sanitarium."

"How does he know that?" Rafe asked.

Liz shook her head. "He hung up before I could ask."

Rafe considered the information. "She could have been involved with the CHIMES project." Rafe slid from bed, grabbed his jeans, tugged them on, and reached for his phone.

Liz stood beside him, the sheet wrapped around her beautiful naked body, her expression torn. Remnants of their lovemaking lingered in her eyes, in the rosy color of her skin where he'd heated her with kisses. He wanted to throw her back down on the bed and make love to her again, this time fast and furious, until he was inside her, obliterating the memory of any other man's touch.

She stroked his arm, turning him toward her, desire darkening her eyes. "We . . . I . . . we could go back to bed."

He offered her a tender smile, although the raging need inside him wasn't tender. That smile fueled his need to have her. If he was honest with himself, she'd always meant more to him than a case or sex.

He didn't want to lose her again.

But those thoughts were dangerous. Everyone he'd ever cared about had died.

That fear made him step away. But he tucked a strand of hair behind her ear as he did. "Not tonight, Liz. I need to call Nick and Jake and tell them about this call. Maybe it will convince Amelia to draw that sketch of Six."

Disappointment flickered in Liz's eyes for a moment, but she accepted his reasoning.

He dropped a kiss into her hair. "Get some sleep. Tomorrow we'll go back to the sanitarium and snoop around."

"We also need to talk to CSI Castor."

Rafe arched a brow. "What about Castor?"

"My friend from Social Services came through. Apparently the son Ester gave up was adopted by a family named Castor. Truitt was also adopted the same year."

Rafe's pulse kicked up a notch. Maybe they finally had some leads and they'd catch this bastard.

———————— , ————————

Liz was tempted to beg Rafe to stay, but she had too much pride for that. If Rafe wanted to be with her, he would join her.

Besides, he was right. This case took precedence. If she allowed her head and heart to get too involved, she might miss something important about the Dissector's profile, just like she had with Harlan.

She crawled back in bed, certain she wouldn't sleep. When she closed her eyes, though, for the first time in ages, she felt sated and content.

And safe. She always felt safe with Rafe.

Darkness hovered around her, normally making her feel uneasy, but tonight she put thoughts of Harlan and this latest unsub out of her mind, allowing the blissful memory of Rafe's hands and mouth pleasuring her to replace the gruesome images that haunted her at night.

Using visualization skills she'd learned in therapy, imagining Rafe's arms around her, his steady breathing on her cheek, she fell into a deep sleep.

Hours later, she woke to see sunlight streaming through the window. A few snowflakes drifted down, melting as soon as they hit the ground.

She felt more rested than she had in ages. But when she reached for Rafe, she found the bed beside her empty. His masculine scent lingered on her pillow, making her miss him already.

Footsteps sounded from the kitchen, and she tensed. It had to be Rafe, not an intruder.

But after the break-in, she needed to be sure.

She tiptoed to the kitchen and saw him pouring coffee for himself. Would it be awkward between them this morning?

Hoping to stall, give herself time to pull herself together, she jumped into the shower. While she washed her hair, she forced her mind back to the case. She needed to work on the profile for the Dissector.

Serial killers normally chose one MO and stuck to it. This unsub had removed one woman's hands, another's eyes.

Seven had been part of the experiment, and she'd targeted men who'd worked for the project, men who'd guarded her, kept her locked up, abused her.

If this unsub was Six, he might be doing the same thing by targeting nurses. The fact that the perp had used Ester's hands to beat her might mean she had abused him with those hands.

And Beaulah Hodge? She'd worked at the sanitarium . . . perhaps with the project? Why had he cut out her eyes? Because they were the windows of the soul—and he perceived her as having no soul?

What exactly had Beaulah done to him?

And who would he target next?

Another nurse?

If they could locate a list of the nurses who'd worked with the project, they could warn the next victim. That is, if that list existed.

She rinsed her hair, toweled off, grabbed her robe and pulled it on, then padded to the kitchen. Rafe was making omelets.

She poured coffee into her favorite oversize mug and leaned against the counter, studying him as he scooped the omelets onto two plates. The toast popped up at that moment, and she took it out, spread butter and jelly on it, and added it to their plates.

Sharing the kitchen with him felt so intimate that she almost forgot that he was only here because a psycho killer was on the loose.

---

Rafe listened quietly while Liz relayed her theory about the unsub. "All the more reason to talk to the director at the sanitarium."

They polished off the food and cleaned up together, a routine that felt so comfortable that Rafe thought he could get used to it.

It had never occurred to him before he met Liz that he'd want to spend all his time with one woman, but with Liz he'd thought about it months ago.

And this morning, when he'd peeked in to watch her sleep.

The very reason he'd have to ask for a new partner when they closed this investigation.

"Did you talk to Jake?" Liz asked as they walked out to the car.

"Sadie agreed to talk to Amelia again. She thinks Amelia bonded with Six because of the way they suffered together. She has to convince Amelia that he's dangerous."

"So Sadie believes Six has been in contact with Amelia?"

"Amelia's definitely been seeing some man," Rafe said as he drove toward the hospital. "Now Sadie believes it's Six."

"I suppose I can't fault her. She's protecting him because, like Seven, he's cleaning up the people who abused the subjects."

Rafe nodded as he veered onto the winding road leading to the sanitarium. "After what they endured, it's difficult to argue with that logic. By the way, Lieutenant Maddison called. Forensics show that the senator was murdered. There was no gunshot residue on his hands, no sign of the weapon, and they still haven't located the driver of the sedan that raced away from the hospital. They also identified the soap found on Beaulah. It's antibacterial hospital soap, but it can be bought almost anywhere, including on the Internet."

"That soap means something to our killer. It triggers sensory details that are painful and reminds him of the people who hurt him."

"He's getting rid of evidence," Rafe pointed out. "That means he's smart and organized enough to plan these murders."

Liz nodded. "Our killer might also have a background in medicine or law enforcement. Castor fits that description."

"Maybe the director can tell us more about Ms. Hodge. Then we'll question Castor."

"We can assume that all the victims hurt our unsub or represent someone who did, but the perp's manner of killing them varies. Each death is personally tailored. There must be a reason."

Rafe nodded. "About the medical background—what if our unsub is some kind of mad scientist? Maybe he's trying different ways of killing, to see which one causes the most pain? Or which method takes the vic longer to bleed out?"

Liz shivered at his theory. "That's a possibility. We can't rule out anything at this point."

"If the bastard was part of the experiment, the Commander could have given him commands, trained him to experiment on other humans."

"That would fit with the experiment as well." Liz wrapped her arms around herself. "Sadistic and cold-blooded, but we know the Commander used mind control to train Giogardi as a hit man."

He glanced at Liz and saw the wheels turning in her head, knew she was diving into the killer's mind. Venturing into the darkness was dangerous for her and left her drained and exhausted.

She hadn't worked a case since Harlan, and Rafe was worried she wouldn't be able to survive going into that dark place again.

———————————

Liz rubbed her arms in an effort to ward off the chill that seemed to pervade the hospital walls as the receptionist led them to the director's office.

The director, Anderson Loggins, wearing a suit that set off his stark features, was attractive, although a small scar at his temple made her wonder if he'd been injured or had had some kind of medical treatment himself.

"Mr. Loggins," Liz said, "we appreciate your seeing us on such quick notice."

"Agent Hood said it was important." He offered coffee, but they both declined, seating themselves across from his desk.

Liz took the lead. "You understand that we're investigating the death of the senator as well as that of two women who've been found murdered in Slaughter Creek."

"Yes, the security team pulled copies of all the tapes on the day of the senator's death." He gestured toward Rafe. "Do you want to see them now?"

Rafe nodded. "Yes. Why don't I look at them while you and Agent Lucas talk?"

Mr. Loggins nodded, punched his intercom, and requested a security guard. A heartbeat later a husky bald man appeared and escorted Rafe into the hall.

When they'd left, Loggins faced Liz. "How else can I help you?"

"I received an anonymous call about the second murder victim, Beaulah Hodge." She paused to see if he recognized the name.

"And that brought you here because?"

"The caller said that Ms. Hodge worked at the sanitarium at one time. I hoped you could find records to confirm that."

He steepled his hands on the desk. He had blunt nails, calluses, and a jagged scar on his right hand that ran deep. "How will that help you?"

"Studying victimology, knowing as much as we can about victims and finding a common pattern among them, can often lead to the killer. Most repeat killers—"

"You mean serial killers?"

"Yes, they establish a pattern and target victims for a specific reason, usually because the victims remind them of someone who hurt or abused them. The first victim, Ester Banning, had a nursing background and was fired from a nursing home for abusing patients. When she left, she applied for a job with a company that provided home health care for patients." She paused. "Our working theory is that both victims worked with the CHIMES project."

"I see. So why did you come to me?"

Liz checked her notes. "Because we believe our unsub is one of the subjects. And if he's targeting nurses who worked with the project, we need a list of those nurses so we can warn them."

His dark gaze shot to hers, a muscle twitching in his jaw. A minute later he stood, walked over to a filing cabinet, and dug inside. "Actually the files for that period burned in a fire a while back. Employee records were lost. But . . ."

"But what?"

"I'm a resourceful man. I managed to find a backup copy of a file regarding the project."

Adrenaline pumped through Liz like a shot of caffeine. "You did? Where?"

"In a file box that had been placed in the basement."

"Can I see it?" Liz asked.

"Yes, of course. Although I'm afraid it's pretty slim. Not a lot of details inside." He removed the folder and handed it to her. "I believe it has the names of the subjects of the experiment. There were seven, correct?"

"Seven that we know of."

His eyebrows rose. "You think there are more?"

"It's possible that there were sister experiments performed in other towns."

"Oh, I see. That makes sense."

Liz opened the folder and skimmed the first page. It was indeed a list of the subjects. There were scattered notes on treatments, shock therapy, pharmaceuticals they'd tested, hallucinogens, sensory deprivation, and mind control techniques. It sounded like something out of a horror movie, bringing back the reality of the pain that victims like Amelia had suffered.

She studied the few names listed, for the first time seeing concrete evidence of the subjects' names, not just the numbers they'd been assigned. Amelia had first given them that clue—she was number three. Seven had no name as far as she knew, other than Seven. Here she was listed as Seven Blackwood.

She zeroed in on the sixth listing.

But just as with Seven, there was no name listed, just the number—as if he hadn't been important enough to have a name.

Unless Blackwood had found a way to erase the names so they would never be found.

# Chapter Sixteen

───── o ─────

Rafe finally managed to get hold of the security tapes from the hospital—damn red tape had nearly made it impossible. He studied the footage of the hallways leading to and from the senator's room, noting very little activity. A nurse popped in to check on the senator during the two hours of footage that Rafe was scanning; he recognized her as Mazie, the head nurse on the floor.

She'd worked at the hospital for years, and had insisted that she didn't know about the experiments when they were running. She certainly had no reason to kill the senator and was middle-aged, not the age of the subjects. But she might recognize Six and be able to offer a description. She also might give them a list of other nurses who'd worked with Blackwood.

He checked the camera inside the senator's room and frowned. The senator seemed to have lapsed into a catatonic state—whether from the narcotics prescribed by the doctor or from depression was unclear. Probably it was both. But the senator was nonresponsive when Mazie checked on him, as well as when a young nurse's aide brought him his meal.

In fact the young assistant spoon-fed the once vibrant, confident senator, who was now as pale and listless as an injured bird.

But the senator hadn't been innocent. He'd allowed the Commander to take advantage of children.

The nurse's aide left the senator sitting in his chair, staring out the window. Rafe scrolled through the footage. Twenty minutes later, according to the time stamp, the door to the senator's room squeaked open and a figure dressed in scrubs, complete with mask and cap, eased into the room.

The figure was tall, broad-shouldered—a man's physique. Keeping his face averted from the camera, he padded so softly that only a slight footfall sounded.

The senator didn't respond at all, as if he hadn't heard the man enter.

Without a word, the man slipped a Glock from inside his scrub suit, gripped the back of the chair, and walked around to face the senator. For a millimeter of a second the senator stared his killer in the eye.

Rafe searched for a flicker of surprise, of fear, for recognition. But the senator simply blinked as if he'd been expecting his attacker. Slowly the killer lifted the weapon, placed the barrel point in the middle of the man's forehead, and fired. The silencer kept the weapon from making a loud noise.

Rafe gripped the chair edge as blood and brain matter splattered everywhere.

It soaked the killer's scrub suit, but the mess didn't faze him. Keeping his face averted again, he backed toward the door and eased out.

Because of the angle of the cameras, Rafe lost sight of him for a fraction of an instant as he ducked into the hallway, but picked him back up as he neared the stairwell.

Looking again at the time stamp on the video feed, Rafe realized that the killer had struck during mealtime to take advantage of the fact that most of the staff would be busy, and the food carts would drown out noise.

Unfortunately there were no cameras in the stairwell, but Rafe caught sight of the killer again as he darted out a side exit door, setting the alarm off.

Frustrated, Rafe knotted his hands into fists. The tapes gave him nothing. Not once had he seen the unsub's face.

Judging from the killer's size and build, and the cold, calculating ease with which he took the senator's life, the man could have been the Commander.

Or a hired gun.

His phone buzzed to announce the arrival of a text: *Meet me at the car asap. I have a lead.*

Rafe turned to the security guard. "I need a copy of this tape to send to the lab. Maybe they can work their magic and tell us more. Can you page Mazie for me?"

The guard tapped a few keys on the computer, then shook his head. "Says here she left early."

Rafe gritted his teeth. "Can you give her a message to call me asap?"

The unsub was targeting nurses who'd participated in the experiments. Mazie might be one of them.

———————— , ————————

Liz met Rafe at his SUV, anxious to show him the file. It provided no new information, but at least it contained the list of subjects, confirming that there had only been seven in Slaughter Creek.

Rafe was waiting in the parking lot when she reached his SUV.

"Did you see anything on the tapes?" Liz asked.

He lifted his sunglasses. "Not much. He wore full scrubs and kept his face averted."

"Maybe a scar or defining feature?"

"No, but I'm sending the tapes to the lab. Maybe they can find something."

"You think the Commander shot the senator?" she asked as they settled into the car and fastened their seat belts.

"Either him or a hired gun." Rafe rubbed a hand across his chin. "The senator appeared to be catatonic. Killer walked right in, stared him in the face, and the senator didn't even react. In fact, he looked up at him but didn't seem surprised."

"He was expecting someone to silence him."

Rafe nodded. "There's something else," he said. "I wanted to talk to Mazie, the head nurse, but she went home early."

"You think she killed the senator?"

"No. The body frame of the killer looked like a man's. But apparently Mazie has worked here for twenty years—right back to when the experiments were going on."

Liz swallowed hard. "Which means the unsub might be after her. And if he's not, the Commander might want to silence her."

"Exactly."

Liz pushed the folder toward Rafe. "Mr. Loggins gave me this file. It lists the subjects of the experiment and the treatments and procedures used on them."

"Jesus." Rafe's face lit with excitement as he skimmed it. "Finally some documentation."

"I'm not sure it'll help much if the subjects are dead, but maybe Amelia's doctor can use the information in her treatment." After all, she was redeemable. Seven had committed too many heinous murders to ever be released or be whole again.

And Six? If he was the Dissector, slicing and dicing women, he needed prison time as well as a psychiatrist.

They had to talk to Castor now to see what his story was, and whether he had an alibi for the time of the murders.

———————————— ' ————————————

Anticipation fueled Rafe as he drove toward the crime lab. He considered calling Lieutenant Maddison and giving him a heads-up, but surprising Castor would be more valuable.

"We need all the background we can get on Castor," he said.

Liz retrieved her tablet from her purse, clicked on it, and frowned. "Damn, we must be in a dead zone, no cell service."

Rafe glanced back at the sanitarium as he wove down the long drive. Live oaks dripping with Spanish moss dotted the background, adding to the eerie feel of the hospital.

He braked, shifting gears as he wove down the mountain, the sharp ridges jutting out over the canyon below. Liz kept trying to get a signal on her tablet, finally managing to connect as they turned onto the main highway leading to the lab. She wanted to find out everything she could about Castor before they questioned him, so she accessed the TBI personnel database and ran a search.

"Brian Castor grew up in Memphis, graduated from college with a degree in premed, then decided to study to become a crimescene investigator."

"Premed would supply him with knowledge of the human anatomy. Any other background information?"

"No prior arrests or record. And nothing in his file about emotional disorders or problems in school."

"He would never have made CSI if he had."

"But most serial killers, especially sociopaths, exhibit violence as children. Killing animals is a common red flag."

"What about his family?"

"It says here they live in Memphis. If we don't get what we want from him, we'll pay them a visit."

---

Rafe parked, and they hurried to the crime lab door.

"Good work, Liz."

"Let's just hope the lead pans out."

They entered the county police building and headed toward the lab. Rafe handed the tapes he'd brought from the hospital to the tech team to analyze, and then they walked to Lieutenant Maddison's office.

Rafe knocked, but the door stood ajar, and Maddison was on the phone, so they waited in the threshold until he waved them in.

"Any news on that DNA from Truitt?" Rafe asked.

"Not yet," Maddison said. "The lab is backed up. And we have another problem. The sample scraping beneath Truitt's fingernails was lost, so we have to collect another one."

Rafe's fists clenched. "How did it get lost?"

"Lab incompetence, but we'll take care of it. One tech has already been fired."

"You need to make this a priority," Rafe said.

Maddison grunted. "Every case is a priority."

Liz explained the reason for their visit, and Lieutenant Maddison's brows flew up in question. "You think one of my men is the Dissector?"

"Ester Banning gave a child up for adoption. Castor's last name shows up in an adoption file at the same time, so he could be her son," Rafe explained.

"And you think he killed her because she gave him away?"

"It's possible that when she did, he wound up in the experiment," Liz said. "That's why we need to question him."

"Do you mean he could be Six?"

Rafe nodded. "He also has a background in premed, his father was a vet, and he worked both crime scenes."

Maddison's face darkened. "So you suspect he insinuated himself into the investigation to cover his tracks. But technically he was already working here before the murders."

"He could have planned ahead," said Liz.

"At any rate, we need to question him," Rafe added. "Even if he isn't our unsub, if he was part of those experiments he could provide valuable information about the participants, hospital staff who assisted, and leaders. He might even know where the Commander is."

Lieutenant Maddison raked a hand through his hair. "All right—let me call him in."

He punched a button on his desk and requested that the CSI come to his office.

"I see your logic," Lieutenant Maddison said. "But I know Brian, and I don't think he killed those women. He's a little strange, obsessive about cleanliness and meticulous in details, but he always seems so controlled."

Liz's expression softened. "True sociopaths can fool the people around them."

A knock sounded at the door, and Rafe opened it to let Castor in. Liz had seen him at the crime scenes, but hadn't paid much attention to him.

And that might be exactly how Castor had wanted it. Another trait of sociopaths—they had an uncanny way of blending in and not being noticed.

Now she noted details. He had a medium build, brown hair combed neatly to the side, an angular face, and eyes . . . eyes that looked right through her when he met her gaze.

Eyes that made her wonder if he'd cold-bloodedly amputated a woman's hands and cut out Beaulah Hodge's eyes.

---

Nick took the call from the secretary of defense before he entered the prison. "Yes, Secretary Mallard, I'm doing everything possible to find my father."

"Keep me posted. I don't have to tell you that we need to have him back in custody. Your father had classified information that he could be selling to a foreign government as we speak."

No pressure there. "Believe me, no one wants him locked back up more than my brother and I do." Their families and loved ones would never be safe until Arthur Blackwood was dead.

"Keep me posted, Blackwood."

Nick agreed, then headed to the door to go through Security

When he finally got to talk to the warden, he was antsy for information.

"Which medical personnel treated the Commander?"

"The physician only worked at the prison for a week. Apparently he was filling in, since we've been short."

Uh-huh. "Where is he now?"

"He disappeared the same day the Commander broke out of prison."

"So this so-called physician might not have been a doctor at all."

"Listen, Agent Blackwood, we do the best we can here."

*Which was shit*, Nick thought.

The rest of his visit went the same. There was no record that the doctor was registered in Tennessee. The clinic nurse gave a description, although Nick guessed that the man might have altered his appearance, as he had his name.

They should have the man's prints on file, but when Nick analyzed them, they matched a dead man's prints, meaning the man had stolen them. Maybe from the morgue.

Finally Nick picked up one tidbit of useful information. The Commander had developed a following using a website to share ideas and support.

He left the prison, more frustrated than before he entered, found a coffee shop with Wi-Fi, and booted up his laptop, anxious to find out more about that damned website.

Five minutes later he was looking at the site, shocked at the depraved individuals who actually proclaimed his father a genius. Some objected to the cover-up, but others, more militant, believed that when the project took place, during the Cold War, desperate measures had been needed. According to them, the United States had to protect itself and keep up with other countries by strategizing and researching biochemical warfare.

Most of the people who'd posted hadn't used their real names, so he phoned the Tech department and asked for assistance.

If one of these nutcases had helped the Commander escape, they had to find him. He—or she—might be able to tell them the Commander's whereabouts and intentions.

———————— , ————————

He paced Amelia's room, furious she hadn't come home the night before.

Where the hell was she? Off with her sister?

Or was there another man?

No . . . Amelia was his. She had been for years. Nothing would stop him from being with her.

Not the police or the Commander.

Not even her twin. Sadie would try to destroy him if she learned they were meeting.

Anger churning in his gut, he drove to the address he had for Ruth Rodgers.

Dark clouds hovered above, and snowflakes swirled in the frigid air. He sat in his car watching and waiting for the bitch to leave the office where she picked up her disability check.

Imagine the old biddy being disabled. She'd fallen on a job and broken a hip lifting a patient, supposedly. More likely she'd slipped while beating one.

He hoped the injury was painful, that she suffered every time she moved.

Ruth was revered as a model of loving-kindness. A foremother of Jesus. A matriarch in the Calendar of Saints of the Lutheran Church. A promoter of well-being.

At least, that was Ruth in the Bible—not the Ruthless Ruth who'd tormented him when he was small.

Ruth with the bitter tongue. With the vile mouth and cold, listless eyes. With the evil smile, like a viper ready to strike.

Ruth, who told him he was an animal right before she strapped him to the chair. Then the Commander showed him pictures of mauled animals, videos of dissections and surgeries and . . . slaughterhouses.

All the time they'd monitored his physical responses.

"Learn to love the pain," Ruth had whispered in his ear. "Pain brings pleasure."

"Watch the animal scream for help," the Commander said in his monotone. "Doesn't your blood burn hot, just watching a live creature squirm and writhe as the blood seeps from its body?"

Yes, it had. Shame had filled him, but over and over, they'd made him watch the same violent killings. Heads being severed. Knives slicing open chest cavities so organs spilled out. Axes chopping off body parts until the animal's blood emptied itself onto the ground.

Eventually the shame had dissipated, and a craving had been born. He'd needed to see the blood. Had begged for more.

Then his training had turned to humans. Anatomy lessons. Postmortem dissections.

He'd been infatuated with the tongue. Maybe because he'd seen Ruth's flit in and out of her mouth as she lashed her ugly words at him. Her berating comments, verbal abuse.

The phrase *bite your tongue* slid into his mind so many times that he'd imagined her biting it until blood dripped down her chin and it hung like a limp piece of tissue, flapping up and down as she tried to speak.

A laugh gurgled in his throat at the realization that his wish would finally be granted.

He followed her to her trailer in the mobile home park outside Slaughter Creek. The trailer looked run-down, the porch that had been added sagging and rotting, the sides splattered with mud and stains from the last winter storm.

Images of the dissections he'd watched as a kid, the mutilations and killings, flashed behind his eyes, and anticipation heated his blood again.

She pulled her rambling old Oldsmobile into her drive and climbed out, batting at the chickens in her yard to make them scatter as she hobbled toward her front door. That bum hip would make it so much easier for him to subdue her.

Other phrases about tongues bombarded him. *Cat got your tongue. Tongue-tied.*

Tongues could bring pleasure when they tasted food. They could give pleasure with kind words.

Or when that tongue worked a man's cock.

But her tongue gave nothing but pain.

He pulled past the trailer, veered down a dirt road, and parked. Tugging a ball cap low on his head, he jammed the scalpel into his pocket and slipped into the woods to wait.

---

Amelia lifted the knife and traced it along the inside of her thigh. Press the tip of the blade, and she could watch the blood flow, watch her pain dissipate as the crimson tide trickled down her leg onto the floor.

*It's a sin to do that to yourself,* Rachel said. *What would God say?*

*What would Sadie say?* another voice whispered in her head.

Amelia recognized that last voice as her own. Amelia's voice— the one that grew stronger every day.

She was still fighting with Rachel, the religious zealot who'd invaded her soul. Or maybe Rachel was her conscience, reminding her of the difference between right and wrong. Maybe Rachel had come to save her from herself.

Amelia threw the knife against the wall, then picked up her paints and began to paint Rachel. Rachel with the fire and brimstone speeches. Rachel with the antisex attitude and the tendency to tell Amelia she was bad.

"I'm not bad," Amelia said, desperate to quiet the ugly voice. "I just want to be normal. To be loved."

She drew Rachel's silhouette in charcoal, coloring in her jet-black hair, her gaunt cheekbones, the way her upper lip curled when she ranted about religion.

God was supposed to be good and loving. But all Rachel talked about was ugliness and punishment. All she did was batter Amelia with judgment.

Amelia's self-preservation instincts kicked in, and she grabbed the knife and tore into the canvas, ripping the nasty-looking face and shredding the canvas into pieces.

Rachel was trying to destroy her. Take over.

Amelia had to fight her, just as she'd fought the others.

A knock sounded at the door, and Sadie appeared with Ayla. Amelia quickly covered the canvas and turned to her sister, her heart thumping erratically. Had Sadie seen the darkness on the canvas?

"Ayla and I are going hiking. Do you want to come with us?"

Amelia saw Ayla's hopeful smile, the innocence of a five-year-old glowing in her eyes.

Amelia had never been that innocent.

Sadie's expression grew worried. "Amelia?"

"Yes, I'm coming," Amelia said. "Just let me change."

Sadie nodded, one hand on Ayla's back as they closed the door. Sadie was so lucky. She'd married the man she loved, adopted his daughter, and now they were having a baby of their own.

She had a real family.

Amelia's heart ached for that. For real love. For a man to hold her at night and whisper her name, and no one else's.

For a baby of her own.

In fact, sometimes at night, she thought she heard a little one's cry. Her own baby's . . .

But that was impossible. She'd never had a child, and never would. She couldn't have a real family. Not until she was whole again.

Not until the Commander was dead and gone forever.

Images of Six pushing her against the wall as he thrust inside her teased her mind. Six . . . should she tell Sadie and Jake about him? Draw that sketch for them?

Had Six killed those women? If so, and if she crossed him, would he turn his rage on her? If she told the police, would they arrest her as his accomplice?

She trembled so badly that she sank onto the bed. No . . . she couldn't go back to prison. Couldn't be locked up in that sanitarium again.

She quickly changed clothes, pulling on jeans, a sweater, and her hiking boots.

No, she wouldn't say anything. She'd keep quiet and hope the police found him without her.

# Chapter Seventeen

———— o ————

Rafe had to agree with Liz. Brian Castor didn't look like a serial killer.

Then again, who did? Ted Bundy was handsome and volunteered at a suicide prevention line. Richard Angelo was a volunteer firefighter and Eagle Scout, but he'd killed twenty-five people. Karl Denke played the organ at his church and was loved by the community. Still, he'd murdered and cannibalized over thirty people.

The list went on and on.

Truitt certainly had the demeanor and the job to fit the profile, though. And if he was Ester's child and had learned that he'd been part of the experiment, he certainly had motive to kill her.

Then again, there was Beaulah Hodge's death. What if Truitt had had an accomplice? Could he and Castor be working together?

"Lieutenant," Castor said, his gaze shooting to Liz and Rafe. "You asked to see me."

Lieutenant Maddison flattened his hands on his desk. "Yes—Special Agents Hood and Lucas need to talk to you."

Castor's brows drew together beneath big square glasses. A tiny mole dotted the left corner of his mouth. His hands were long, the tip of his pinkie finger on his right hand missing, light hair dusting the tops of his hands. "I'm assuming it's about forensics on the Banning and Hodge cases. Is there a problem?"

*Intuitive*, Rafe thought. "Yes. We need to discuss the Slaughter Creek experiments."

Castor shut the door and claimed a seat, his interest obviously piqued. "You believe the two are related?"

Rafe nodded. "Evidence is pointing in that direction."

"Mr. Castor," Liz began. "We'd like to know more about your background before you joined CSI."

Castor looked confused. "I don't understand what my background has to do with this case."

"Please," Liz said. "It's important."

Castor glanced at Maddison, hoping for a way out, but Maddison simply gestured for him to answer.

"I grew up in Memphis," Castor said. "Majored in premed in college, but got interested in forensics and law and switched directions."

"Your family still live in Memphis?" Liz asked.

Castor crossed his leg over his knee. "Yes." Alarm creased his face. "Why? Has something happened to my parents?"

"No," Rafe said, rushing to quell the panic in the man's voice. "They're fine."

Liz kept her voice level. "Do you have any brothers or sisters?"

Castor shook his head no. "I'm an only child."

"Did your parents ever live in Slaughter Creek?" Rafe asked.

"Not that I know of."

Rafe cleared his throat. "Do you remember visiting the town when you were young?"

Castor shook his head again.

"Were you ever hospitalized as a child?" Liz asked.

Castor blinked, a nervous twitch tugging at the corner of his mouth. "I had a tonsillectomy when I was ten. Now what the hell does my tonsil surgery have to do with finding this killer?"

Liz exchanged a curious look with Rafe.

Even if Castor hadn't received treatment at the sanitarium, the Commander could have used another facility. The other doctors involved could also have volunteered at another free clinic.

"Maybe nothing."

"I thought you had the killer in custody."

"We had to release our main suspect because there isn't enough evidence to charge him," Rafe said. "Besides, it's possible he had an accomplice."

Liz gestured toward his hand. "What happened to your finger?"

Castor looked down at his mangled appendage and then folded his fingers. "An accident. I was helping my father with an addition to the clinic when the saw slipped."

"That must have hurt," Liz commented.

Castor shrugged. "Lot of damn blood."

Rafe measured his words, gauging Castor's response. "Do you know if your parents ever had contact with Arthur Blackwood?"

Castor's eyes flared with uncertainty. "Why would they? My mother's a schoolteacher, and Dad's a veterinarian."

"But you were adopted?" Liz asked softly.

Castor's jaw tightened, anger reddening his cheeks as he stood abruptly. "How do you know that?"

Lieutenant Maddison gestured toward the chair. "Sit down, Brian."

"We've done some research," Liz filled in.

Rafe indicated the file from the sanitarium. "We spoke with the director of Slaughter Creek Sanitarium. This file contains information about the experiments and what they did to the children."

The mole at the corner of Castor's mouth twitched, but he sank back into the chair. "What does that have to do with me?"

"See if any of it rings a bell." Rafe shoved the folder into Castor's hands.

Castor glanced at Liz, then back at Rafe and Maddison, before he opened the file. Shock widened his eyes as he skimmed the contents. His hand began to shake, and anger mingled with dis-belief when he looked back up.

"Good God, you think I was one of the subjects?"

———————————

Liz silently studied Castor. The shock on his face looked genuine, but she would refrain from forming an opinion until she was more certain.

Some sociopaths were extremely convincing actors. She couldn't afford to make a snap decision. Lives depended on her objectivity and professional skills.

"That's what we want you to tell us," Rafe said.

Castor raised his hands, as if the file had burned him. "Hell, no, I grew up in a good family."

"The first victim of this serial killer, Ester Banning, gave up a baby around the time you were adopted by the Castors. That means that child might have motive to kill her."

"That's far-fetched." Perspiration beaded on Castor's brow. "And it's not me. I love my parents."

Liz raised a brow. "Did you receive treatment at the hospital or at a free clinic in Slaughter Creek?"

Castor jammed his hands into his pockets. "I already told you I didn't."

"Was your father in the military?" Rafe asked.

"No. And if you're suggesting that he worked with that mon-ster, you're way off. Dad helps animals. He would never hurt any-one, or condone what Blackwood did."

Liz considered his vehemence. "How about male relatives? A cousin, maybe?"

"No. None." He shifted impatiently. "Now you need to do more research. I can search for other Castors in Tennessee if you want."

"Not a good idea," Lieutenant Maddison said emphatically. "Under the circumstances, Brian, it's best if you temporarily remove yourself from this case."

Fury darkened Castor's face. "You're pulling me?"

"I'm just telling you to take a few days off," Lieutenant Maddison said in a low voice. "I can't believe this. One more thing before you go," Maddison added, his voice softening. "We'll need a DNA and blood sample."

Castor balled his hands into fists. "Thanks for standing up for me, Lieutenant."

"I am," Maddison said. "But that means we have to do this by the book. The only way to clear you is to compare DNA and blood samples to the killer's."

Castor cursed again as he strode out. The door slammed behind him, his anger resounding as his feet pounded the hall.

"I'm sorry we upset your CSI," Liz said. "But we had to ask those questions."

"I understand." Lieutenant Maddison tapped a few keys on his computer, hit print, and his printer spewed out a page. "Here's Castor's parents' address and contact information. I suggest you speak to them and clear this matter up asap so the man can return to work."

Rafe took the sheet of paper and stood, and he and Liz walked outside together. "Castor could have been part of the experiment and never known it," Rafe suggested.

Liz considered his comment. "That's true. But if he's innocent, that means the experiment left him unscathed, not negatively affected, as it has all the others."

"Maybe they perfected their training with him." He paused. "Or he's hiding it."

Liz opened the car door and slid inside. Rafe did the same and started the SUV.

"Let's have a chat with Brian's parents," she said. "If Brian worked with his father at the vet clinic, maybe his parents encouraged him to go into police work because of his interest in science."

"You mean his interest in dissecting animals?"

Liz nodded. "Yes. Killing animals is a sign of sociopathic behavior and a precursor to becoming a serial killer."

———————— , ————————

The drive to the Castors' took almost two hours. Rafe called the deputy to check on Truitt, but there had been no signs of him going or coming during surveillance. Rafe ordered the deputy to check the house and call him back once he'd verified that Truitt was inside.

They stopped and picked up lunch, a hailstorm slowing them down as they drove.

On the off chance that there might possibly be another Brian Castor, Liz searched databases on her tablet for other Castors who lived in Tennessee with a son named Brian. "There's one family who lives in Nashville, but their only son is deceased and his name was Joe. Another couple has twin boys, but they're only five years old."

"Anything else?"

"An elderly preacher in western Tennessee, but he has no children."

Rafe turned up the defroster and wipers. "A dead end. Maybe we do have the right family."

Older farmhouses and trailers dotted the mountains, but as they approached Memphis, traffic thickened, gas stations and other commercial buildings popping up. Two miles outside town, he spotted the vet practice, right next to the Castor's house.

Hail battered the windshield as he parked. Liz tugged her coat around her before they got out.

The lights in the clinic were off, so Rafe parked at the house, noting that the place had recently been painted. A pickup truck and a red Toyota were parked to the right.

"This won't be easy," Liz said as they walked up to the house. "No parent wants to hear that the police suspect their son of being a serial killer."

"If they hid what he is, they deserve to be confronted."

Liz's eyes darkened. "True."

Mrs. Castor answered the door, tugging a bathrobe around her. "Yes?"

Rafe and Liz both flashed their badges. "I'm sorry if it's late, ma'am, but we need to talk to you and your husband," said Liz.

Panic flickered in the woman's eyes. "Dear God, is something wrong? Did something happen to Brian?"

"No, ma'am, he's fine," Liz reassured her. "We just need to ask you and your husband some questions."

"What about?"

Rafe put one foot inside the doorway to prevent her from closing it on them. "Please get Dr. Castor, and we'll explain."

Mrs. Castor fiddled with the edge of her robe, then gestured for them to follow her into a den. The room was cozy, with a fire roaring in the stone fireplace, a border collie sprawled on a braided rug in front of it. Cooking and pet care magazines mingled on the coffee table.

Dr. Castor sat in a chair with an open book, reading glasses perched on his nose. He looked up in surprise when he saw them.

The couple appeared to be late forties, both fit. Photographs chronicling Brian's youth decorated one wall above a table that held trophies he'd received from science club and chess tournaments.

A child's teddy bear's pride of place, right in the middle, indicated that it must have been much loved by its owner.

Liz paused and rubbed a hand over the bear, an odd expression darkening her face. The gesture struck Rafe as odd. He'd never pictured Liz with kids—or himself, for that matter.

But an image of her with a baby on her hip flitted through his mind, and his lungs squeezed. Had Liz ever thought about a family?

He stiffened, wondering where in the hell those thoughts had come from.

Although he enjoyed volunteering at the Boys' Club, Rafe hadn't ever considered having a kid of his own. His childhood certainly hadn't prepared him for anything but the life he lived now.

Certainly not for a family, or a happily-ever-after with a woman.

Jumping from one dysfunctional house to another had helped make him tough. Knocked reality into his head early on. No one ever stayed around. People left. People died.

No use getting attached.

"What do you want?" Dr. Castor asked impatiently.

Rafe crossed his arms. "We need to know if either of you had any contact with Arthur Blackwood, or any knowledge of the experiments that took place in Slaughter Creek."

Rafe's phone buzzed: the deputy. He stepped from the room. "Yeah?"

A drawn-out sigh. "Hell, I looked all over the house and the slaughterhouse. Truitt is gone."

Shit. "Find him," Rafe said. "And when you do, get that damn DNA sample."

If Truitt's DNA matched Castor's, they'd know they were related.

And that might help them prove whether the men were working together.

---

He paced the floor of his killing room, inhaling the acrid scent of blood and death from his other victims.

The scent intoxicated him, fueled his energy.

"Ahh, Ruth. . . . You do remember me, don't you?"

The wrinkles around the heartless woman's eyes sank deep into the grooves of her sagging face as she stared up at him. Her body was old now, lumpy and soft. Age spots splattered her skin like ants on a dirt mound, and her teeth had yellowed and blackened with snuff stains.

He remembered watching her pinch a bit of the foul-smelling tobacco and stuff it into her cheek. She'd leave it there, sucking and enjoying the juice until she had to spit. She always kept a spit can with her, a crude tin can that she covered with tinfoil.

Those black teeth had looked nasty when she'd snarled at him, holding him down. But she had firm, strong hands. A man's hands.

Steady hands that had taught him to whack up an animal without blinking an eye. And that tongue . . .

The tongue—a muscular hydrostat on the floor of the mouth of most vertebrates. The tongue manipulates food for mastication. Helps in language. The primary organ of taste. The upper part covered in papillae and taste buds. Eight muscles make up the tongue—intrinsic and extrinsic. Extrinsic ones are anchored to the bone.

The lingual artery, a branch of the carotid artery, sends blood to the tongue.

He would target the carotid artery. Watch the blood seep and spurt.

Yes, now it was her turn to suffer.

She made a disgusting sound in her throat, part laugh, part challenge, as if the evil had permeated her soul a long time ago, feeding her spirit like a sick beast.

"You do know who I am?" he asked again.

Her eyes flitted over him, eyes so dead with meanness that he realized she knew him but refused to admit it.

"You're going to hell for what you did." He slapped her face so hard she cried out.

"Why did you do it?" he asked. "Why did you hurt us?"

"I had orders," she said, those blackened teeth snapping like a turtle's beak. "If I hadn't, they would have killed me."

"You were scared?" he asked with a harsh laugh. "I don't buy that, Ruth."

"You were lost anyway," she hissed. "No one wanted you. No one loved you. Even your own mother threw you away."

He raised the scalpel and waved it in front of her.

In a last-ditch effort to save herself, she struggled with the ropes holding her down. "You're a sick monster," she spewed.

This time he grinned. "You should know. You created me." He gripped her jaw and pried open her mouth. She tried to bite him, but he slammed his fist into her jaw. The bone cracked and she cried out in pain, her body jerking.

He grabbed a pair of pliers and shoved them into her mouth to keep it open, then jabbed the sharp tip of his scalpel into the skin around her tongue.

Blood spurted, washing down his hands like a river. He could bathe in her blood, though, and it still wouldn't erase her horrible words.

The rage seething inside him burned like a fire out of control as he carved out her tongue.

Tears streaked her face, her cheeks paling, shock robbing her of color as her body turned cold. He leaned closer, holding her bloody tongue in front of her face as he whispered in her ear. "Now no one else will ever have to listen to your vile words again."

Laughter rumbled from his chest as he dropped the tongue into a jar. Another piece in his collection.

# Chapter Eighteen

———— o ————

Rafe stepped back into the room with a grimace. Dr. Castor leaned forward in his chair, his face grim. "Why would you think we knew anything about Arthur Blackwood? And what in the world does he have to do with our son?"

As he spoke, Rafe noted the books on surgical techniques and dissections on the bookshelf to the right of Dr. Castor. "We identified all but one of the subjects," Rafe said.

The couple exchanged confused looks. "What are you saying?" Dr. Castor asked.

Rafe decided to cut to the chase. "Is it possible that your son was one of the subjects?"

Mrs. Castor gasped. "You think we put our little boy in that experiment?"

"That's preposterous," Dr. Castor said angrily.

"Did Brian ever receive treatment at a free clinic in Slaughter Creek?" Liz asked.

Dr. Castor stiffened. "No. We used a pediatrician here in Memphis when he was little. Then our family doctor. Why?"

"Because some of the subjects were originally affected by vaccines they received at the free clinic in Slaughter Creek," Liz explained. "Later they experienced emotional problems as a result and were referred to the mental hospital, where they were used as test subjects."

Mrs. Castor massaged her forehead. "Our Brian didn't have any health problems, and he certainly never spent time at the sanitarium."

"We would never have let a doctor do the things to him that that Blackwood maniac did," Dr. Castor said.

"Commander Blackwood is dangerous," Rafe said sternly. "He tried to kill everyone who knew about the project. So if you know anything about it, it would be in your best interest to tell us."

"In exchange for your cooperation, we can offer you protection," Liz added.

Anger blazed in the doctor's eyes. "I'm telling you one more time—we had nothing to do with that project. And neither did Brian."

Liz changed tactics. "Has Brian ever exhibited signs of violence?"

"Brian?" Mrs. Castor said, wide-eyed. "God, no. He loves animals. He worked with my husband all through high school."

"Brian was tenderhearted," Dr. Castor said. "When one of our patients was in trouble, he'd stay and watch the animal all night just so it wouldn't be alone."

"Did you lose any of those patients?" Liz asked.

"A few," Dr. Castor admitted. "But that's part of the business."

"You never suspected that he might have helped them along?" Liz pressed.

Dr. Castor's nostrils flared. "You mean, did he euthanize them?"

"Yes."

"Brian would never have done that without talking to me," Dr. Castor said.

"No autopsies on the animals to prove that?" Rafe asked.

Dr. Castor removed his reading glasses with a trembling hand. "No. There was no need."

"Brian is a good boy," Mrs. Castor insisted. "He volunteered at rescue shelters for animals and helped find them homes. He even applied to med school, but later he decided to go into police work."

"Why did he change his mind?" Rafe asked, fishing for more information. Something that would catch Brian in a lie.

"A friend of his was killed," Dr. Castor said. "A young woman. Brian was so torn up about it that he dogged the police until they solved the crime. Turned out the girl's former boyfriend was stalking her."

Rafe glanced at Liz, his jaw tight. The couple seemed sincere, but all parents were capable of lying through their teeth to protect their child.

———————·———————

Liz considered the information. If Brian was a psychopath, had he hidden those tendencies from his parents?

Or were she and Rafe mistaken about his identity?

"He never had to see a counselor?" Liz asked. "No problems at school?"

"He did see a counselor for a while his freshman year, but that was because of personal matters," Dr. Castor said.

"What kind of personal matters?" Liz pushed.

Mrs. Castor sighed wearily, as if resigned. "Because Brian had learned he was adopted."

Liz nodded.

"He was upset about it?" Rafe asked.

Mrs. Castor twisted her fingers together. "At first, yes. He asked a lot of questions about his birth parents, but we'd been told they died in a car accident when Brian was three months old."

Of course that could have been a lie.

Mrs. Castor wiped at a tear trickling down her cheek. "We wanted a child so badly that when we heard, we adopted both boys."

Liz tempered her voice to be gentle. "What do you mean, both boys?"

Mrs. Castor looked over at her husband as if she were debating how to answer.

"What happened?" Rafe asked the father.

Dr. Castor rubbed his temple. "Brian had an older brother, who was four when we adopted them . . ."

Truitt had been adopted at that age.

"But we decided we couldn't keep him," Dr. Castor said. "That we'd taken too much on ourselves. We had to let him go back to the agency."

Something about that didn't sound right. "What was his name?"

"Jeremy," Mrs. Castor said.

Jeremy. Could he be J. R. Truitt?

"Why exactly couldn't you keep him?" Liz asked. They obviously had enough money.

Dr. Castor stood. "Look, that was a long time ago. We really don't want to talk about it anymore. Now I think it's time you left."

He motioned toward the door. Liz and Rafe stood, but Liz paused before moving. "One more question. Does Brian know he has a brother?"

Dr. Castor shook his head. "Not that we know of. We thought it might upset him, so we never told him."

"What happened to him?" Rafe asked.

The couple looked away, obviously disturbed by the question. "We have no idea. It was too painful for us," said Mrs. Castor.

What about the child? Liz thought. "Who handled the case?"

"We've already told you enough." Dr. Castor gestured toward the door again. "Now let us be."

Liz would have to call Sienna again. The Castors were definitely keeping something from them.

Something that might offer insight into the case, possibly confirm that Jeremy and J. R. Truitt were one and the same.

And exonerate—or cast more doubt on—CSI Brian Castor.

---

Rafe phoned Nick and filled him in on what they'd learned as he left the Castors' and drove toward the station.

"Any word on the Commander?" Rafe asked.

"No, and I'm getting heat from Secretary of Defense Mallard to find him. I have a meeting with a friend of mine from the CIA," Nick said. "The Commander's followers created a website. We're investigating them to see if they helped him escape or are hiding him now."

"Keep me posted."

Liz was talking to her friend Sienna when he hung up. "Yes, Sienna, the Castors' originally adopted brothers. The baby was Brian, but there was another child. I need everything you can find on that adoption and what happened to the brother Jeremy." A pause. "Thanks."

She hung up and turned to look out the window while he phoned Lieutenant Maddison and got Brian Castor's home address.

He slowed as the SUV skidded on black ice. "Castor lives in those apartments near the crime lab."

Liz stared out the window as they drove, her expression pensive.

"What are you thinking, Liz?" Rafe asked.

She angled her face toward him. "Just wondering if Brian found out about his brother. And if Jeremy and J. R. Truitt are the same person."

He was wondering the same thing. "If so, Brian could be angry at the Castors for giving up on his brother and for keeping secrets."

"Or the older brother could be furious that Brian was adopted, and he could be framing Brian."

"That's a possibility." They definitely needed more information. Rafe turned in to the apartment complex, a new development perched on the side of the mountain that featured decks overlooking the woods. He parked, and they both tugged their coats tighter to fight the wind as they hurried up the sidewalk to Castor's building.

Rafe knocked, bracing himself for animosity from Brian. Hell, if Brian had no knowledge of his brother or the project, this was going to be a hard blow.

But his gut told him Castor knew more than he'd revealed.

Footsteps sounded inside, and the door opened. Brian adjusted his glasses when he saw them on the doorstep. He was also holding his cell phone, anger flaring in his tight expression. "Yes, Mom, they're here now."

Rafe grimaced. They should have known the Castors would warn Brian they were coming.

Brian said good-bye to his mother and then crossed his arms, his stance belligerent. "More questions?"

"A few," Rafe said.

Liz offered him a smile. "Can we come in, Brian?"

He blew an exasperated breath between his teeth. "I guess I don't have a choice."

Rafe bit back a comment, and the two of them followed Castor inside. Steely gray leather furniture dominated the room along with chrome and glass tables, striking Rafe as impersonal.

Except for photos on one wall, of hunting expeditions where he'd bagged a deer.

Odd for a vet's son who supposedly liked to rescue animals.

"I see you're a hunter," Rafe said.

Brian shrugged. "A couple of the guys at the academy took me once. They say hunting blows off steam."

"I don't understand how killing anything relieves tension," Liz said.

Brian glared at her. "Is that why you came? To ask me about my hunting?"

"No. You were on the phone with your mother," Rafe cut in. "You know the reason we're here."

———————— , ————————

Liz studied Brian's posture and body language, analyzing his behavior for clues to his psyche.

Brian's mouth twitched, a nervous tic that Rafe had mentioned earlier. But he seemed resigned as he invited them in.

They followed him to the den and took seats on a sofa across from him. Rafe gestured toward a desk in the corner with high-tech computer equipment. A file was open with articles detailing the Slaughter Creek experiment.

"You're doing research?" Rafe said.

Brian shrugged. "I figured if I was going to be accused of something, I might as well learn all I could about it."

"We haven't accused you of anything," Liz said. "We're simply trying to figure out connections, and your name came up."

"Your mother said a friend of yours died, that that's the reason you decided to become a CSI instead of a doctor?" Rafe asked.

Brian slanted him a cold look. "Yes."

"Her death changed your mind about medicine?" Liz asked.

Brian released a wary breath and then angled his head at Liz. "Yeah, just like your mother's murder made you decide to choose police work."

Liz forced herself not to react. Brian was trying to throw her off guard.

He angled his head toward Rafe. "And you? You grew up in the system, too, didn't you, Hood? One of your own foster sisters died. My guess is that you felt guilty, so you joined the TBI. Maybe you're the serial killer, not me."

"Let's talk about your family," Liz said.

"What if I say no?"

Rafe shrugged. "We can do it here or down at the sheriff's office. When did you find out you had a brother?"

For a brief second pain flickered in Brian's eyes before he masked it. "A few months ago."

So he had known. "How did you find out?" Liz asked.

Brian clenched his hands together. "One day I was helping my dad clean out the garage and found a box of old pictures. There was one of me as a baby and this other kid. He was about four." Brian scraped a hand through his hair. "That's when I realized they lied to me."

"Did you ask them about him?" Liz asked.

"Yes. At first Dad got mad and didn't want to talk about it. But he admitted that they gave my brother back, said he had emotional problems."

"What kind of emotional problems?"

"That he was violent." Brian cursed. "Hell, he was only four. How can you tell that at four?"

"Some mentally ill people exhibit signs at a very early age," Liz pointed out.

"Did you find your brother?" Rafe asked.

"No. The social worker who handled our case wasn't around anymore."

"Did you find anything on him?" Liz pressed.

Brian fisted his hands by his sides. "I don't know where you're going with this, but I think he's been through enough."

Rafe cleared his throat. "What did you learn, Brian?"

"That he was put it an institution," Brian snapped.

Liz glanced at Rafe, her mind ticking away the possibilities.

"Where?" Liz asked.

"I don't know. But what the fuck? Who locks a four-year-old away like that?"

Liz had no answer that would satisfy Brian. "We have to find out where he was and what happened to him. He could be our killer."

Brian glared at her, but didn't offer any more information.

Liz swallowed hard. "I understand you may have compassion for him. You may even feel guilty that you had the better life. But if he is subject Six, and he mutilated those women, he needs to be stopped."

"Have you had any contact with him?" Rafe asked bluntly.

Brian's gaze shot to Rafe. "No."

"Brian, please," Liz said softly. "If you're hiding him, you'll be considered an accomplice to murder. The loyalty you feel for him may not be returned. It's possible that he resents you, that he may try to get revenge on you. He may even be setting you up."

"I can take care of myself," Brian said. "Now we're done here."

"May I use your restroom before we go?" Liz asked.

Brian frowned. "I guess so. Second door on the left."

Liz walked down the hall. The first door led to a small bedroom that doubled as an office. Dozens of books on medical and surgical techniques filled the bookshelf, along with books on crime-scene investigation. A clear glass jar on one shelf held colored marbles.

They made Liz think of Beaulah Hodge's missing eye.

She examined the desk and found files about the Slaughter Creek project, about the murders orchestrated by Blackwood, about Amelia, and about the senator's arrest. Another folder held articles about adoptions and a paper trail chronicling Brian's adoption.

But there was nothing about his brother.

A bulletin board hung above the desk with photos of all the victims of the Slaughter Creek project. He'd added photos of Ester Banning and Beaulah Hodge.

Pulse pounding, Liz glanced at the desktop computer screen. Articles on amputations and eye surgeries filled the screen.

Brian had drawn lines connecting some of the photos and articles on the bulletin board; in another section she noticed a picture of a woman in her mid-fifties with shaggy brown hair and pale skin.

Liz leaned closer and skimmed the notes Castor had made about her. She was the social worker who'd handled his adoption.

Her name was Rusty Lintell.

And she was dead. Murdered two years ago.

About the same time Brian decided to become a CSI.

---

Rafe tried to mentally place himself in Brian Castor's shoes. But their pasts were different.

At one point he'd attempted to find out where his real parents were, but that had only opened up a boatload of pain. His father had murdered his mother when he'd caught her trying to leave him, and had died in prison.

For the longest time, Rafe had wondered if he'd turn out like his old man. If genetically he'd been born a bad seed and would one day snap and murder someone.

But he'd met a cop who volunteered with homeless boys at a shelter, and that cop turned his thinking around. First he got Rafe involved in the Boys' Club, where he made friends with other kids like himself. Then he encouraged Rafe to channel his rage into tracking down men like his father.

Every time he got justice for a victim, he was getting justice for his own mother.

It was the one connection he'd had with Liz. He understood her drive to find her mother's murderer.

What would he have done if he'd discovered he had a sibling somewhere? A brother he'd been denied knowing? A brother who'd suffered horrendously at the hands of adults who should have taken care of him?

Liz walked back in, her expression troubled. "Thanks for talking with us," she told Brian. "If you remember anything else that might help, give us a call."

Brian looked confused that she was dismissing him, but Rafe followed her cue.

When they were headed back toward her place, Liz explained what she'd seen. "We need to review Castor's phone records and put a trace on his cell. Then I want to talk to the sheriff who investigated the social worker's murder."

Rafe's cell phone buzzed, and he pressed answer.

"Agent Hood, Mazie hasn't shown back up at work, and she isn't answering her phone."

Worry pinched Rafe's gut. "Give me her address. I'll go check on her."

The guard recited it, and Rafe spun the car around.

---

Shadows darkened the landscape as they neared the outskirts of Slaughter Creek again. Hoping the head nurse at the sanitarium might have information, Rafe wove through a tunnel of trees on a long, winding drive toward Mazie Paulsen's house, the sleet turning to rain. Thunder rumbled and lighting zigzagged across the tops of the trees in jagged lines.

Trees swayed with the force of the wind, pinecones and debris scattering in the breeze. Raindrops splattered the windshield, a gray fog sweeping across the land and woods, making visibility difficult.

The SUV hit a pothole and slid, tires grinding in the mud. "I hope we don't get stuck up here," Liz said with a shiver.

Rafe maneuvered the vehicle onto the graveled portion of the road, steering it around a bend until they reached a clearing. Mazie lived on the side of the mountain in a small cabin nestled amid pines and oaks.

Rafe glanced around for a vehicle, but didn't see one.

"It doesn't look like anyone's home," Liz said.

Rafe pulled to a stop and cut the engine, his gaze sweeping the outside of the cabin. The place was small but looked well kept and offered a spectacular view of the mountain ridges. You could even see the town from the peak, and the road that led to the sanitarium.

Liz climbed out, but she seemed cautious as well as they walked up to the front porch. A porch swing creaked in the wind, several hand-painted roosters carved from wood decorating the porch. A weathervane flapped back and forth on the hill to the right.

Birdfeeders swayed in a nearby tree, and a deer grazed at the edge of the woods, as if he'd come to Mazie's to be hand-fed.

Liz peered into the front windows, a frown puckering between her eyes. "It's dark inside. No lights. Doesn't look like she's home."

"Maybe she got spooked by the Commander's prison escape and ran," Rafe said.

"Let's check the inside. Then I'll do some research and find out if she has some family she might stay with." She jiggled the doorknob, and Rafe heard it screech open.

He threw up a hand to caution her and pulled his gun, and she did the same. Shouldering his way to the front, he took the lead. Liz glared at him as if to protest, but he didn't give a damn. If someone was waiting inside to ambush them, he'd rather the culprit meet his six-four, 220-pound body than Liz's five-three, 110-pound frame.

The wood floors squeaked as he crossed the threshold. He played his flashlight over the space. The living room adjoined the kitchen, a wooden breakfast bar crafted from a tree trunk separating the areas.

But he forgot the architecture when he noticed that the place had been tossed. Papers from a corner oak desk were scattered among magazines on the floor. The leather furniture had been ripped apart with a sharp knife, the pillows torn, kitchen cabinets spilling out their contents.

Liz opened the pantry door. "Clear."

He moved left and checked the master bedroom while she started up the steps. The bedroom was empty, the bedding tossed as well, pictures overturned, frames broken.

Seconds later Liz returned and appeared at the bedroom door. "It's clear upstairs. Two rooms, no furniture in either one."

"There are signs of a struggle in here." He gestured to the overturned lamp, the dark handprint on the wall.

A print that looked like blood.

Liz knelt to examine the floor. "She was hurt, Rafe. There's a lot of blood here."

Liz was right. She'd obviously been injured.

The question was—was she still alive?

---

He cranked the engine and drove out toward Slaughter Creek, specifically to the place where that TBI agent Liz Lucas lived. He'd done his research on all the players in the Slaughter Creek investigation.

He'd seen that looker Brenda Banks when she'd done the story on Seven. She'd even made Seven sound sympathetic.

Now she was talking about him. The Dissector, that's what they were calling him.

He laughed at the name. It suited him. Made him stand out. Made him sound a little like Hannibal, except that he didn't eat his victims.

He just destroyed them by stripping them of the very organ that they used as a weapon.

Special Agent Rafe Hood worked with the Blackwood brothers. But they were chasing the Commander now.

Lucky for him the police were splintered.

And Miss Lucas. Ah, she was a beauty. Soft-looking blond hair swept her shoulders like silk. Her big luminous eyes shimmered with dark memories of her mother's death.

And of the man who'd almost destroyed her.

Ned Harlan. The Blade.

A smile curved his mouth. Liz was back, though, working his case. He was honored that she considered his mind worthy of dissecting.

Honored because she wasn't some damn fake. She'd lived with a maniac like Harlan and understood his drive. She would understand him as well. And she would make him famous. Make him a hero.

The truck bounced over the fucking ruts in the road, and he swerved to avoid a dog that ran out in front of him. No use killing a defenseless animal tonight.

Not when he had better prey.

For a second, he thought he spotted the blue lights of a police car swirling, and he slowed, holding his breath until the car passed.

Thankfully it was just a white car, and it roared on.

The steady drone of the engine ticked over the sound of his own breathing as the truck ate up the miles.

Liz Lucas had security. But security could be breached, especially with the woods backing up to the property. Not everyone knew about the dirt road on that side.

He parked on the far side of the woods, hidden deep in the copse of trees lining the deserted dirt road that used to take miners into the mountain. Now no one used it anymore.

Adrenaline pumping, he dragged the old biddy from the back of the truck and hauled her through the woods. At the edge of the property, a long screened-in porch ran the length of the profiler's house.

He scanned the backyard before he left the woods, then dragged the body up to the back porch steps. Then he situated her on the stairs, as if she were waiting for Liz to come home.

An animal growled from deep in the woods. Night had fallen, darkness cloaking the woods, reminding him of the long nights he'd spent alone trapped in darkness as a child. Only the sound of the others' cries had drowned out the silence.

Amelia's voice, whispering that she was scared.

Don't worry, darling, he murmured. Soon all our monsters will be dead.

And you and I will never have to be afraid of them again.

# Chapter Nineteen

———————— o ————————

While Rafe searched Mazie's cabin, Liz dug through her nightstand, searching for a clue as to where the nurse might have gone—some sign that she wasn't dead. And if she was, where was the body?

But Liz found no family pictures, no travel itinerary, no deeds to any other property.

"She doesn't seem to have a computer, and I can't find a purse or cell phone," Rafe said.

Liz scowled as she removed a folder inside the drawer and flipped it open: several news stories about the sanitarium and the CHIMES project, news of the senator's and the Commander's arrests.

Her finger brushed something stiff, and she realized that it was a business card Mazie had jammed between the panels. She tugged it out, her pulse quickening. The business card belonged to Brenda Banks.

"Look at this," she told Rafe. "I think Brenda may have talked to Mazie."

Rafe raised a brow. "Maybe that's where Brenda got the scoop on Blackwood and the project. We suspected she had a source."

"We need to talk to her," Liz said. "Maybe she's heard from Mazie."

Rafe collected a sample of the blood on the floor and bagged it to send to the lab. "I'll call Maddison to process this place. Maybe we'll lift a print and ID who was here."

Two possibilities sprang to mind. Six was targeting Mazie, as he'd done with Ester Banning and Beaulah Hodge. Or . . . the Commander or one of his men was determined to keep Mazie from revealing any more secrets.

Liz stepped outside to call Brenda while Rafe phoned Maddison. Three rings later, she answered. "Brenda Banks speaking."

"Brenda, this is Special Agent Liz Lucas."

"What can I do for you?"

Liz knew reporters guarded their sources, but she hoped Brenda would trust her. "Special Agent Hood and I are at Mazie Paulsen's cabin. I found your business card and wondered if you know where she is."

A pregnant pause "No—why would I?"

"Because I think you talked to her about the CHIMES project and the arrest of Blackwood and Senator Stowe."

A heartbeat passed. "I questioned her because she worked at the hospital."

"And she was employed at the time of the project?"

"Listen, Liz," Brenda said. "I don't feel comfortable talking about this. Whatever Mazie told me was strictly confidential."

"I understand that," Liz said. "But I think that something may have happened to Mazie. There are signs of foul play."

"Oh, God," Brenda said softly. "And Commander Blackwood is on the loose."

"Exactly. If she confided about the experiment, she's probably in danger." Liz paused. "That is, unless he already found her. We found blood in her bedroom."

"No one knows that she talked to me," Brenda said earnestly. "I've kept her identity secret."

"Maybe the Commander is just finishing up with everyone who knew about the experiment. There's also the possibility that the Dissector found Mazie."

"Why would he go after her?"

Liz measured her words. "Brenda, this is off the record, so you cannot print any of it, understand?"

"I understand," Brenda said. "You can trust me, Liz."

Liz rarely trusted anyone, but Brenda and Nick were together both personally and professionally, so if Nick trusted her, she supposed Brenda was all right. She explained her theory about the unsub killing nursing staff who either hurt him or were involved in the project, but refrained from mentioning J. R. Truitt and Castor.

"What about family?" Liz scavenged through the pictures that lay on the floor, crumpled and torn, their frames shattered. "There's a picture of a teenage girl and boy in her house. Were they her children?"

"I don't know, but I'll see what I can find out," Brenda said.

Liz ended the call and stepped back inside. Rafe had yanked on latex gloves and was examining a bullet casing that he held between his fingers. "Look what I dug out of the wall by the bed."

Liz walked over to study it. "Looks like the same caliber as the bullet that killed the senator."

Rafe dropped it into an evidence bag. "Which means that whoever killed the senator either shot Mazie or has her now."

---

When they arrived at Liz's, after spending all evening processing the scene at Mazie's house, the sound of dogs barking echoed from the back.

Already jumpy after the earlier break-in, Liz pulled her gun and eased around the side of the building.

Rafe's senses were instantly on high alert, and he removed his own gun from the holster and followed her. The wind shook the trees, causing rain to drip down.

A German shepherd hovered by the porch, barking at something on the steps. Rafe slowly brought his hand up to stroke the dog's back, murmuring soft words to quiet him.

Liz came to an abrupt stop. "Oh, my God. There's a body on my porch."

Rafe grimaced. Blood stained the dead woman's face and chin, and her mouth hung open as if she'd been posed. He inched closer, patting the dog to pull him away.

The woman had obviously been murdered, her tongue cut out.

The Dissector had struck again.

And this time he'd left his victim at Liz's door to flaunt his kill.

# Chapter Twenty

———————— o ————————

Liz's stomach rolled at the sight of the blood streaking the woman's mouth and chin. Her lips had turned a nasty purple, and bruises discolored her face, as if the killer had used some kind of tool to hold her mouth open.

She half expected the body to be Mazie's, but it wasn't.

Rafe yanked the dog away and sent it running into the woods as Liz snapped a photo of the victim. "What exactly did you do to our unsub to make him remove your tongue?" she asked the corpse.

Was that man Brian Castor? Had he dumped this woman's body on her doorstep earlier today because he was pissed they'd questioned him?

Or was this Truitt's work?

Rafe examined the woman's hands, arms, and legs for injuries. But other than scrapes and bruises from the ropes the killer had bound her with, she hadn't sustained any other wounds. The unsub had cut out her tongue for a reason, just as he'd targeted the other victims' hands and eyes.

"You think she knew something—that the missing tongue is a message that he didn't want her to talk?"

Liz shook her head. "Some killers do that, but this is different." The chill of the night washed over her, making her shiver. "It seems like he cut off victim one's hands because she'd hurt him with them—that's the reason he beat her with them. Vic two lost her eyes because she must have used them to inflict pain on him. The same with this woman's tongue."

"Jesus. What next?" Rafe asked.

"We need to catch him before there is a next."

Rafe punched Maddison's number. "I'm calling the crime lab. Guess they'll be working overtime again."

Liz studied the woods behind her home. The creek was only a few feet away, bordered by trees. The other two victims had been left near the water, but this body had been left at her door.

To show her that the killer knew he was beating them at the game.

---

Nick finally had a lead on his father.

He'd worked with tech all day on that damned website for the Commander's followers. One name stuck out as a possible accomplice to his escape. The crazy woman had professed undying love for his father. The thought made him grind his molars.

But he'd tracked her down, and she was in a wheelchair.

An extremist militant group voiced their support for the experiments. Paranoia about other government secret projects was evident in the posts, and conspiracy theories abounded. Some contributors had military backgrounds and connections.

The mountains were the perfect place for the group's headquarters—and the perfect place to hide the Commander.

Nick phoned Brenda to check on her, grateful she'd agreed to have dinner with her parents. At one time her father, the mayor, had disapproved of Nick, but they both loved Brenda, and more than anything they wanted to keep her safe. If Brenda knew he'd phoned the mayor to ask him to watch her tonight, she'd be furious.

Love made a man do crazy things.

Gears ground as he climbed the mountain, the switchbacks and ridges leading him into the dark, deserted forests. Storm clouds rumbled again, and the roads were coated with the earlier hail, forcing him to crawl along the narrow road.

His phone buzzed. Carl Mallard, the secretary of defense, again. Damn, the man was putting the heat on him. He punched connect. "Agent Blackwood."

"Tell me you know where Commander Blackwood is."

"I think I may have a lead." Nick explained about the militant group.

"That does sound like just the sort of group he would turn to. Where the hell did you say they meet?"

"They're in the mountains. I'm on my way there now," Nick said. "I'll keep you updated."

"Good. I'd like something to report to the committee when we meet this week. No one wants a devious man like Blackwood on the loose."

Nick agreed, and hung up. Pines and oaks swayed in the wind, the branches bending with the weight of the earlier rain, tossing twigs and pine needles across the road. He steered the SUV up a side road. Icy mountain water trickled along the tall stone ridges, running down the embankment. The moon tried to fight its way through the clouds but failed miserably, making the area look even more desolate.

His GPS showed he was a half mile from the group's base camp, so he slowed, debating whether he should confront the group or slip in and do surveillance.

Surveillance won.

He veered into a space between several trees, cut the engine, and climbed out, grabbing his binoculars and his camera with a telephoto lens. Tucking his gun into his holster, he strode through the woods toward the camp.

The sound of gunfire made him pause. Several gunshots.

What the hell was going on?

Barbed wire fencing surrounded the area, barring curiosity seekers, and NO TRESPASSING signs had been tacked up along the fence line in several areas. Nick tried to cut through the fence with a small pair of wire cutters, but the wire was too strong. He hurried back to the SUV and retrieved his military bolt cutters, using them to clip a small section, enough to allow him entry.

Twigs snapped beneath his boots as he inched through the woods. Finally he spotted an old building that looked as if it might have once been some kind of fishing/hunting camp. Three other metal buildings had been erected, and there were campfires spread around the site.

He counted at least four men in military uniforms with assault rifles guarding the camp; there'd be more inside the buildings, he suspected. A group of preteen boys holding weapons and wearing camouflage were lined up, waiting their turn to shoot at makeshift targets.

An obstacle course for physical training had been built to the right. Nick used his night binoculars to peer through the trees. Two men in uniforms were unloading boxes full of semiautomatic weapons and hauling them into one of the metal buildings.

A limb crunched behind him, and suddenly Nick felt a gun barrel at the back of his neck.

"Who the hell are you?" a voice growled. "And what are you doing on private property?"

Nick froze. He knew these men's mindsets. Violence, taking lives—they considered it their honor to serve their country.

Was the Commander here? Maybe he was actually running this place, training a new wave of boys to kill for him.

They'd probably been taught to do anything to protect the mission.

Killing a federal agent wouldn't faze them.

———————— , ————————

Liz took several deep breaths to stem the nausea washing over her. But the darkness drew her in. She was in the killer's mind, watching him tie the woman down, raise the knife, and carve out her tongue while she struggled to escape.

Next came images of the victim crying for help. The woman had looked into her killer's eyes and seen only evil there as he ripped out her tongue.

Liz glanced up at her porch, fear slithering through her. She pulled her gun. "I'm checking the house."

"Wait and let me call for backup," Rafe said.

"I can't let him get away again." Liz climbed the steps, bypassing the body, then reached for the door to the porch. Her alarm had been set, but appeared to have been turned off.

Rafe punched Lieutenant Maddison's number and asked him to get a team out to the house as he followed her up the steps.

Liz gave the door a gentle push, and it squeaked open.

"You left it unlocked?" Rafe asked.

Liz shook her head. "No. The alarm was set."

Rafe hissed between his teeth and entered the porch behind her. She surveyed the screened-in area, but saw nothing out of place.

Slowly she inched inside the kitchen, scanning left and right, but nothing looked amiss. Rafe gestured that he'd go left, and she went right, toward her bedroom. Rafe's footsteps were soft, but she could hear him combing the kitchen and extra room.

Suddenly Liz smelled garlic.

Her heart hammered against her breastbone. Gripping her gun with clammy hands, she fought the churning in her belly and inched into her bedroom, searching the room for signs of an intruder. The chair where she'd tossed her nightgown was empty now.

The killer might have taken it for some perverse reason.

Breathing deeply to calm her fear, she opened the closet door, but her clothes were still hanging as she'd left them, shoes stacked in the bins.

She crossed the room and checked the bathroom, but there was nothing out of place. Makeup on the vanity. Body wash and shampoo in the shower caddy.

Relieved that no one was inside, she turned and walked back into the bedroom—then froze, her throat closing, as she glanced at her pillow.

Another white rose lay in the middle.

───────────── , ─────────────

Rafe darted to Liz's room in case the unsub had hidden inside, waiting to ambush her. Déjà vu of nearly losing her to Harlan assaulted him.

If he hadn't been so damn determined to keep his distance after they crawled into bed together, he would have been with her the night she was abducted, and she never would have been hurt.

He'd never forgive himself for that mistake.

"Liz?"

Her back was to him, but it looked as if she'd stuffed something under her pillow.

"Was someone here?"

She turned around, her face ashen, eyes washed out. Something was terribly wrong. He rushed across the room and wrapped his hands around her arms. "Liz, what is it? You look like you saw a ghost."

"I think Harlan is alive, that he's been in my house."

Rafe's body tensed to high alert. Not the Dissector . . . Harlan. "Did you see him?"

She shook her head, a heavy sigh escaping. "The smell. Garlic." She pressed a hand to her face. "Don't you smell it?"

Rafe frowned, trying to detect the odor. But if there was garlic in the air, it was so subtle he didn't recognize it. "I'm sorry, no, I . . . I don't."

Was this case triggering traumatic memories to the point that she was imagining Harlan's return?

"The MO of the Dissector fits with the victim outside," he said, pointing out the obvious.

Liz pulled away from him, her lips pinched in anger.

Then Rafe saw the bottle of pills on her nightstand. Antianxiety medication. The bottle was half empty.

Liz had lied to the chief when she told him she'd stopped taking them.

───────────── , ─────────────

Liz couldn't shake the memories of her attack.

Months ago, when Harlan had raised the knife to her neck and sliced her, Rafe had swept in to fight him. The next few minutes had been a blur as she'd lapsed into unconsciousness.

When she woke up in the hospital, bandaged and medicated, she'd held her pain deep inside. And her secret . . .

It was the only way.

Rafe stroked her arm. "Are you all right, Liz?"

She nodded. A lie. She wasn't okay. She wouldn't be until Harlan was locked away. Or dead.

God, she wanted him dead.

Had he killed the woman on her doorstep, or had she caught the attention of the Dissector now? The account of her ordeal had been all over the news a few months ago. This new unsub could have read about it. He could have left the white rose just to make her think Harlan had returned.

A knock sounded on the door, and Rafe rushed to answer it. She heard him talking to Lieutenant Maddison and CSI Perkins.

Their voices faded away as they went back outside so Rafe could show them the body.

Liz waited until she heard the door close, then took the rose and bagged it. If Harlan had left it, he might not have bothered to wear gloves. He wanted her to know he'd been at her house—that he was counting the minutes until he had her in his clutches again, until he killed her.

The rose would prove that she wasn't crazy or imagining things. That someone had really been there.

The anguish that had overpowered her after the attack flooded her again. She wanted to retreat to that faraway place, lost in her silence and denial, where no one could hurt her again.

She wanted to curl up in Rafe's arms and feel his hands on her and his arms around her. She wanted him to love her and make the pain go away.

But how could she ask that, and not confess the truth? If he knew the truth, he'd be devastated that she'd kept it from him.

───────────── , ─────────────

Amelia added the final strokes to her painting of Six, then stared into the bottomless pit of his eyes, willing herself to understand him. His physical appearance changed every time she saw him. He was a master of disguise, an intelligent man, well versed in medical practices and skilled with a knife. He had a photographic memory.

He would never forget it if she betrayed him.

Evil flared in his eyes, yet a deep agony gleamed there too, as if he were two different people.

Just as she had been all her life. Fragmented.

Crazed with the horrors of what they'd endured and the memories of the Commander's punishment.

Driven to survive no matter what.

*Ting. Ting. Ting.* The wind chimes tinkled.

She'd seen how he'd suffered.

Knew the horrors he'd endured. The sensory deprivation experiments. The constant barrage of pictures of mutilations and sex scenes that followed. Scenes that aroused him.

Disturbed by the memory, she crawled into bed and closed her eyes. Rachel's voice grated at the back of her mind.

*You're evil, Amelia. A sinner. Sinners go to hell.*

"I'm not evil. Go away." Determination mushroomed inside her. She'd forced little Bessie to disappear, and Viola, and Skid. And now this Rachel person was here. Rachel the religious fanatic.

Rachel had to leave too.

Cold air seeped through the window of the cabin, making the room feel icy.

Suddenly she sensed someone in the room.

Six. She smelled his musky odor. Felt his hands reach for her as he slipped into bed behind her.

"I missed you, Amelia."

Amelia inhaled, her body aching for physical comfort. But her mind told her that Six's loving wasn't real love. That it was all-consuming. Poisonous.

Smothering.

He eased her hair back from her face and whispered against her ear, "You'd never tell anyone about us, would you? You know I love you."

Amelia clutched the sheets in the dark, half terrified, half excited by his touch.

She wanted to be loved so badly. To be whole and have a family like Sadie. But she couldn't imagine Jake ever holding Sadie down and scaring her.

Six nuzzled her neck. "Amelia?"

*Make him leave. He's a pervert!* Rachel shouted. *You're both sinners.*

Amelia closed her eyes, willing strength into her voice and trying to quiet Rachel. But the metallic scent of blood wafted around her.

*Repent your sins,* Rachel said again. *If you don't tell Sadie, you're nothing but a murderer yourself.*

God help her. She'd been hoping all along that Six wasn't the killer the police were looking for. But she smelled blood on him.

Maybe Rachel had known all along . . .

Tears blinded Amelia. What was she going to do? If she turned against Six, he would kill her, too.

# Chapter Twenty-One

———— o ————

L iz slipped the bagged rose to CSI Perkins. "I need you to see if you can lift any evidence from this. Someone broke in and left it in my house."

Perkins took the bag. "Sure. Do you have a suspect in mind?"

Liz lowered her voice. "Yes—Harlan. But most everyone in the department thinks he's dead, so I want to verify it before I mention it."

Perkins adjusted his glasses. "I'll let you know what I find asap."

The lights of a van appeared around the corner of the building, and Rafe grimaced. "It's Brenda Banks. Can you deal with her while Maddison and I search the area?"

Liz nodded, knowing Rafe and Maddison were looking for the woman's tongue. They wouldn't find it, though. The unsub had kept it as his trophy.

She envisioned a room full of jars with various organs in them, and bile rose in her throat.

Brenda stormed around the corner, her cameraman in tow. Liz hurried to stop her from getting too close.

"Brenda, you can't show the vic's photo. We haven't even iden-tified her."

"I'm aware of that, but Agent Lucas, this is the third gruesome murder this week. The citizens of Slaughter Creek have a right to know that there's a psychopath on the loose."

Liz inhaled sharply, trying to curb her temper. Brenda was right. But the fact that they hadn't solved the case yet and that this victim was lying on her very own doorstep grated on her nerves.

And made her guilt mount.

How many more women had to die before they stopped this unsub?

"What body part did he take this time?" Brenda asked.

Liz glared at her. "I'm not going to answer that. In fact, you've jeopardized the case by labeling him the Dissector in the first place."

"I'm just doing my job," Brenda said.

Liz took a deep breath. "And making our jobs more difficult."

"Then give me something, and I'll get out of your way." Brenda shoved the microphone toward her.

"All right, a short interview." After all, she had to address the public, or they would panic.

Brenda looked surprised. "That would be great." She leaned closer. "By the way, have you or Rafe heard from Nick?"

Liz folded her arms. "No. . . . Why?"

Brenda worried her bottom lip with her teeth. "He texted that he had a lead on the Commander, and that he was going to check it out, but I haven't heard from him."

Liz offered her a smile. "I'm sure Nick is fine. He may be doing surveillance and simply not be able to call."

"I suppose." Brenda finger-combed her hair, then turned toward her cameraman and gestured for him to start rolling. "This is Brenda Banks, reporting from a residence outside Slaughter Creek, where the body of another woman has just been found." She tilted the microphone toward Liz. "This latest victim was left at the home of

Special Agent Liz Lucas, who has been investigating the case of the Dissector. Agent Lucas, do you have any suspects?"

Liz forced a calm to her voice as she addressed the camera. While she didn't want to alarm residents, she also wanted them to be cautious.

"It's true that a body was left on my property tonight. The victim was a white woman in her late forties to fifties, but we haven't identified her yet."

"But you think she was murdered by the same person who killed Ester Banning and Beaulah Hodge?"

"That is our working theory," Liz said. "We have questioned a couple of persons of interest, but we're still pursuing other leads."

"Do you think this latest serial killer case is connected to the CHIMES experiment?"

"I'm not at liberty to discuss specifics, but we are asking residents to be diligent about their safety and to phone us if they have any information regarding these crimes."

Brenda licked her lips. "Agent Lucas, why do you think the perpetrator left the body at your house? Do you think it has to do with the fact that you were the lead investigator in a serial killer crime related to your own mother's murder?"

Now she was getting way too personal. "He left the victim here to make a statement to the police, to boast that he's escaped detection. He's challenging me to find him." She looked directly into the camera. "And trust me, I will find you."

Liz hadn't realized that Rafe had come up behind her. He jerked the microphone away from Brenda and shut it off.

"What in the hell are you doing, Liz? Inviting the bastard to come after you?"

---

Rafe struggled to temper his reaction. The last time Liz had been in front of the camera on the Harlan case, she'd made a similar statement.

And Harlan *had* come after her—and nearly killed her.

The Dissector could do the same thing.

She lifted her chin defiantly. "I'm doing my job, Rafe." She gestured behind her toward the body. "Ignoring the fact that he literally left a victim on my doorstep would only piss him off more. He wants to think he's getting to us."

Rafe bit back an argument. She was the profiler, and she was right. But he didn't like it one damn bit.

Brenda and the cameraman were watching them, so Rafe pulled Liz to the side. "We have to do something, Rafe," she said. "Just think about it. That the killer's appearance on the personal property of an agent means he's escalating. He's taking chances."

Rafe recognized the determination in Liz's voice. She'd spoken with the same intensity right before he'd nearly lost her to that other bastard. "Then he'll make a mistake, and we'll catch him. You don't have to throw yourself in front of the bus to do that."

Liz shifted, hands on her hips. "But we need to stop him before any more women die."

CSI Perkins approached them, his flashlight probing the woods. "We didn't find the tongue."

"The killer took it." Liz angled her face away from Brenda so she wouldn't hear. "Just as his name suggests, he's keeping the body parts as his trophies."

Rafe walked over to Dr. Bullock. "Cause of death?"

"Bled to death, like the others. She died sometime yesterday— late afternoon, early evening. I'll let you know what I find when I do the autopsy."

Maddison joined them, notepad in hand.

"We need an ID," Rafe told him. "Run her prints, and if that doesn't turn up anything, plug her picture into facial software recognition."

Liz gestured toward her phone. "I'll email her picture to the head of HomeBound and the director of the sanitarium, see if either of them recognizes her."

Liz stepped away to text the photo, and Maddison lowered his voice. "Is Agent Lucas all right, Hood?"

"Yes," Rafe said. "She's strong."

"But I know what she went through before, that she had to go into therapy."

"Therapy is routine for any agent who was abducted, terrorized, or injured."

Maddison shrugged. "Still, should she be working this case?" He pointed toward the dead woman. "Especially considering the killer is getting personal with her."

The nagging worry in Rafe's belly was turning into a damned ulcer. Hell, Maddison was preaching to the choir. "I don't like it either. I'll take her somewhere safe after we're finished here."

The ME called Maddison's name. They were ready to transport the woman's body to the morgue, so Rafe walked around front to find Liz. Brenda and her cameraman were packing up as he slipped into Liz's house.

"Mr. Samson, I just sent a photo of another victim to your HomeBound office," Liz said. "Please let me know if you recognize her." She hung up, then dialed another number. "Mr. Loggins, I sent you a photo of a woman who was found murdered outside my house tonight. Please let me know if you recognize her and if she worked for the sanitarium. She looks to be late forties to fifties, and could have been involved in the Slaughter Creek experiments."

Liz pocketed her phone as Rafe entered. "It's late, Rafe. Maybe we'll hear something in the morning."

"Pack a bag," Rafe said. "You're not staying here tonight."

Liz opened her mouth to speak.

"I'm not arguing, Liz," Rafe said firmly. "It's late, and we're both exhausted. We'll hit the ground running tomorrow, but let's go to my place and get some sleep."

Uncertainty flared in Liz's eyes. "To your place?"

Rafe shrugged, although he couldn't resist giving her a devil-ish look. "You'll be safe there with me, Liz."

She gave him a doubtful look, but disappeared into her bed-room to pack.

# Chapter Twenty-Two

———— ◦ ————

Rafe veered onto a graveled road leading into the woods. "You moved here?" Liz asked.

"Yeah. I rented a cabin."

Rafe parked, and she studied his house. Icicles had begun to form along the overhang of the roof. Rafe started around to her side of the car, but she forced herself out. She'd stood her ground; she couldn't back down now.

Rafe retrieved her bag from the back of the SUV, and she followed him up the stone path. The rustic log cabin looked primitive against the dark woods, but when he opened the door and they entered, it felt new and cozy. Whitewashed wood floors complemented knotty pine walls and ceilings. Comfortable chairs and a tan sofa formed a sitting area around a stone fireplace that ran from floor to ceiling. Skylights brought in light, although tonight winter clouds shrouded the moon and stars.

Stainless steel appliances and a granite counter gave the cabin a modern feel, yet a braided rug reminded her of days gone by.

"This is beautiful," she said, hoping to ease the awkwardness between them.

Rafe gestured toward the bathroom. "If you want, there's the shower."

Liz rubbed at the back of her neck. "Thanks, I think I will."

His gaze met hers, dark emotions glittering. Emotions she was afraid to explore.

"Are you hungry?"

She shook her head. "A drink would be good."

He nodded, and she grabbed her bag from him and ducked into the bathroom. She closed the door and leaned against it, the night's events playing on her nerves.

They'd found a dead woman at her house. Someone had left a rose on her bed. And now she was here, alone with Rafe.

She stripped, her body trembling as she stepped beneath the warm spray of water.

But when she closed her eyes to rid the tension, the image of a man cutting out a woman's tongue rose in front of her.

———————— · ————————

Rafe felt the stench of death on him as Liz disappeared into the shower. He could still smell the blood, the decomposing body, the sweat from the victim. The room was cold, too, so he lit a fire, then poured shots of bourbon for himself and Liz.

Deciding he needed to wash away the odor himself, he showered in the master bathroom, his gut knotting every time he thought about the fact that Liz could have been home when the killer had left that body on her porch.

She was a damn magnet for trouble.

Or maybe it was the death curse following him, reminding him that anyone he got too close to would end up dead.

Something had spooked her inside her house, too, specifically in her bedroom.

Something she was hiding from him.

Something besides the fact that she was still taking antianxiety medication.

Maybe she was afraid he'd have her removed from the case.

Hell, he *wanted* to do just that. Because he wanted her safe, dammit. And she would never be safe doing her job.

Just like he wouldn't be.

Still, it was different . . .

A dark laugh caught in his throat. Yeah, Liz would love that sexist thinking.

He towel-dried his hair and yanked on jeans and a clean shirt, although he didn't bother to button it.

Tension vibrated through him as he stepped from the bedroom. The guest bathroom door was cracked, steam oozing out in a cloudy, sensual haze. He imagined her naked, and his pulse kicked up a notch.

He caught sight of Liz in the mirror as he paused at the door. She'd dressed in a camisole tank and boxer pajama shorts.

The steam from the shower created a halo around her, making her look sensual and so damn beautiful that his blood stirred. "Are you okay, Liz?"

"Yes," she said.

But her voice broke, making her sound vulnerable as if she needed someone to hold her.

He wanted to be that someone.

Her sigh punctuated the silence stretching between them.

He inhaled deeply, vying for control, but when he got a whiff of her body wash and shampoo, he felt himself swiftly losing control.

"You could have been there when he left that woman," he said, his voice cracking.

"But I wasn't," Liz replied quietly.

Emotions blending with need, Rafe tipped her chin up with his thumb. Desire darkened Liz's eyes, and the memory of making love to her flashed back in delicious tempting snippets that made him harden.

"Rafe," Liz whispered.

"Shh," he murmured. "I can't help it, Liz. I tried to forget how it felt to be with you, but I can't."

Her sweet sigh of acquiescence fueled his hunger. "Neither can I."

Her softly spoken admission shattered his last shred of restraint, and he cradled her face between his hands and did what he'd wanted to do the moment she'd walked back into his life.

He closed his mouth over hers and kissed her.

———————— , ————————

Liz had wanted Rafe's arms around her for months. Ever since she'd pushed him away at the hospital . . .

"Liz?" Rafe teased her lips apart with his tongue, drawing her back to the moment and the desire rippling through her. She'd missed him, missed this.

No man had ever given her orgasms like Rafe.

He probed deeper with his tongue, and she moaned, raking her hands up his back to draw him closer. Rafe was all strong, sinewy muscle, his body hard as a rock. His hands glided everywhere, teasing her to life with erotic sensations that she hadn't felt since the last time he'd touched her.

She wanted more.

He deepened the kiss, hands roving over her hips and down her legs. She wrapped a leg around him, sliding her foot up and down his thigh. He hadn't buttoned his shirt, and she slid her hands inside, stroking his chest until he groaned and pushed her against the wall.

He dipped his head and trailed kisses down her neck, suckling the sensitive skin behind her ear as his hand cupped her breast. Her nipples hardened to peaks, aching for his mouth.

Rafe seemed to read her mind. He kissed his way down her throat, then lifted her camisole and teased one nipple with his fingers while he closed his mouth around the other. Liz moaned his name, frantic to have him naked, to feel his bare skin.

His breath sent a chill rippling through her as he moved his mouth to the other breast, and she clung to him, willing him to take her to bed.

"God, Liz, I've wanted you," he growled.

She smiled as she dipped her head and took his nipple between her teeth. He moaned, then picked her up and carried her to his bed.

For a fraction of a second, she remembered the scar, covering it with her hand.

"Don't hide from me, Liz," he murmured as he pulled her hand away and kissed the jagged line.

His tenderness made tears pool in her eyes. Then he made her forget everything but him when he stripped her pajamas and tossed his shirt and jeans to the side. He kissed her again as he slid between her thighs, and she opened for him, needing him more than she needed air.

Last time, at her house, he'd pleasured her and taken nothing for himself.

This time she wanted to please him.

She rolled him over to his back, and cupped his thick length in her hands.

"Liz," he groaned.

"Let me," she whispered. She trailed her tongue down his torso and abdomen, circling his cock with her lips and mouth. He dug his hands into her hair and threw his head back, and she loved him with her mouth until he yanked her up on top of him and gripped her hips.

"Wait," he said in a strained voice. He reached inside the nightstand, grabbed a condom, ripped the wrapper open with his teeth, and rolled it on. Liz watched, tempted to tell him that they didn't need it, but she held back.

No explanations now.

They both needed to feel, to be alive. To hold each other and forget the horror that had been on her doorstep.

That more horrors would come tomorrow, and the next day, and the day after that.

He framed her face with his big hands and kissed her again, and Liz forgot about everything else as pleasure overcame her.

She straddled him and sank onto his rigid length, closing her eyes and savoring each inch as he penetrated her. Erotic sensations overcame her, and she braced her hands beside his chest and rode him.

Rafe teased her clit with his fingers as she built a rhythm, their bodies sliding against each other, slick skin against slick skin, sex against sex, until she felt the tremors of her release clawing at her.

Liz whispered his name as the colors blinded her and she soared over the edge.

———————— , ————————

Rafe groaned with pleasure as his release seized him. Liz's sweet body moved against him, creating an erotic friction that made him crave her again.

She clung to him, riding him until the waves of pleasure started to recede, and he rolled them to the side and cradled her in his arms. Their bodies were still joined, their breathing erratic, the room filled with their heated lovemaking.

Liz kissed his neck, and he tightened his hold, stroking the fine softness of her back. Memories of the dead women tried to intercede, but just for tonight, he banished them.

They would tackle work tomorrow. Tonight he wanted to savor the fact that Liz was alive and naked in his arms.

Where he wanted her every night.

He tensed; the thought had come out of nowhere. The idea of waking up to her every morning stirred primitive instincts and hunger.

But fear rode on its tail.

Liz's breathing steadied, and he realized she'd fallen asleep. He threaded his fingers into her hair, amazed at the silkiness, enchanted by the soft purr she emitted when he kissed her cheek.

But the scar on her neck reminded him that she could be taken from him any minute.

Shaken by the realization that he was losing himself in her again, he left the bed, disposed of the condom, and tugged on a pair of sweats. He walked into his den and paced the room, desperate to wrangle his emotions under control.

The wooden animals he'd carved for the Boys' Club were lined up on his bookshelf, waiting for his next visit. He took his knife off the shelf, then stepped onto his back porch and dropped into the chair he kept outside.

Remembering Benny's little face, he knew he had to make something special for him.

Night sounds crept around him, the animals foraging in the woods, the trees rustling, as he selected a piece of wood. One of his mentors at the club had taught him how to whittle. Something about carving an object out of a raw piece of wood helped relieve his stress.

Then he'd realized that the young kids at the Boys' Club liked his crude pieces, so he kept up the hobby.

Tonight he carved a deer, whittling and smoothing the wood until he felt himself relaxing.

But he thought of Liz in his bed, and his sex hardened again.

He'd broken his own rules by getting involved with her. By caring so much for anyone.

But there was something about Liz that made it impossible not to care.

―――――――――― ・ ――――――――――

Sweat soaked the back of Nick's shirt. The bastards who'd taken him at gunpoint had refused to let him go. Instead they'd tied him up, tossed him into a chair in some kind of interrogation room, and beaten him until he was so weak he'd passed out at one point.

"You know I'm an agent with the TBI," Nick growled. "Just tell me where the Commander is, and we can make a deal."

The big burly guy in camouflage, who appeared to be the leader of this militant group, crossed his beefy arms. "We told you we don't know."

"I don't believe you. I saw your posts on that damned website. You support what he did. You helped him escape."

"That's because pussies are running the government now. Someone has to take action to defend this country."

"Commander Blackwood is not doing anything for the country," Nick said. "He took advantage of innocents in a crazy experiment that even the government realized failed. Why else would they cover it up?"

"The same reason they lie to the public and don't tell the citizens about terrorist attacks they know are imminent."

More conspiracy theories.

"You think teaching those young boys to kill is protecting our country? You're brainwashing them to commit murder based on your own paranoia."

The man clenched his assault rifle. "You must have been a disappointment to your father."

Nick opened his mouth to argue, but the asshole raised the weapon and slammed it against his head. He grunted in pain, his head swimming. Another blow came, then another. Nausea threatened, and he passed out again.

When he stirred, he struggled with the wire they'd strapped around his hands. Two of the big guys stood watching him.

He had to get out of here. Save himself. Bring Jake and backup to disband this group.

The wire cut into his wrists, and he twisted and fumbled to undo it until blood dripped down his fingers.

One of the soldiers took his fists to him again. Another blow and another, and Nick spit blood at his attacker's feet. Driven by his survival instincts, he lunged from the chair and slammed his head into the man's gut, knocking him backward. Head-butting him, he dug his elbows into the man's chest, striving to render him unconscious.

Seconds later, two of the militants rushed in and dragged him off their leader. Nick cursed and threw a kick at the bigger guy, but another blow to the head made him fall to his knees.

Before he could recover, they hauled him out of the room into the dark. Nick scanned his surroundings, using his weight to slow the men down.

"We going to kill him?" one of the men asked the other.

"Probably. But we'll wait for our orders." A low laugh. "Not that anyone will ever find him out here."

Nick summoned his energy and pushed to his feet again, but they had the advantage and shoved him into a hole in the ground.

He blinked to orient himself, but it was so damn dark he couldn't see, and he toppled down a set of stairs and landed with a thud at the bottom. He ate dirt as he rolled to his back, and the darkness swallowed him.

Above him, the wooden door slammed shut and hammers pounded.

Fuck. They were nailing him into this godforsaken hole in the ground. Then they'd probably pack up, move their headquarters, and leave him here to die.

# Chapter Twenty-Three

—————— o ——————

For the first time in ages, Liz slept peacefully. No nightmares to terrify her. Instead she dreamed that she and Rafe were living together in a beautiful cabin in the mountains, happy and content. Snow fluttered down, Christmas music played in the background, and the tree sparkled with white lights.

Three stockings hung from the hearth—one filled with rattles and baby bibs in anticipation of the baby they'd have.

She jerked awake, then rolled over, but the space beside her was empty. Rafe's head print still remained on the pillow, and she inhaled his masculine scent, missing him already.

Stretching to relieve the kinks in her muscles, she ducked into the shower, almost hating to wash off the scent of Rafe's lovemaking.

But she and Rafe had a job to do.

She dressed in jeans and a denim shirt, then dabbed powder on her cheeks to cover the dark spots beneath her eyes that betrayed the sleep she'd lost this week.

A little lip gloss, and she hurried to meet Rafe.

The scent of coffee and bacon wafted toward her, and she found him sipping from a mug while he flipped the bacon in the pan. She was tempted to run her hands over his back and greet him with a morning kiss.

But the look he gave her when he glanced over his shoulder made her pause. Just like he had the last time they'd gotten close, he already seemed to be pulling away.

"Smells good in here," she said, testing the waters.

He shrugged. "Figured we'd need breakfast before we hit the road." He gestured toward the cabinet above the coffeepot. "Mugs are up there."

She offered a tentative smile, opened the cabinet, and chose a handmade mug. He placed the bacon on a plate lined with a paper towel, then scooped eggs and toast onto more two plates, carried the food to the table, and set it by the orange juice he'd poured. Butter and jelly waited on the table.

"Thanks," she said, suddenly feeling awkward. Early morning sunlight filtered through the trees, glittering off the soft coating of snow on the ground, dappling golden lines across the oak table. The scene felt cozy, so intimate, that she ached to reach across the table and squeeze his hand.

To kiss him and beg him to come back to bed, where they could forget about murders and dead bodies and focus on loving each other all day.

But being needy would only drive Rafe away and prove to him that she wasn't ready to be back at the bureau.

"Where should we start this morning?" she asked.

Rafe spooned a bite of his eggs into his mouth and chewed. "The sheriff who handled the Lintell woman's murder. See if Brian Castor or his brother were persons of interest in that case."

A strained silence stretched between them as she ate. Finally, Liz couldn't stand it any longer. "Rafe, about last night . . ."

He threw up a warning hand. "Forget about it, Liz. It's normal to need a tension release."

Anger hit her. "Is that what we were doing? Just releasing tension?"

His level gaze showed no emotion. "Of course."

Liz gripped her coffee cup. She certainly didn't intend to declare her feelings when he obviously didn't reciprocate them.

He rose to clear the dishes, and her gaze strayed to the bookshelf, where a dozen or more wooden carvings filled the shelf. On the table, a deer stood, staring at her. She hadn't noticed it last night.

Not that she'd noticed much. Her nerves had been frayed, her senses on overdrive. All she'd thought about were Rafe's hands and mouth on her.

"Do you carve the wooden animals yourself?" she asked.

An odd expression flared in Rafe's eyes, almost as if he was embarrassed. "Yeah. It's a hobby."

"They're beautiful," Liz said. Primitive and rough looking, just like him. "Do you sell them?"

"I make them for the kids at the Boys' Club."

Liz's heart skipped a beat. "You volunteer with the Boys' Club?"

Rafe shrugged. "Yeah. One of my social workers took me when I was a kid. I met an older guy who mentored me and kept me out of trouble." He ran his finger over the head of the deer. "He taught me how to whittle."

Liz's heart melted. Rafe had always held his emotions close to the vest. He was so dedicated to his job, so good at tracking down evil, that she'd never imagined him with children at all, much less volunteering to spend time with them.

He set the deer back on the table, with a sigh. "There's a little kid there now, Benny, about four, just lost both parents. I thought he might like it."

Tears nearly blinded her. Beneath that tough, steely veneer, Rafe was tenderhearted.

He might want a family of his own some day. Something she could never give him.

Rafe stepped onto the porch to phone Jim Laredo, the sheriff who'd investigated the social worker's murder.

The subject of his volunteer work made him feel raw, exposed. Maybe because he related to the troubled kids so well—to their personal tragedies, to the violence they'd suffered at the hands of people who were supposed to love and care for them.

Sheriff Laredo answered on the third ring, his breath rattling. Rafe explained that he needed to talk to the sheriff, and Laredo gave him directions to his house.

His cell phone rang just as he hung up. "Agent Hood."

"Rafe, it's Jake. Have you heard from Nick?"

"No," Rafe said. "Brenda asked Liz the same thing last night, but neither of us have talked to him."

"Hell," Jake muttered. "Brenda's frantic. He didn't come home last night. And he's not answering his cell. Can you get the techs to trace his phone for a location?"

"Sure." Trepidation mounted in Rafe's belly. Nick had been chasing a lead about the Commander. Maybe he'd gotten too close and stumbled into trouble.

He had no doubt the Commander would kill his sons to protect himself and his secrets.

They hung up, and Rafe punched the number for the lab and requested the trace. "Call Sheriff Blackwood if you find him."

Liz returned from the bedroom with her purse, her face strained, and they headed out to the SUV together. The memory of the erotic pleasure they'd shared teased him, tempting him to love her again.

Not going to happen now. He had to focus.

Sun fought with the storm clouds in the gray sky, the temperature dropping to the thirties as they drove around the mountain toward the neighboring town of Patchy Rock. A saloon, a saddle and tack shop, and a western boot store flanked one side of the street. Signs advertising trail riding and a dude ranch were tacked all over town. Other signs announced a whitewater rafting company and outpost a few miles on the other side of the mountain.

Apparently Sheriff Laredo had retired ten years ago and moved near the outpost, so Rafe passed through Patchy Rock and wound onto the country road leading to the river.

Farmland sprawled between the town and outpost. A junkyard and flea market sat on top of a hill, along with a country store boasting Native American crafts.

Two miles down the road, Rafe made the turn to Laredo's. The former sheriff lived in a small cabin nestled at the foot of a hill, near a creek that flowed into the river. Rafe parked, and he and Liz waded through the weeds to the man's front door. When Rafe knocked, a dog barked, its toenails clacking on the floor inside.

"Hang on," a man shouted.

A minute later the door swung open and a short, chubby man with wiry hair greeted them. "You got to be those feds."

Laredo rubbed a hand over his belly, which strained against a dark gray T-shirt. "Come on in. I pulled up that file after you called. Been a couple years, and my memory ain't what it used to be."

They followed him inside to the den, a small room overloaded with hunting and fishing magazines. Pictures of three children, ages toddler to teenager—obviously grandchildren—sat on top of a pine table, behind a plaid couch.

"Nice-looking family," Liz commented.

Laredo gave them a blustery grin. "Yeah, I'm right proud of 'em. Just wish my Haddie was still around to enjoy them. Lord, how she loved little ones."

Liz bit her lip, a wave of sadness showing in her eyes, but it disappeared a second later.

"Do you remember the Lintell case?" Rafe asked as they claimed wooden chairs around a round pine table.

"It was about two years ago." Laredo opened the file on the table and skimmed it. "The Lintell woman was a social worker for the county. She did school and home visits for a while, then took a job placing kids in foster homes and arranging adoptions."

"How exactly did she die?" Liz asked.

Laredo jammed a pair of reading glasses on. "Stabbed in the chest with a steak knife."

"A knife from her own kitchen?" Rafe asked.

The sheriff nodded. "Never found the weapon, though. Assumed the killer took it with him and got rid of it."

"What about other forensics?" Liz asked.

Sheriff Laredo used his finger to find his place on the page. "A stray hair, short. Dark. Male. Never matched it to anyone."

Rafe folded his arms on the table. "Did you have any suspects?"

"No one who panned out. Neighbor said she heard shouting and saw a black Jeep leave the place the night before the murder, but nothing on the day of the murder."

"Did you trace the Jeep to anyone?"

"Yeah, some drug addict girl who had her kid taken away because she was a junkie."

"A good motive for murder," Liz said.

Sheriff Laredo shrugged. "Yes, it was. Except that at the time of the murder, the girl was in a cell."

"I imagine she wasn't the only one angry with Ms. Lintell," Rafe said.

Laredo made a low sound in his throat. "Naw, the woman had a tough job. But everybody she worked with said she was fair. She tried her best to get the druggies and alcoholics to clean up so they could get their kids back. Believed in family and worked hard to reunite the birth parents. She was a foster herself." He hesitated. "She always followed up with the families to make sure they took good care of the kids she placed."

"But one of the foster parents or birth parents could have had a beef with her," Liz said.

"Goes with the job. But there wasn't enough evidence to pin down the killer. And nobody wanted to dole out names, especially in adoption cases."

Rafe knew the drill. Everyone guarded their secrets. The addicts who got clean wanted their kids back but had to prove themselves. The adopted parents wanted privacy and to know that their children couldn't be jerked away and given back to the parents who'd screwed them over in the first place. And confidentiality issues with adoptions were always an issue.

"How about a man named Brian Castor?" Rafe asked. "Did his name come up in your investigation?"

The sheriff looked back over the file. "Matter of fact, it did. Found a note at Lintell's house with Brian Castor's phone number on it."

"Did you question him about Lintell's murder?"

"Yeah, but he had an alibi. Was out of town at some premed function. A couple of other students verified it."

Students could have lied for him. "Did you learn anything about Brian's brother?"

Sheriff Laredo shook his head. "Not much. According to Lintell's notes, his name was Jeremy. There was something else that was weird, though."

"What?" Liz asked.

The sheriff lit a cigar. "Crime tech found DNA on the victim they thought belonged to the perpetrator."

Rafe's heart jumped a beat. "Whose was it?"

"That was the strange thing. DNA had an odd genetic marker to it."

"What do you mean?" Liz asked.

"Lab said it looked like the person's DNA had been altered."

Rafe clenched his jaw. "We found a similar drop of what we believe is the killer's blood on Ester Banning."

"Were any of the Lintell woman's body parts removed?" Liz asked.

Sheriff Laredo shook his head.

Liz frowned. "Maybe she was his first kill, then he got a taste for it and perfected his MO."

"We need to compare those samples," Rafe said. "If they match, we're looking at the same killer."

---

He taped pictures of the major organs of the body along the wall by the shelf holding his trophies. The brain, lungs, bladder, small intestine, large intestine, kidneys, heart . . .

The heart pumped blood through the body and gave it life.

But there were other expressions about the heart.

*Brokenhearted.* What did that mean? Was the heart broken? Or were feelings just hurt?

*He loved her with all his heart.* But the heart was an organ, a physical entity. It had nothing to do with love.

*He was good-hearted.* That meant he was kind and loving. But did kind and loving really have anything to do with blood pumping through the body?

*He had no heart.* Which meant the person was evil.

That saying he believed in.

The woman he wanted to take next had no heart. Not like a mother should. She had taken him in, then thrown him away. She only loved one of her children.

And that child hadn't been him.

So she'd sent him to an institution where that monster the Commander had poked and prodded him, turned him into a number instead of a man.

She had to pay.

He removed the photograph he carried of her from his pocket and studied it. She was younger than the others. Maybe mid-forties now. An attractive woman, with wavy brown hair, green eyes, and a smile for the camera and the man beside her. Yes, she looked at him with doting eyes and a puffed-up chest.

But she'd forgotten *him* as if he'd never existed.

Soon she would remember everything.

And if she cried for help or forgiveness, he'd carve out her heart. Then everyone would know she didn't have one.

# Chapter Twenty-Four

───────── ◦ ─────────

S heriff Jake Blackwood studied his brother's computer, searching for clues as to where Nick might have gone.

The fact that Brenda had shown up at dawn at the cabin where he and Sadie, Ayla, Gigi, and Amelia were staying had freaked the hell out of him.

Worse, if Nick hadn't found a way to contact Brenda, Jake was damn worried, too.

Determined to get answers, he scoured Nick's history on his laptop. The last open file was a website for a group supporting the Commander—apparently the bastard had garnered followers.

Jake's gut tightened with disgust.

It seemed that Nick had researched several names, hunting for more information on individual forum posters.

A militia group calling themselves the SFTF—Soldiers for the Future—caught his attention with the force of a brick in his gut. Many of the comments boasted about the government needing cutting-edge thinkers like the Commander, citing dozens of examples of suspected terrorist activities, conspiracy theories, alleged experiments, and military acts by enemy countries.

He clicked for more information but couldn't determine the group's physical location. But he did find photos of preteen boys being trained as guerilla soldiers.

Had Nick discovered the location for this place? Was that where he'd gone?

Jesus, why hadn't he called Jake for backup?

He scrolled through a group of photos of military tactical training exercises, stirring memories of the rigorous training exercises the Commander had forced on him and Nick.

Another photo made his blood freeze. He leaned closer, studying the face. The photo was grainy, the man's face smeared with mud for the training exercise, but Jake recognized him.

Chet Roper.

Jake had served with the man.

His pulse thrumming, he entered Roper's name into the police database and ran a search.

Seconds later he fisted his hands by his side. Dammit to hell. Roper was a guard at the state prison.

Jake punched the number for the warden and asked if Roper was on duty.

"Yes, he's here today."

"Don't let him leave," Jake said. "I think he may have helped Arthur Blackwood escape. I'm on my way."

---

The deputy phoned that Truitt was still missing, but Mazie Paulsen's car had been found on Windmill Road. Rafe and Liz drove straight from Sheriff Laredo's cabin to the site.

"How did you find it?" Rafe asked the deputy.

"A lady called in," he explained. "Said she passed it on her way into the mountain, but she wouldn't leave her name or number. Said she didn't want to get involved."

"How about caller ID?"

"A pay phone from a convenience store a few miles down the road. I talked to the owner, but he claims he doesn't remember the woman."

A dead end.

Liz walked over to examine the red Toyota. The front end had crashed into a ditch, glass had shattered all over the interior, and blood soaked the driver's seat.

"This is strange," Liz said. "First we find Mazie's place trashed and blood inside. Now her car and more blood."

The deputy shaded his eyes with his hand. "Maybe someone attacked her at her house, and she escaped. She could have been driving too fast, or maybe she crashed because she was weak."

Liz leaned closer to look at the blood. "Then where's the body?"

"Maybe her attacker was following. He ran her off the road, then abducted her."

"You're probably right." Liz walked around the car and checked the trunk.

Rafe examined the tires, then the tire prints in the dirt and the skid marks on the black asphalt. "Odd. I don't see tire marks for a second vehicle."

"Call a crime unit," Rafe told the deputy. "We need to process the car for evidence."

Liz rubbed her forehead in worry. "I'm going to call the Castors. If the son they gave up is Six, he may eventually decide to punish them, like he punished the nurses."

"Mrs. Castor in particular," Rafe said. "She was supposed to be a mother to him, like she was to Brian. She could be his end game."

Liz stepped aside to make the call, and Rafe and the deputy searched the area in case the killer had left Mazie's body in the woods.

---

Liz paced beside the road. "Mrs. Castor, I'm sorry to disturb you again, but we need to talk."

"How dare you interrogate my son as if he was some kind of criminal?" Mrs. Castor said in a shrill voice. "Brian is a good boy. He would never hurt anyone."

"You should have told us his brother had emotional problems," Liz countered. "We're looking into the possibility that he resurfaced. That he may have a vendetta against your family. Has Brian spoken with him?"

"No. If he had, he would have told us."

"Maybe not," Liz said. "He was angry that you and your husband kept secrets from him."

Fear laced Mrs. Castor's voice, "You think Jeremy might hurt Brian?"

Liz silently debated whether to tell the woman her suspicions. "At this point, I can't really say. But we think he may be responsible for killing three women, and that he is extremely dangerous."

"You mean he's that horrid killer they're calling the Dissector?" Mrs. Castor cried.

Liz hated the names people gave serial killers. Naming them seemed to glorify them, which fed into the demented minds of the killers. Made them into legends, which was exactly what they wanted.

"We're working on that theory," Liz said calmly. "So far his victims have been nurses. We suspect that they treated him during the experiment, and now he's taking revenge."

A long pause, fraught with tension. "This is our fault," Mrs. Castor said. "If we'd kept Jeremy, maybe we could have gotten him help, some therapy, and none of this would have happened."

Liz inhaled deeply, her chest aching. The Castors were obviously nice people; they had done the best they could in a difficult situation. "This isn't your fault, Mrs. Castor. And I certainly didn't call to blame you. But I did want to warn you. It might be best if you and your husband went somewhere for a few days until we solve this case."

"All right. Brian can leave town with us."

"Mrs. Castor, Brian can't leave town now. He may be able to help us catch Jeremy."

"How? If Jeremy resents Brian, he might try to hurt him."

Or they could be working together. "We'll make sure he's protected," Liz assured her.

Even if they had to lock him up to do so.

---

As Rafe drove toward Castor's apartment, Liz's phone buzzed.

"It's Anderson Loggins from the sanitarium," she said before stabbing the connect button. "Agent Lucas speaking." A pause. "Yes." Another pause, and Liz's mouth twisted into a grimace. "Okay, thanks."

She hung up and turned to Rafe. "Loggins passed the latest victim's photo around, and one of the janitors recognized her. Her name is Ruth Rodgers. She worked at the sanitarium when Blackwood was director."

Rafe chewed the inside of his cheek. "At least now we understand the victimology."

He pulled up at Castor's place, and they hurried up to his apartment. But when they rang the bell, no one answered.

Rafe pounded on the door while Liz canvassed the area, but no one responded.

"I don't see his car," Liz said.

"His parents probably warned him we were coming."

Liz punched in a number. "Lieutenant Maddison, it's Agent Lucas. Have you heard from Brian Castor?"

Rafe peeked in the front window but the rooms were dark. Still, enough daylight flickered in to show him that nothing looked amiss. No furniture overturned. No bloody body.

Unless it was in a room he couldn't see.

"Thanks," Liz said. "Let us know if you hear from him."

Rafe removed a tool from his pocket and picked the lock.

"You're breaking in?" Liz asked.

"It's a reasonable search. For all we know, he could be inside, hurt."

Liz pulled her gun and followed him in. They combed each of the rooms, but Castor wasn't there, and neither was his body. Rafe noted Castor's collection of articles on the experiments and books on dissection, and his research into his family.

"He certainly has the background knowledge and motive, doesn't he?" Liz commented.

Rafe nodded as he dug through the files on Brian's desk. Nothing new, although it was interesting how much work Brian had done on his own researching the Dissector.

Liz checked the man's nightstand. "Look at this, Rafe. It's a gas receipt."

Rafe walked over to examine it. "Castor bought gas the day the Commander escaped from prison. And the station where he gassed up was only three miles from the state prison."

———————— ' ————————

Jake explained to the warden that he'd found Chet Roper's name associated with a militant group.

"You think this group has something to do with Arthur Blackwood?"

Jake showed him a printout of some of the posts. "You tell me."

The warden skimmed the page. "Jesus, I've heard of these kinds of groups. They're dangerous. But Roper? Hell, he's been one of the best guards I've ever had. In fact I had him keeping an ear out to help determine how Blackwood planned the escape."

"Perfect for him," Jake said wryly.

The warden grimaced. "I'm sorry, I . . . didn't see it."

Because Roper had covered his tracks. "The group he works with is training boys to be soldiers," Jake said. "It sounds like Roper is right in the middle of it."

"Bunch of freaks," the warden said. "Roper's been tough on the inmates, but that goes with the job."

"I need to talk to him."

The warden punched his intercom and requested that his receptionist page Roper.

"While we wait on him," Jake said, "check and see if a man named Brian Castor visited the Commander." He might have come to find out about Jeremy.

"As I've said before, the only visitors he had were you and your brother, the prison shrink, and the cops and feds on the list."

Jake stewed over that. "All right. Can you check and see if Castor visited anyone else? Maybe he communicated with the Commander through another inmate."

"I suppose that's possible." The warden clicked a few keys on his computer, then pulled at his chin. "Says here that he saw an inmate named Harvey Yates."

"I want to question him."

The warden released an exasperated breath. "I'm afraid that's not possible."

"Why not?"

"He's dead. Was stabbed during the prison breakout."

Jake silently cursed. "My father, cleaning up after himself."

A knock sounded on the door, and the warden yelled, "Come in."

Roper entered, his brows furrowing when he saw Jake. "Blackwood?"

"Hello, Chet," Jake said.

Roper looked back and forth between the warden and Jake, but showed no reaction. "What's going on?"

"Sit down," the warden said. "Sheriff Blackwood needs to ask you some questions."

Roper folded his big arms. "What about?"

"Do you know Brian Castor?"

"No—should I?"

"I think he might have communicated with Blackwood through another prisoner."

"That'd be news to me."

"What happened the day of the prison break?"

"I've already been through this a dozen times," Roper said. "It was chaos. Commander Blackwood stabbed Yates and then got away."

The warden shoved the file Jake had given him toward Roper. "Sheriff Blackwood found posts you made to a group called SFTF."

"What I do on my own time is my business," Roper said, his tone clipped.

"Not if you're selling guns, or if you helped Arthur Blackwood escape."

Roper's eyes flared with distress. "That website simply promotes free speech. That's not against the law."

"Fostering paranoia and pushing conspiracy theories is dangerous," Jake said.

"And teaching young boys to shoot and think like guerilla soldiers is wrong."

"What's wrong is our country coddling kids while other countries prepare them to defend themselves and their fellow citizens from attack."

Jake hated the mindset of people like Roper. But he couldn't arrest the man without evidence he'd committed a crime.

His phone buzzed, signaling a text from Rafe.

*Trace on Nick's phone came through. The GPS coordinates are for the SFTF compound.*

If Nick was there, and not answering his phone, he had to be in trouble.

"My brother, Nick, went to talk to your group," Jake said. "He hasn't been seen or heard from since."

Tension vibrated in the room as Roper's hands tightened around the edge of his chair.

"Come on, Roper." Jake stood and gripped Roper's arm. "You're going to help me get my brother back."

———————— , ————————

Rafe was still contemplating why Castor would help the Commander escape as he and Liz ate an early dinner. They hadn't bothered with lunch, waiting until they got back to Slaughter Creek to eat.

Tech had also called in the trace on Mazie's phone. They'd located it, but when the deputy went to check it out, he found the phone had been left in a Dumpster at a gas station.

"There's no way Castor would have helped the Commander escape," Liz said.

"Not unless he helped him escape so he could kill him."

"That could be true," Liz said. "But he probably just wanted to know whether his brother was in the experiment."

Rafe's phone buzzed, and he tossed some cash on the table to pay the bill as he answered it. "Hood."

Liz excused herself to go to the restroom while Jake explained that he was at the prison.

"If Nick went to the compound to snoop around, they may have taken him hostage."

"Any luck at the prison?"

"Just that Chet Roper, an ex-soldier who works as a prison guard, may have helped the Commander, but I have no proof. I'm bringing him with me to the compound."

"I'll meet you for backup."

"Thanks. We'll connect at my office and go from there."

Rafe hung up just as Liz returned. "That was Jake. We traced Nick's phone to the militia compound in the mountains. Jake thinks Nick's in trouble, and I'm going to provide backup."

Liz tossed her purse over her shoulder. "Then let's go."

Rafe caught her arm as they stepped outside. "Jake and I are going to handle this."

Liz's pulse quickened. "But you need me, Rafe. If Nick's in trouble, I can help."

A muscle ticked in Rafe's jaw as they walked to his SUV. "No way. It's too dangerous."

Steam emanated from Liz's glare. "I'm not a rookie, Rafe. I'm a seasoned agent. Your partner."

"I know that, but this militia group is made up of men. Angry, belligerent, violent men."

Liz's face fell. "Rafe, you can't keep treating me like I'm not a professional."

The thought of one of those men putting his hands on Liz made Rafe's stomach knot. He knew he was being selfish. Sexist. But Liz had been beaten and nearly murdered by one crazy man. He couldn't take the chance of her being caught by a group of them.

---

Liz slammed the door to her house, furious at Rafe. As soon as they solved this case, she would request a new partner.

She'd thought she could earn Rafe's respect again, but obviously it was futile. Rafe would never see her as anything but a weak female who'd screwed up the last case.

He didn't trust her to back him up. And partners had to have trust, above anything else.

She flipped on the news to listen to while she studied her notes, not surprised to find Brenda Banks giving an update.

"Senator Stowe's death is now under investigation. Police are also looking for this woman, Mazie Paulsen"—the camera cut to a photo of the middle-aged nurse—"who worked at Slaughter Creek Sanitarium. At this point Ms. Paulsen is missing. Blood was found in her abandoned car as well as at her residence, leading police to suspect foul play. If you have any information regarding her disappearance, please contact the police."

Liz's cell phone buzzed. An unknown number. She pressed ANSWER. "Agent Liz Lucas."

"I have information about your case."

Liz tensed. The voice sounded disguised. "Who is this?"

"Meet me at Smoky's on Union Road."

"Tell me your name—" But the caller hung up before Liz could finish the sentence.

For a brief second she considered phoning Rafe for backup, but he'd made it clear how he felt about her going with him and Jake to find Nick.

She'd check this lead out on her own.

She grabbed her purse and weapon, then hurried outside, surveying the driveway as she climbed in, just in case someone was watching her. Everything seemed quiet tonight.

Maybe too quiet.

She slid into her car and drove toward Union Road, well aware that the barbeque pit was off the beaten path and that she might be walking into a trap. Judging from the vehicles in the parking lot, it was a popular truck stop and biker joint.

She tugged her jacket around her, one hand jammed in her pocket, fingers wrapped around her gun as she entered. A group of bikers were playing pool in the back, while several truckers chowed down on barbeque plates. The place reeked of beer, sweat, mesquite, and smoke, but she knew some of the dives had the best food in the mountains.

Not knowing who to look for, she assumed the caller would find her, so she took a barstool at the counter. The waitress narrowed her eyes as Liz sat down, then slid a folded scrap of paper in front of Liz.

Liz opened it and read the scrawled writing. "Back booth in the corner."

She stuffed the note into her pocket, then wove through the throng of bikers, ignoring the leers and whistles. By the time she reached the back booth, she was sweating. Her nerves intensified when she noticed that the booth was near a back entrance.

A good place to sneak out—or abduct someone.

Fingers gripping the gun inside her pocket, she moved closer, then claimed the booth and waited.

# Chapter Twenty-Five

———————— o ————————

L iz clenched her teeth as a woman eased into the seat across from her.

She wore dark glasses, a blond wig, western clothes, and big hoop earrings. A Dolly Parton look-alike.

"Thank you for coming," the woman said in a whisper.

"Who are you?"

The woman lifted the dark glasses enough for Liz to see her face.

It was Mazie.

She was alive.

"Were you followed?"

"No," Liz said. "What's going on? The police have been looking for you. We thought you were dead."

"I know. I had to do that, make everyone think I was gone, to save myself." Mazie angled her body to hide her face from the patrons in the bar.

Liz leaned closer. "Someone's after you?"

Mazie nodded, but stayed silent until the waitress had stopped to ask for their orders.

Liz ordered a beer to keep from standing out in the crowd. "Who?" she asked when the waitress had left.

Mazie fiddled with the salt shaker. "I'm not sure—probably people working for Commander Blackwood."

"You worked with him on the experiments?"

"No," Mazie said emphatically. "When Amelia Nettleton was accused of killing her grandfather, I put it all together." She looked miserable. "Then the senator was murdered right there in the hospital, and I was terrified I'd be next."

"What is it you know that would get you killed?"

Mazie rubbed her forehead. "When I was feeding the senator one day, he was talking out of his head. I figured it was the medication, but he rambled on about there being more subjects than the police thought."

"You mean more than seven?"

Mazie nodded.

"Who are they?" Liz asked.

Mazie shook her head. "I don't know. It's been so long ago. They were just children then. I don't know if I'd even recognize them as adults."

"Did you ask the senator?"

"Yes, but he became agitated and incoherent after that."

Liz stewed over that information. "Loggins gave us a file with a list of the subjects. We suspect that the sixth subject, the only one unaccounted for, is the Dissector."

Mazie adjusted her glasses as a chunky man in jeans and a flannel shirt walked by and stared at them. "That's possible."

"Do you know how many more?" Liz asked.

Mazie shook her head again.

Liz swallowed hard. That meant there wasn't just one subject missing. More were unaccounted for. How many more?

Mazie worried her bottom lip with her teeth, then clutched Liz's hand. "Now I've told you all I know, can you help me?"

Rafe and Jake checked their weapons as they parked beside Nick's car near the compound.

"This proves Nick came here," Jake said.

But he hadn't left. Not a good sign.

Nick glanced inside the car, but everything seemed normal.

Roper growled his protests at being forced to accompany them, but Rafe had given him a choice of cooperating or being arrested for aiding and abetting the prison escape. Rafe had relieved him of his gun and his phone, so he couldn't warn the group they were coming.

Still, Jake handcuffed Roper to keep him from trying to run ahead.

Night had fallen. The ground was frozen under the earlier hail and snow, and wind lashed through the trees, making the branches sway. Rafe and Jake used flashlights to pick out a trail. The silence was broken only by their footsteps and the occasional rustle of animals scurrying through the forest.

They came to a place where the path split in two. Rafe poked Roper in the back with his gun. "Which way?"

Roper gestured to the right, and Jake led the way, Rafe bringing up the rear, with Roper between them. They reached a barbed wire fence, finding a section that had been cut.

"Must have been where Nick snuck through," Jake said.

After they'd trudged on another two miles, Jake pointed up a hill to a clearing. Rafe spotted some buildings and campsites, but the place appeared to be deserted.

No trucks or jeeps were parked anywhere in the camp, either.

"Damn," Jake said. "It looks like they packed up and left."

Rafe nudged Roper with the barrel of his gun again. "You warned them, didn't you?"

"I told 'em not to kill the agent. That would only bring heat."

"So you knew he had my brother?" Jake confronted Roper, his face menacing.

"He trespassed," Roper said. "He shoulda left us alone."

Jake jerked Roper by the collar and pressed his gun to his temple. "Did they kill my brother?"

———————— , ————————

Outside, the wind howled and tree limbs swayed as Liz hurried toward her car. She had promised Mazie she'd talk to her superiors about getting her into WITSEC. Brenda could run the story about Mazie's murder as a cover.

But she had to talk to Rafe about the plan and tell him what she'd learned. Meanwhile, Mazie needed to lay low.

Still, Liz phoned Brenda and left a message, asking her to meet her. Her phone buzzed just as she ended the call, and she clicked to connect.

"Agent Lucas, this is Maddison. I ran that comparison on the blood found on Ester Banning and the sample from the Lintell murder, like you asked."

"And?"

"It was a match. Both had the same altered genetic makeup."

That meant that whoever killed Rusty Lintell had also killed Ester. Only he hadn't taken any organs from Lintell. For some reason, he'd added that to his MO later.

Liz thanked Maddison, then ended the call, eager to tell Rafe. Footsteps crunched behind her, and she fumbled with her keys, anxious to get into the safety of her car.

Suddenly someone grabbed her from behind. She tried to swing around to fight, but a crackling pop sounded, and something zapped her neck.

A stun gun.

Her body convulsed as wave after wave of voltage jolted through her.

Liz stirred from unconsciousness, her body throbbing. She opened her eyes, but wherever she was, it was so dark that she couldn't see anything.

At least she was moving.

She struggled to sit up, but her legs and arms were bound, secured so tightly that the circulation in her hands and legs was being cut off. Or maybe she was still numb from the stun gun.

The stun gun—that was the Dissector's MO.

God . . . he had her.

She had to find a way to escape.

The vehicle she was in bounced over ruts in the road, jarring her teeth. Gears ground, the car shaking, indicating that it was a five-speed and that the shocks were worn out.

She tried to scream, but duct tape covered her mouth.

Her mind raced. She had to stay cool. Figure out where he was taking her. How long she'd been in the car. How far they'd traveled.

She strained, listening for clues. Other cars? No . . . a train? Airplane?

Tears pushed at the backs of her eyelids, but she blinked them away. No time to cry. She had to think. . . .

No. He wouldn't take her to the Smokies. The Dissector wanted attention. He had left all his previous victims in Slaughter Creek so the town would know he'd killed again.

Although she didn't fit his normal victimology, he probably thought she was getting too close. He'd needed to stop her from exposing him.

The car bounced again, vibrating as he switched gears. Maybe they were crossing a railroad track.

Her ears popped, a sign that they were climbing. But there was no telling how long she'd been unconscious. He could have left Slaughter Creek and be deep into the Smokies by now.

Miles of forest and nothingness. No one would find her there.

———————— , ————————

Rafe handcuffed Roper to the fence and gestured to Jake. "Let's check out all the buildings. Maybe Nick's inside, or maybe we'll find something to indicate where the camp moved."

Jake's dark look mirrored Rafe's thoughts. If Nick was inside, he was probably dead. If the group was as smart as he expected, though, they might have buried him to cover their tracks.

Or taken him with them.

Although the place looked deserted, they both pulled their weapons, braced to fire in case a couple of the militants had been left behind to ambush them.

Jake went to check the two smaller buildings while Rafe inched up to the main building. He eased inside, noting the concrete floors, bare tables, and walls on which marks indicated that whatever had been hanging there had been hurriedly ripped off—probably bulletin boards and whiteboards holding information for training sessions.

He combed through the main room, searching cabinets and then moving to the other rooms off the hall. More meeting rooms, he guessed, or bedrooms, although the space had been literally stripped of everything.

Frustrated, he stepped back outside. Jake was coming out of the neighboring building, his face grim. Sensing that Jake had found something, Rafe went to join him.

"Nothing in the main building. Place has been cleaned out."

"The outbuildings are empty. But I found blood in the last one." Jake wiped sweat from his forehead. "There are also signs that they tortured Nick."

"They probably took him with them."

Jake rubbed his head again. "The last thing they'd want is to take a fed with them."

Rafe considered his comment. "Then let's keep looking. Most of these camps have built-in shelters and escape tunnels, in case they're attacked."

Jake snapped his fingers. "You could be right. This used to be an old mining area."

The two of them split up again, Jake taking the northern perimeter while Rafe took the south side. He examined the space surrounding the main building, looking for a secret basement, but found nothing. A small square building behind it looked as if it had probably served as a warehouse, most likely for the guns the group was accumulating.

Metal stakes surrounded a large tree, and he noted another area that looked as if it had been used for target practice. Several rounds of spent ammunition littered the ground and the trees were pocked with bullet holes.

Roper leaned against the fence, his eyes sweeping the area. Rafe stopped to study him for a moment. The bastard kept glancing at a clump of brush and weeds choking the side of one trailer.

Rafe's heart sped up, and he jogged toward the trailer. Using his flashlight, he examined the brush, then began to pull it away. Branches and brush had been ripped from trees and bushes and piled up as if someone had thrown them there.

Rafe heaved for a breath as he tossed them aside, removing layer after layer until he found a wooden trapdoor leading into the ground.

"Jake, come here!"

Rafe knelt to pry the door up, but it was nailed shut. Jake ran toward him.

"Get a crowbar or ax, something to break this up!" Rafe shouted.

Jake jogged back to the building where he'd found the blood, then returned with an ax. He hacked at the trapdoor until the wood splintered.

"Nick?" Jake shouted as they worked to pry the remnants of the wood loose. "Are you down there?"

Harlan's cynical laugh made Liz tense.

She had survived the last time he'd kidnapped her. She'd find a way to survive now.

She had to, or the Dissector would keep killing more women.

The vehicle rumbled to a stop, gravel skidding and spinning beneath the tires below. She tensed at the sound of the car door opening and slamming shut, fighting for courage as she heard the crunch of footsteps on the gravel—her abductor, making his way to the trunk of the car.

She fought again against her bindings, desperate to free herself—or at least remove the blindfold, so she could see the Dissector's face.

The trunk screeched open, and Liz held her breath as the man lifted her and carried her across a path. Cold winter air assaulted her, and she heard the sound of a creek rippling over rocks.

Rafe shone his flashlight into the hole as Jake climbed down the steps. The hole looked like a bottomless pit.

Seconds later Jake dropped to the floor with a thud. "He's here!" he shouted. "And . . . he's alive. But I need help. He's barely breathing."

"I'm coming down." Rafe lowered himself onto the steps and inched down, using his flashlight to locate Jake as he neared the ground. Jake was stooped beside his brother, checking him for injuries.

Jake patted Nick's face. "Nick, can you hear me?"

Nick moaned, and Rafe heard Jake's hiss of relief. "We're going to get you out of here," Jake murmured. "Just hang in there, brother."

Rafe scanned the inside of the hole, noticing shelves built along one wall. Probably they'd held canned food, water, and weapons, but they were empty now. They'd obviously cleared out the place before throwing Nick down here to die.

"We should get an ambulance," Rafe said, wincing at the sight of the blood and bruises covering Nick.

"No," Nick groaned. "Just get me out of here."

"You got it, Nick." Jake reached for Nick's arm, Rafe slipped his hand under the other one, and they lifted Nick to a standing position. Nick was weak and leaned on them, but he limped to the steps.

Together they helped Nick climb the steps, and finally he slumped onto the ground, heaving for fresh air.

"What happened?" Jake asked.

"Too many of them. They trapped me." Sweat mingled with drying blood on Nick's face. One eyelid was cut, bruises darkened his features, and he pressed a hand to his chest as if it hurt to breathe. He probably had broken ribs and maybe internal injuries.

"Are they working with the Commander?" Jake asked.

"I think so," Nick said, his voice gaining strength. "Did you search the compound?"

"Yes," Jake told him. "They cleaned everything out."

"Fuck." Nick tried to sit up, swaying slightly.

"Did you hear them discuss their plans or talk about the Commander?"

Nick coughed, then spit blood onto the ground. "I didn't get a chance. They beat me and then threw me in that pit."

Rafe jerked his head back toward the fence where he'd left Roper. He half expected the man to have gotten away, but the handcuffs had held.

"I think I know how we can find out." He removed his gun from the holster as he strode toward Roper.

If the asshole didn't talk, he'd beat the truth out of him.

# Chapter Twenty-Six

———— o ————

Rafe jammed the barrel of his weapon into Roper's temple. "Where's the Commander?"

Roper jerked at the handcuffs, rattling the wire fence. "I don't know."

"I don't believe you," Rafe said, teeth clenched.

Roper's menacing glare met Rafe's. A battle of wills.

"You're finished with your job," Rafe said. "You're going to jail as an accomplice to the prison escape, which involves murder charges. How do you think the prisoners you abused over the years are going to enjoy having you in their cell block?"

Fear flickered in the man's eyes. "Who said I abused any of them?"

"Are you saying you didn't? Because I know how guards work. Those inmates were the perfect guinea pigs for you to impose your beliefs on, for you to exert your authority over."

"Fuck you."

"No, you're the one who's fucked." Rafe cocked the trigger. "Where's the Commander?"

Roper's cheeks turned ruddy with rage. "I told you, I don't know."

"What *do* you know?"

Roper averted his eyes for a moment, infuriating Rafe, who jerked him by the collar. "I asked you a damn question, you bastard. Either answer me, or we'll go to that building where your friends tortured Nick Blackwood and treat you to the same hospitality he received."

Roper flashed a wild-eyed look at Rafe. "You wouldn't do that."

Rafe gave him a menacing smile. "You have no idea what I'm capable of."

Roper stiffened. Rafe kept the gun trained on him as he unlocked the handcuffs from the fence. Roper tried to jerk free, but Rafe slammed the butt of the gun into the man's head. Roper staggered at the force of the blow, and Rafe handcuffed his hands behind his back.

"Walk, asshole." He nudged Roper in the back with the gun, forcing him toward the building where they'd held Nick. Jake looked up and saw him, said something to Nick, then headed toward them.

"You're not going to let this crazy fucker torture me, are you, Sheriff?" Roper shouted.

Jake laughed. "Are you kidding? I'm going to help him."

Roper stumbled, but Rafe shoved him inside the concrete building. Darkness filled the room, the scent of blood heavy in the air. Rafe pushed Roper toward the tub of water, forcing the man to his knees.

Jake grabbed a dirty towel from the rags hanging by the tub, then pressed the cloth over his face. He grabbed the water hose and aimed it at Roper's face, drenching him. Roper jerked and fought, spitting and coughing, but Jake kept it up until Roper sagged, nearly unconscious.

Rafe removed the rag and jammed the barrel of his gun against Roper's temple. "Where is the Commander?"

"Go to hell!"

"Why are you protecting him?"

"Because he made me who I am," Roper snarled. "I will always obey my Commander. Always."

Rafe and Jake exchanged glances.

"You're Six?" Jake asked cautiously.

Roper shook his head with a grin. "Ten."

Rafe went cold. "Ten? There are only seven subjects," he said, his hand suspended midair.

"Apparently not," Roper said, his tone mocking.

Rafe clenched the man by the neck. "Where is he?"

Roper spit at him. "You'll never find him."

Rafe tossed the towel over the man's head again, and Jake repeated the process with the water, over and over, until Roper passed out. Then they revived him and started again. Finally Roper caved.

"They're meeting in the hills," he rasped.

"Who's meeting?" Rafe growled.

"I don't know. They used code language, but it's someone big. Someone who started the experiments."

"Where are they meeting, exactly?" Rafe pressed.

Roper coughed, his head lolling sideways. "The main hospital."

———————— , ————————

Liz opened her eyes, surprised to realize that her abductor had removed the blindfold and freed her hands and feet.

Pain ricocheted through her temples as she pushed herself up to stand. She swayed and caught a wall with one hand, determined to remain conscious.

She was in a room in a house somewhere, in the dark—but she had no idea where.

And no idea if anyone even knew she was missing.

Self-recriminations whispered in her head. She should have called Rafe from Smoky's. But after the way he'd dismissed her, she'd stubbornly set out on her own.

Brenda . . .

When Liz didn't make it to meet her, surely Brenda would figure out that something was wrong.

She rubbed her hand along the wall, fumbling for an opening, but when she reached a window, she realized it was nailed shut, boarded up.

Despair threatened to overwhelm her, but she tamped it down. She had to keep her wits about her and figure out a way to get out of here.

Footsteps sounded outside the door, and suddenly it screeched open. She sucked in a breath as a dark figure limped toward her. Faint light from somewhere in the house streaked his face, revealing a jagged scar that ran the length of his right cheek, from the crown of his head to his neck. His hair was shaved, a tribal tattoo swirling across his skull.

Dammit. Shadows made it impossible for her to fully see his face.

———————— , ————————

Rafe handcuffed Roper inside his SUV and locked the door while he, Jake, and Nick hurried up to the hospital entrance.

They divided up and canvassed the staff, showing photos of the Commander to see if anyone had spotted him.

Finally they met with the chief of Security. "We have reason to believe Commander Blackwood is planning to leave the country today. Alert all guards and employees to be on the lookout for him. Warn them that he's extremely dangerous; they shouldn't approach him or let him know he's been recognized."

"Of course," the guard said.

Nick offered to watch the security cams in the building while Jake and Rafe hurried to the elevator to go to the roof. The hospital had a helipad to facilitate medevacs and transfer patients to trauma units.

They checked the face of every nurse and doctor along the way, searching for the Commander.

Jake's phone buzzed, and he snatched it up. "Yeah? We'll check it out." A pause. "Nick thinks he spotted the Commander on the fifth floor, surgical wing."

Hope whipped through Rafe. This time if they caught Arthur Blackwood, they'd make damn sure he never saw the light of day again.

The elevator doors swished open, and he and Jake raced out. A sign for the surgical wing pointed to the left, and they jogged down the hall. Jake stopped to speak to the nurse at the nurses' station, and Rafe met a doctor exiting the wing.

"We're looking for Commander Arthur Blackwood." He showed the doctor the photo on his phone. "We think he may be in disguise here, that he's planning to get away via the helipad."

"I've been in surgery, doing a liver transplant," the doctor said. "I haven't seen anyone but the staff in the OR."

Rafe's phone buzzed with a text from Nick.

*The secretary of defense is with the Commander. They're heading to the roof.*

He read it and then showed it to Jake.

The secretary of defense.

Carl Mallard.

Shock waves hit Rafe. "Hell, Mallard has been pressing Nick to find Blackwood all along. Now I know the reason."

"He was keeping tabs to see what we knew," Jake said in disgust.

Rafe tapped his foot impatiently as the elevator climbed. "Back when the experiments took place, he was making his way up the political ladder. That experiment could have catapulted him to the top with the military."

"And could end his career now," Jake said.

As the elevator doors slid open, they rushed to the stairwell leading to the roof.

Just as they made it onto the roof, a man in scrubs, a lab coat, and a mask helped another man onto a chopper.

Rafe and Jake ran toward it, but the men jumped in, and the chopper lifted off.

Just as they did, though, Rafe saw one of the men turn—Carl Mallard, the secretary of defense. He was definitely on board.

The force of the chopper lifting nearly knocked Rafe down. He had his gun aimed to fire, but the chopper was too fast. The blades spun, the noise drowning out Jake's voice, as it flew across the parking lot.

Suddenly a loud boom exploded in the air, and flames lit the sky.

The chopper burst into flames, spinning and whirling as pieces of it crashed into the woods.

———

Liz's hands shook as she removed her jeans and shirt and pulled on the little black dress her kidnapper had tossed into the room for her to wear. The thought of sitting with him, talking with him, letting him touch her, turned her stomach.

But if she kept her cool, maybe she could find a way to escape. Reminding herself she'd been trained in self-defense and attack moves, she zipped the back of the dress and brushed it over her hips.

The red heels he'd tossed into the room came next. They fit perfectly, as if he'd known all her sizes.

*He does. He's been in your house.*

What body part did he plan to take?

Footsteps pounded outside the door, and the door opened. Liz swallowed back revulsion as the hulking figure appeared in the doorway.

A shudder coursed up her spine

"Come. I have something to show you."

Liz kept her hands at her sides but slowly walked behind him. Keys jangled from his pocket as he limped forward. The lights were off, but candles flickered from a wooden table in the kitchen area, giving her just enough light to see that they were alone.

She quickly glanced around, searching for possible escape routes. They appeared to be in an older cabin. The floors were rustic, the walls knotty pine. A fireplace glowed, wood crackling.

The windows were boarded up, locks on the door.

The scent of garlic wafted to her, making her stomach curdle, and she spotted a cutting board on the butcher block counter, a sharp kitchen knife resting atop it beside meat that looked raw, bloody.

He shoved her into a chair, and once again she scanned the room for a way out. There were multiple locks on the wooden door that led outside. Locks that needed a key.

A key that was on that key chain on his belt.

"You said you had something to show me?" she asked, gauging the distance to the knife.

"Yes." He gestured to the left at a computer he'd set up on the sideboard, then flicked a remote. A video appeared on the screen.

Liz gasped. Her mother was in the same room where Liz was now.

"Please, I have a daughter," her mother pleaded. "She needs me."

Laughing bitterly, Harlan gripped her mother by the hair and held her head back as he forced her to look at photos of his other victims. Three other women he'd killed, the blood running down their necks, their eyes wide with the horror of death.

"You helped the whores keep their kids so they could put them to work on the street. You threw other kids in foster homes where the parents beat and raped them."

Liz's mother shook her head in denial, tears streaming down her face. "No! I tried to help them."

"You didn't help them—you gave them over to animals like Blackwood. Then you had to get nosy."

Liz's gaze shot to her abductor. His face was scarred, his skin puckered and ridged. But it was him.

Harlan.

# Chapter Twenty-Seven

—————— o ——————

The explosion rocked the night, fiery bits of the helicopter flying in all directions, the bulk landing in the woods by the hospital.

Rafe and Jake had both been blown backward by the blast. Nick raced onto the roof, his expression shocked.

"Did you see the Commander get in the chopper?" Jake yelled over the noise.

Rafe hesitated. "I'm not sure. Mallard was in there, though."

Nick ran a hand through his hair. "We have to confirm that the Commander is dead."

"I'm calling Maddison," Rafe said as he punched Lieutenant Maddison's number.

Nick and Jake both walked to the edge of the roof, looking out at the debris and burning parts scattered across the woods. Two security guards raced outside.

"What happened?"

Jake relayed the situation to the guards. "We need a list of the staff on board, as well as the pilot of the chopper."

"What's going on now?" Lieutenant Maddison asked.

Rafe filled him in.

The guards jumped into action, radioing the central security station to explain.

Nick's phone buzzed, and he stepped aside to answer it.

"I'll dispatch teams to the area asap, along with explosive experts," Maddison told Rafe.

"I'll call the chief and tell him about the secretary of defense. We'll get warrants and search all his properties and computers to confirm his involvement."

"You think it was accidental?" Lieutenant Maddison asked.

"This was no accident," Rafe said. "I'd bet my life on it."

"Who would you guess was responsible?"

"They had too many enemies to pick just one."

Maddison ended the call to dispatch the team.

Nick approached him. "Rafe, that was Brenda. She's worried about Agent Lucas."

Rafe jerked his head up. "Why? What's wrong?"

"They were supposed to meet at the sanitarium about some lead she had regarding the experiment."

"What kind of lead?"

"Something about there being more than seven subjects. But Liz hasn't shown, and she isn't answering her phone."

"Is Brenda at the hospital now?"

"Yes, but no sign of Liz anywhere."

Dammit, what was going on?

He checked his phone and saw a message from Liz. "Rafe, it's Liz. We have to talk. Call me as soon as you get this."

He sucked in a breath and punched Liz's cell number, anxiety knotting his gut as it rang and rang. But no one answered.

Dammit to hell. Liz might be in trouble.

---

"What are you talking about?" Liz asked Harlan.

"Your mother, she caught on to what the Commander was doing to the children."

Liz's mind raced. "You killed my mother because she found out about the experiment?"

He nodded, his sinister laugh filling the air. "She knew about me, and planned to expose me."

"Expose you as a killer?"

"And one of the Commander's pet subjects. I know you've been looking for me."

"You're Six?"

Harlan simply grinned, but a scream from the taping jerked Liz's head back to the video. On the screen Harlan raised the knife to her mother's neck. The terror on her mother's face made her tremble. With one quick swipe, the monster slashed her throat.

Liz gasped as blood flowed down her mother's neck and the life drained from her. She jerked her head away, unable to bear any more.

Her mother had begged him to spare her life for her daughter, just as Liz had begged him for hers.

But he'd killed her mother anyway to protect the Commander.

She met his cold, sadistic look with one of hate. The emotion fueled her courage, and she lunged around the table and grabbed him by the throat. Her fingers dug in, squeezing, choking, but he was a big man, and he swung his fist into her stomach, just as he had the first time he'd kidnapped her.

Her breath rushed out at the blow, and her grip loosened enough for him to push her arms away and come after her. Liz leaped to the side and raced for the knife on the butcher block counter. If she could get it, she'd stab him to death without blinking an eye.

But he caught her by the shoulders just as her fingertips brushed it. Liz swung an elbow back to dislodge him, but he aimed a blow at her kidneys, and her legs buckled as pain disabled her.

Gulping back a sob, she fell to her knees but kicked her right foot backward, hoping to connect with his knee. Another blow to the back of her head knocked her to the floor. She tasted blood, and the room spun.

He grabbed the knife from the counter, pulled her head back by her hair, and pressed the blade to her neck.

Liz's life flashed in front of her.

Harlan was going to kill her, and she'd never get to tell Rafe that she loved him.

———————— , ————————

Rafe drove like a maniac, the lights of other cars flashing by in a blur as he sped past them. The fifteen-minute drive took him ten minutes but felt like a hundred.

Nick veered toward the road that snaked up into the mountains toward the sanitarium, but he decided to check Liz's house first.

He waved his badge out the window toward the security guard as he slowed near the gate. "Have you seen Agent Liz Lucas?" Rafe asked

"No."

"How about anything suspicious?"

The guard's brows knitted together. "No, why? What's going on?"

"I'm worried about her," Rafe said. "I'll check her house."

The guard waved him through, and Rafe pressed the accelerator. A minute later he parked by Liz's, jumped out, and jogged toward her front door. A lone light burned in the hallway. He rang the doorbell and knocked a dozen times, but no one answered.

His heart hammered as he raced around to the porch. They'd found one woman's body here already.

An image of Liz lying dead, mutilated, flashed in front of his eyes, and he froze, his lungs straining for air.

Liz couldn't be dead.

He flexed and unflexed his hands as he fought for calm. Post-poning the search wouldn't help.

He climbed the porch steps, shining his flashlight across the lawn and steps. Nothing stuck out, so he opened the screened door and inched inside, gun at the ready.

He waved the flashlight across the porch but everything seemed in order. So far, no blood . . .

He wiggled the doorknob leading to the interior, cursing at the fact that it was unlocked. Not a good sign.

Inching through the door, he panned the living area and kitchen, but no one was inside. Shoulders tense, he listened for sounds of an intruder.

Footsteps? A breath? The wind whipping a branch against the house. Windowpanes rattling.

Moving quickly, he checked the laundry room, then went to Liz's room. If she'd been abducted, had it been from here?

There were no signs of a struggle.

But something in the middle of Liz's bed caught his eye.

The red scarf she'd worn earlier.

On top of it lay a pair of silver earrings, the silver rings encas-ing glass that changed colors in the light.

Liz's mother had worn earrings like these.

The earrings had gone missing when she was abducted. Police thought the killer had taken them.

God . . . Sweat broke out all over Rafe's body. Liz had said she'd smelled garlic in her house. That she'd found white roses in her car.

And a pair of earrings just like her mother's missing pair lay on her bed.

He yanked latex gloves from his pocket, photographed the earrings, then gently picked them up in the palm of his hand.

God. Liz had been right all along. Harlan really was back from the dead.

Liz forced herself to draw a shallow breath. If she moved too quickly, Harlan would sever her carotid artery and she'd bleed out in minutes.

She had to beat the son of a bitch.

He tightened his hold, the blade pricking her skin. "Don't worry, I'm not ready to kill you yet," he murmured against her ear.

What did he have in mind?

He reached for a rope from the duffel bag in one of the chairs. She tried to run again, but he slashed her arm with the knife. Liz cried out in pain as he shoved her into the chair.

This time he tied her arms and feet to the chair. Blood dripped down her forearm onto the wood floor, and she gritted her teeth to keep from crying as it began to throb.

Breathing heavily now, as if he'd taxed himself, he angled his computer toward her again.

"We have more movies to watch."

Liz blinked back emotions as he punched play, and pictures of his other victims appeared on the screen.

Apparently he'd videotaped each one of them from the time he'd kidnapped her to the time of her death. He'd kept them in the same room where she was now.

He'd forced them to dress like whores and called them names and made them eat his poison food.

His job had been to clean up after the Commander. But he'd taken a perverse kind of pleasure in punishing the mothers who'd given up their children. Even if those women hadn't known they were turning their kids over to Blackwood.

---

Fear immobilized Rafe for a brief second. Was Liz still alive?

His phone buzzed. Nick. "Did you find Liz?"

"No, she's gone," Rafe said in a gruff voice. "I think Harlan has her."

A tense heartbeat passed. "How do you know?"

"I'm at her house. The earrings that Liz gave her mother, the ones that went missing with her, they're here on Liz's bed."

"Jesus." Nick sighed. "I'll get a team together."

Rafe hung up, his mind spinning as he tried to decide where Harlan would take Liz. Details of the case nagged at him. Harlan had kept his victims for three days before killing them. Long enough to beat them and punish them for what he considered their transgressions.

At first police hadn't known where he'd kept them, but three months after Rafe threw Harlan into the river, they'd located the house. It was miles from nowhere, tucked so deeply in the foothills that no one could hear the girls scream for help.

The police had searched for evidence, but Harlan was missing, presumed dead, so they'd put the evidence into a file and stored it at the TBI.

Harlan might take Liz to that house.

Rafe jogged out to his SUV, tires screeching as he drove across the parking lot. He slowed at the security gate just enough to tell the guard to call him if he saw Liz or anything suspicious, then hung a sharp left and roared toward the mountains.

# Chapter Twenty-Eight

———————  o  ———————

Rafe fought images of Liz bleeding and beaten, as he flew up the mountain. Ridge after ridge swallowed him as he drove deeper into the hills. More rain fell, slowing him as he negotiated the switchbacks.

The engine rumbled, gears grinding, rain swishing off his tires. He turned up the graveled road, bouncing over ruts and potholes, keeping his lights on bright to show him the way.

Driving on autopilot, he swung around a curve, then dodged a clump of tree limbs that had fallen into the road. Through the leafless trees he spotted the dilapidated house on top of the hill. His headlights illuminated the road, but he flipped them off, not wanting to alert Harlan if he was at the house.

He prayed Harlan was there. If not, Rafe had no idea where to look. Harlan could be anywhere in the acres of wilderness.

He swung the SUV to the right and parked between some trees. He grabbed his gun, then slowly opened his car door and closed it, scanning the property ahead.

Rain sluiced down his neck and jacket, mud squishing beneath his boots as he wove behind the trees toward the house.

His flashlight illuminated the way enough for him to see that the house had been boarded up. But a car was parked to the side, under a giant oak.

Why had Harlan brought Liz here? Didn't he know the TBI had found the place after his disappearance?

Wind blew rain across the path, and the answer hit him.

He could be setting a trap.

All his senses straining, Rafe continued up the path, scanning the outside until he neared the house. There was a rustle behind him, and he pivoted.

He raised his gun but didn't have time to fire it. A shadow moved, the butt of a gun slammed into his head, and he fell to the ground.

Another blow, and he tasted dirt and blood. Then the world went dark.

———————— , ————————

Liz watched in horror as Harlan dragged Rafe inside the house and hauled him into a chair.

Fear engulfed her as he sagged unconscious in the chair. Blood dripped from the side of his head, where Harlan had struck him.

Harlan made quick work of tying Rafe to the chair, then filled a pitcher with water, walked over, and dumped it on Rafe's head.

Rafe jerked his eyes open and looked up, disoriented for a moment.

"Rafe?" Liz said, striving for calm. "Are you all right?"

Slowly he angled his face toward her. "Yeah. Are you?"

Liz nodded.

"Well, well, well, isn't this a happy little reunion?" Harlan said in a singsong voice.

Rafe pulled his gaze back to Harlan, but Liz saw him visually sweep the room, sizing it up, looking for escape routes just as she had.

Unfortunately they'd have to free themselves before they could fight Harlan.

Harlan stepped over to the computer, with a sinister grin. "Looks like you're in time to watch the show with us, Hood."

Rafe's look could have cut glass. "Show?"

Liz gritted her teeth as Harlan pressed the play button. Her own face flashed onto the screen.

"Stop it!" Liz said as she realized that he'd filmed himself beating her during her captivity.

Rage filled Rafe's eyes as he stared at the scene. Harlan had tied her up just as he had now, and was telling her how he'd killed her mother and the other women because they were bad mothers.

Then he'd attacked her, sending blow after blow to her midsection. Liz had sobbed, begging him to stop.

"Please don't," she cried. "I'm pregnant. You'll kill my baby!"

Rafe's body went completely still at her cries. He inhaled sharply before cutting his gaze toward her.

"Liz?"

Tears blurred her vision. "Rafe, I—"

"Why didn't you tell me?" he asked, his voice raspy with pain.

"I . . ." Liz's throat clogged with emotions. "I'd just found out . . . I didn't have time . . ."

"Enough lies!" Harlan slashed the ropes restraining Liz in one quick motion, then dragged her up from the chair and hauled her toward the door.

His shrill laugh rent the air as he raised the knife to Liz's throat.

---

Rafe struggled with his bindings as Harlan teased Liz's neck with the tip of the blade.

He'd managed to reach inside his back pocket for his knife as the bastard forced him to watch that video of Liz begging for her life.

Liz had been pregnant with his baby.

The realization both stunned and enraged him. Hurt that she hadn't told him mingled with fury that Harlan had robbed them of the chance to meet their child.

He would not get away with it.

Blood trickled down his arm, but he ignored it, sawing faster as the bastard pushed Liz toward the door.

"Maybe we should go down to the river. You know that's where I left your mother."

Liz suddenly threw her foot up and kicked Harlan in the knee, at the same time jabbing her elbow into his side. Harlan grunted and loosened his grip slightly, and she spun around and swung at his arm, sending the knife skittering across the floor.

Liz dove for it, but Harlan grabbed her leg, and she fell face forward onto the floor. She kicked at him, trying to dislodge his hand, but the asshole yanked her backward and crawled on top of her, straddling her back.

Rafe jabbed his hand with the knife and cursed, but one more slice of the knife, and his hands jerked free. Pulse hammering, he slashed the ropes around his feet and lunged for Harlan.

He yanked him off of Liz, threw him to the floor, and sank his knife deep into his belly. Harlan's eyes widened in shock, and he emitted a gurgling sound.

The man's blood soaked Rafe's hands as he dug the knife deeper.

---

Liz pushed herself up from the floor, her lungs straining for air. She drew in a deep breath, relieved that Rafe had subdued Harlan. That the bastard was the one finally feeling pain.

A horrible thought, but she couldn't help herself. He'd killed her mother and baby.

He deserved to die.

Rafe looked up at her, the emotions in his eyes mirroring her own.

Liz didn't hesitate. She grabbed the knife from Rafe and thrust it again as deep as she could into the man's belly.

"Where have you been hiding all this time?" she growled.

Harlan's eyes fluttered closed, and then he opened them again. "Watching you," he said in a choked voice. "All those women I carved up . . . All for you."

"You're the Dissector?" Liz asked.

Harlan nodded and then coughed, the sound feeble, as Liz twisted the knife again and watched the life drain from him.

———————— , ————————

Rafe met the ME outside and directed him to Harlan's body.

He watched as he loaded Harlan into the back of the ambulance. But he couldn't bring himself to look at Liz, knowing she'd kept something as important as her pregnancy from him.

Lieutenant Maddison and his crew pulled up, and Liz went to fill them in.

God, she'd been through hell, but even with blood on her neck and bruises on her face and arms, she looked beautiful.

Dammit. He'd almost been too late, and Liz had nearly died because of it.

But she had survived.

If Harlan was telling the truth, they could tie up both cases with his arrest, and she'd finally be safe.

Then . . . what?

What was he going to do?

He'd lost his head over her again. But how could he forgive her for not telling him about the baby?

Worse, how could he forgive himself for not being there to protect her and his child?

Liz explained to Maddison and the CSI team what had happened. "Let's search this place for evidence to confirm that Harlan was the Dissector. If we find the body parts he took, we can nail him."

CSI Perkins gestured toward the dead man, his brows furrowed. "You think he was lying?"

Liz shrugged weakly. "I just don't want to miss anything."

"Don't worry," Lieutenant Maddison assured her. "We'll be thorough."

Liz wanted to explain about the pregnancy, but she sensed Rafe closing down, and she was exhausted. Now the ordeal was over, her adrenaline was waning fast.

She should've been content. Relieved.

But Harlan's confession bothered her. Something wasn't quite right about it.

# Chapter Twenty-Nine

————— o —————

Tension stretched between Rafe and Liz as he drove her back to her house. She relayed what Mazie had told her.

"So Harlan worked for the Commander too?" Rafe said.

Liz nodded. "Apparently. According to him, there are others."

Rafe's hand tightened around the steering wheel. "That fits with what Roper told us. He's Ten."

Liz went cold. There were ten?

That meant Eight and Nine were still unaccounted for.

"I promised Mazie I'd help her go into the witness protection program," Liz said. "Even if the Commander is dead, she still could be in danger."

Rafe agreed, and Liz made a mental note to phone her superior and arrange the new identity for Mazie.

They also needed to meet with the press, but she wanted more evidence to corroborate Harlan's confession before she released a public statement.

Rafe pulled in to her complex, his expression tormented as he walked her to her door. "You finally found your mother's killer and got justice for her." Emotions darkened his eyes. "You can leave the bureau now."

Liz squared her shoulders. "You want me to quit?"

"If you don't quit, I'm going to request a transfer."

Did he think she was that incompetent, or did he just hate her now? "Is this because you think I messed up with Harlan?"

The anger in his voice was searing. "For God's sake, Liz, he killed our unborn child. A baby you didn't even bother to tell me about."

Liz's heart thumped wildly. Regret, sorrow, anger, and a dozen other emotions filled her, leaving her voice weak. "I know what he did. I've had to live with it for the past few months." In fact, that was the reason she'd fallen into such a deep, dark depression. The reason she'd needed the medication.

Her hand shook as she unlocked the door and stumbled inside.

Not only had she lost her baby and her chance of ever having one, but she'd lost Rafe for good as well.

---

Rafe gripped the steering wheel, battling the emotions pummeling him.

He had been scared to death when he'd seen Harlan holding that knife to Liz's throat. And this was the second time in a year.

He couldn't stand to see her in danger again.

The anguish on her face when he'd mentioned the baby wrenched his heart. God . . . if he'd found her sooner last time, maybe he could have saved their child.

Maybe he'd have a son or daughter now. A real family.

Something he'd never had.

He pinched the bridge of his nose to regain control, then backed out of the parking spot. Too upset to sleep, he headed toward the helicopter crash site, figuring that Jake would still be there with the crime-scene investigators.

They had certainly kept Lieutenant Maddison's crew busy the past few days.

Thirty minutes later, he reached the site. Emergency vehicles, police cars, crime-scene investigators, and rubberneckers were parked along the road. Two uniformed officers were trying to keep the curiosity seekers away from the scene. Lights still flickered here and there in the woods, workers combing the area and collecting the debris for analysis.

He spotted Jake talking to a dark-haired guy wearing a CSI vest and hurried toward him.

"Rafe, you're back?" Jake asked.

"Yeah." He relayed the night's events. "Harlan is dead. And he confessed that he is—was—the Dissector."

Jake rubbed at the back of his neck. "You believe him?"

"I want to," Rafe said, hating the doubts in his head. "What reason would he have to confess to murders he didn't commit?"

"He's a psychopath," Jake said. "Maybe he wants the attention."

Rafe inhaled sharply. "You could be right. We'll review all the evidence we have and hope it supports his confession. The crime-scene investigators are looking for the missing body parts at the house where he held Liz."

"Good work," Jake said.

"Any luck on Truitt?"

There was still the possibility he was one of the secret subjects.

"My deputy is still looking. He found out Truitt had an assault charge three years ago, but the charges were dropped. He went to talk to the woman Truitt was accused of attacking."

"What about you? Did you find the bodies of the Commander and the secretary of defense?"

"We've recovered the pilot's body, but the others were blown to bits. The lab will have to look at teeth and DNA to confirm who was on that chopper."

Jake gestured to the investigator, who was holding something in an evidence bag. "We found a finger. I'm certain it was my father's."

Rafe peered at the bag. "Why do you think that?"

"The signet ring. He got it in the military and never took it off."

Relief filled Rafe. Harlan and the Commander were both dead. Now they could close both cases and end the reign of terror haunting Slaughter Creek.

───────────── , ─────────────

Liz removed the baby blanket she'd kept in the closet, not bothering to fight the tears.

It had been a horrible night.

The trauma of having Harlan's hands on her made her shudder, and she stripped off the dress he'd forced her to wear and threw it into the trash. She jumped into the shower and scrubbed herself until her skin was almost raw, but still she felt his hands on her, his breath bathing her face as he held that knife to her throat.

He's dead, she reminded herself as she dried off, pulled on pajamas, and poured herself a drink. She walked to the den and looked through the French doors to her screened porch, but in her mind she saw Harlan gasping for his last breath.

She should be comforted by his death. Her mother had finally gotten justice, and Liz would never have to worry about him stalking her again.

She tossed down the drink, then crawled into bed and hugged the covers and baby blanket to her.

Once she'd believed that finding and killing Harlan was the most important thing in the world.

But now she'd achieved that, she realized how empty her life was.

The fact that Rafe blamed her for losing their child made fresh tears fill her eyes.

She'd won by ending it with Harlan.

But she'd lost Rafe, and any chance that they might have of a future.

The next morning Liz arranged protection for Mazie, then met with Brenda for the press conference. Jake, Nick, and Rafe showed up as well, but they all looked exhausted, as if they hadn't slept.

"This is Brenda Banks coming to you live from the courthouse in Slaughter Creek. We have Sheriff Blackwood here, along with Special Agents Nick Blackwood, Rafe Hood, and Liz Lucas."

She turned to the stage where all of them stood. "Sheriff Blackwood, would you like to begin?"

Jake stepped up to the mic. "For days the police have been searching for Commander Arthur Blackwood, who escaped from the state prison. Last night Agent Nick Blackwood and Agent Hood discovered that he was meeting with the secretary of defense at the hospital and planned to escape via helicopter. The chopper exploded in midair above the wooded area by the hospital. The pilot died in the explosion, along with Secretary of Defense Mallard. Law enforcement agencies are now investigating the possibility that the secretary of defense was connected to the Slaughter Creek experiments."

Nick stepped up next. "The TBI is working in conjunction with other law officials and agencies to determine the part that the secretary of defense may have played in the Slaughter Creek experiments and the deaths of those associated with the project. We also have detained the man responsible for Senator Stowe's death. His name is Chet Roper. He belonged to a militant group called SFTF, and he's admitted to tying up loose ends for the Commander and the secretary of defense by killing the senator."

Rafe stepped up to the podium next, and Liz joined him. "We also apprehended the serial killer Ned Harlan, known as the Blade, last night. He was killed while being arrested."

He stepped away to give Liz access to the microphone, but averted his gaze.

*If you don't quit, I'm going to request a transfer.*

The other reporters and locals who'd met to hear the news announcements grew restless, whispering among themselves, drawing Liz back to the case.

"Before Ned Harlan died, he confessed to the murders of Ester Banning, Beaulah Hodge, and Ruth Rodgers. Police and crime-scene investigators are still investigating, but at this point, we believe the man everyone called the Dissector and Harlan were one and the same."

Reporters' hands shot up, and Liz stepped back to let the Blackwood brothers and Jake respond.

But unanswered questions nagged at her.

They hadn't recovered the body parts at that house. Had Harlan just confessed to get attention?

If he had, the Dissector was still out there.

He wouldn't like someone else taking credit for his kills.

Which meant he would be hungry for another victim, just to prove to the police and TBI that they were wrong.

---

Six clapped his hands over his ears as they finished that stupid broadcast. Brenda Banks had gotten all the major players on-screen at once.

But that fucking profiler Liz Lucas was the one he couldn't tear his gaze from. *She* was supposed to be the best? The one who understood people like him?

Amelia was the only one who understood him.

If Agent Lucas was really that smart, she'd know Harlan was lying. He could use her mistake to his advantage, though, lie low and wait awhile for his next kill.

But he had better plans. He clenched the phone he'd stolen from Amelia in his sweaty hand.

He wasn't like Harlan. He only took the lives of bad people, like the nurses who were supposed to take care of people but tortured them instead.

Heat simmered in his blood. There was one other who'd hurt him.

The Castor woman.

The truth hit him like a fist in the chest—he knew why she hadn't been home.

That fucking profiler had warned her that he'd come for her.

Fuck. He wanted the Castor woman's heart.

But Liz Lucas had gotten in the way. The damn woman had to pay.

She was smart.

He wanted her brain.

The brain . . .

Facts filled his head. The brain is responsible for movement and control, emotions and feelings, the senses, language and communication, thinking and memory. The skull is called the cranium. The four main sections of the brain are the cerebrum, the cerebellum, the pons, and the medulla. Thought processes are controlled by the cerebrum; muscle coordination and body equilibrium, by the cerebellum. The pons receives and sends impulses from the brain to the spinal cord. The medulla regulates breathing, heartbeat, and vomiting.

Six clapped his hands over his ears again—stop, stop, stop! But the sayings about the brain screamed in his head.

*She has the brains of a gnat.*

*Going to beat her brains out.*

*He'll blow her brains out.*

*He wants to pick her brain.*

*They were going to rack their brains.*

*She has shit for brains.*

*He's brain dead.*

*An idle brain is the devil's workshop.*

*The scarecrow went to Oz to get a brain . . .*

The singsong voice of the scarecrow echoed in his head—*If I only had a brain . . .*

Laughter bubbled in his throat. When he had the Lucas woman's brain, maybe he'd study it.

Maybe he'd even give it to the scarecrow.

Then he'd take the Castor woman's heart, and his collection would truly be complete.

# Chapter Thirty

———— o ————

After the press conference ended, Rafe considered the details that still needed tying up. The fact that they hadn't found the organs let doubts creep in.

And they still hadn't found Truitt.

"I'll follow up with the ME," Rafe said.

Nick cleared his throat. "I'll confer with the agents who searched the secretary of defense's house."

Jake looked sheepish. "If you guys don't need me, I'm going to the cabin to see my family."

Liz smiled at the hungry way he said it. Jake obviously adored Sadie and his daughter. They were lucky to have found each other. She'd heard the story about Sadie leaving town after high school, and she knew they'd had to overcome obstacles to be together. But in the end, their love had been strong enough to get them through.

Her heart throbbed with a dull ache. She wanted that kind of love with Rafe.

But what did she have to offer?

If he wanted a child, she couldn't give it to him.

He didn't even want to work with her.

She had to accept it.

Her heart heavy, she turned to leave. But just as she reached her car, her phone buzzed with a text.

She slid into the driver's seat, then checked it. Maybe Rafe had changed his mind and wanted her to accompany him to talk to the ME.

But the text was from Amelia.

*I'm ready to talk. Meet me at the old drive-in outside town.*

Liz's pulse jumped. Maybe Amelia was going to tell her Six's identity now.

For a millisecond she considered calling Rafe to fill him in, but he'd dismissed her so easily that she refrained.

She quickly texted back that she'd meet Amelia, threw the car into gear, and drove from the parking lot.

She couldn't rest until she tied up the loose ends of the Slaughter Creek case and made sure that Harlan was actually the Dissector.

---

Rafe stepped into the morgue with the ME, Dr. Bullock.

"Harlan definitely died from the knife wound," Dr. Bullock said as he uncovered the body.

Rafe stared at the man's ugly face, thinking how peaceful he looked in death, while in life he'd been a monster.

"It hit the main artery in his heart, and he bled out."

Ironic that his heart had bled out when the man had no heart.

"You good with the chief?" Bullock asked.

Rafe nodded. "Self-defense. Harlan had a knife to Agent Lucas's throat." And he'd killed their child.

Now he understood Liz's depression after the attack.

All his fault—he should have saved her *and* the baby.

Dr. Bullock scratched his forehead. "You know something else? I got word that Harlan was an organ donor. He specifically donated his brain for study."

Disgust filled Rafe. "How arrogant. He thought we'd want to study his demented mind."

"Might not be a bad idea," Dr. Bullock said. "There are studies being done on the brains of serial killers."

Rafe released a breath. "Let's move on."

Dr. Bullock gestured toward another steel table, and they walked over to it. A partial skeleton, organs in various dishes, tissues. "There were three bodies in that crash. The pilot and two others."

Rafe thought back to the roof. He'd seen the secretary of defense. Had the other man been Blackwood?

"The other two bodies were blown to bits, and parts were burned beyond recognition in the fire. So far, I've identified organs belonging to the secretary of defense, along with a hair sample that belonged to him." He shoved his glasses up his nose and indicated the finger in a separate dish. "This finger definitely belonged to Commander Blackwood. I also found hair samples and clothing with his DNA."

"Which meant he was there in the fire."

Nick and Jake would be relieved at the news. Now their families could feel safe.

"What about the DNA from the Ester Banning and Rusty Lintell scenes? Did it belong to Harlan?"

Bullock shook his head. "I'm afraid not."

Rafe went stone cold.

If Harlan's didn't match, that meant he hadn't killed Lintell and Banning.

He'd lied about being the Dissector.

Which meant the sadistic mutilator was still out there, hunting . . .

———————— ⸱ ————————

Liz pulled up to the drive-in, her senses honed. It had been shut down for years.

As a teen she and her friends had spread blankets on the hoods of their cars or in the back of pickup trucks and shared popcorn and sodas while they watched the latest flick. Occasionally someone snuck in beer, and it turned into a party.

She'd forgotten about that time because it happened before her mother's death. After her death, finding her mother's killer had consumed all her thoughts.

The place was deserted now, had been for ages, but the metal posts that had held the speakers were still there, rusted and swaying as the rain poured down around them. The screen was torn, by weather or vandalism. And the shed where they'd bought refreshments was boarded up.

She scanned the parking lot, wondering why Amelia had chosen to meet here. It must be because she didn't want anyone else to know she was spilling secrets.

Odd though, that she hadn't turned to her brother-in-law, Jake.

Suddenly a vehicle rolled toward her, its brights on, and she opened her car door and stepped out. Still, her training kicked in, and she pulled her gun from her purse and slid it into the holster inside her jacket. If this was a setup, she'd be prepared.

The car stopped and the driver got out, but the headlights blinded her.

"Amelia, is that you?"

Tension coiled inside her as the shadowy figure approached. She had a bad feeling and drew her gun, but the figure lunged toward her, and for the second time in two days a stun gun zapped her, sending her body into spasms of pain.

She struggled to remain upright, but the voltage was too high. She collapsed into the dirt and fell into unconsciousness.

---

Amelia studied the newscast as the TV replayed the interview with Brenda, Jake, Nick, and the other agents, Rafe Hood and Liz Lucas.

Brenda looked beautiful as always. She had been a good friend to Amelia, even when she was all mixed up and the others were fighting in her head.

But they showed a picture of a man with a scar on his face and eyes that looked like demon eyes, and her stomach twisted into a knot. The man was Ned Harlan. He had confessed to being the Dissector.

Deep inside, she'd been afraid Six was guilty. Not that he'd ever hurt her, but the Commander had done things to him that had warped his mind. He did have a violent streak.

And all the women who'd died had been nurses who'd tormented the children in the sanitarium. Nurses who should have helped them and loved them and reported what was going on.

Had she been wrong about Six?

God, she hoped so . . .

Her nerves on edge, she grabbed her cell phone and punched his number in. The phone rang three times before he answered.

"Six, it's me."

"What do you want, Amelia?"

He sounded as if he was distracted. Angry that she'd phoned.

"I needed to hear your voice. Did you see the news?"

"Yes. Agent Lucas is here with me now."

A muffled sound followed, as if he'd covered up the phone, and then a scream rent the air.

Amelia gripped the phone in a panic. Agent Lucas was with him . . .

"What are you doing?"

"I have to go, Amelia." He lowered his voice to a whisper. "As soon as I'm finished, we can be together."

He disconnected the call, and Amelia paced the room. The voices started in her head again. Rachel's. *You're a whore. And now you're helping him kill a woman.*

Amelia pressed her hands over her ears. "No, stop it."

*You stop it, Amelia. You're the only one that can. The only one who knows where he has the woman.*

A sob wrenched Amelia's chest. She didn't want Agent Lucas to die. Liz Lucas had never hurt her or Six. She hadn't been part of the experiment.

*He's going to kill her now if you don't call someone*, Rachel whispered.

Amelia's heart pounded so loudly, she heard the blood roaring in her ears. Rachel was right.

She had to do something. She had to save Agent Lucas.

Heart heavy, she ran outside to get Sadie.

———————— , ————————

Rafe was just leaving the morgue when his phone buzzed.

"Agent Hood, I got an address for that woman Truitt was accused of assaulting."

"Text it to me," Rafe said. "I want to see if Truitt is there."

The deputy texted him the address, and Rafe crossed the mountain to the neighborhood where the woman lived. Her house was a weathered clapboard one-story hanging off the side of a ridge.

When he pulled up, chickens were roaming in the yard, and a mangy dog barked from where it lay beneath an oak, although it didn't bother to get up. A pickup and Pathfinder were parked in front.

He climbed out, hurried up to the door, and knocked. The door screeched open, and a chunky woman in a faded shirt and jeans poked her head through.

Rafe identified himself. "I need to talk to you about J. R. Truitt."

She cut her eyes to the side, nervous. "He didn't kill them women."

Rafe raised a brow. "Is he here?"

"No. But he was, and he's all tore up, and scared you're gonna lock him up."

Rafe gritted his teeth. "I'll only lock him up if he's guilty."

"He ain't."

"Aren't you the one who filed charges against him for assault?"

She fidgeted with a strand of her hair. "That was a mistake. Back then, J. R. was drinking, and we got into it. But he quit drinking after that night, hasn't touched a drop since."

"Where is he?"

"I don't know. He called a little while ago, all upset. Said he lost his mama and me, and now the police thought he was cutting up women."

Women never ceased to amaze him. This one actually felt sorry for the man.

"Do you have any idea where he'd go?"

She shook her head. "Just don't hurt him when you find him. He's not a bad man."

Dammit, they needed that DNA test.

His phone buzzed, and he checked the number. Jake.

He punched connect. "Agent Hood."

"Rafe, it's Jake. Listen, Liz is in trouble."

Rafe's blood turned cold. "What happened?"

"Amelia just told me Harlan is not Six. She called Six a few minutes ago and heard Liz scream."

Terror immobilized Rafe. "Where are they?"

"Amelia says she can lead us there. She thinks he's the Dissector."

"We can't take Amelia with us."

"She insists. She claims she can talk him down."

A war raged in Rafe's head as he rushed back to his SUV. Taking a civilian into a dangerous situation was against everything he believed in. But Liz's life was at stake.

And if Six and Amelia were close, she might be helpful.

"All right."

"Meet us at my office and we'll ride together."

Worry knotted every muscle in Rafe's body as he sped toward the sheriff's office. Images of what Six had done to the other women tormented him.

He was sadistic. He had a hand, an eye, a tongue—what did he plan to take from Liz?

The thought of him cutting her up made him clench the steering wheel in a white-knuckled grip. Liz had already suffered too much.

Tires squealed as he swung in to the sheriff's office. Jake pulled in about the same time, his siren wailing, blue lights rotating.

Rafe jumped out and climbed in the front seat. Amelia was seated in the back, twisting her hands, looking nervous and scared.

"Amelia, thank you for telling Jake," Rafe said, his voice racked with emotion.

Amelia nodded, her eyes clouding over. "I didn't know . . . didn't think he really would kill them."

"The nurses?" Rafe asked.

She nodded. "He can't help it," she whispered. "It's what they did to him."

"It's okay, Amelia, we can talk about it later. Just tell Jake where to go."

"There's an old house where he's been hiding," Amelia said. "I met him there before."

"Where is it?" Rafe asked.

"In the mountains off Route Four."

"That's not too far from here," Jake said.

Sweat broke out all over Rafe's body. Any distance was too far if Liz was in danger.

Rafe's phone buzzed, and he pressed answer, praying for good news.

"Agent Hood, it's Dr. Bullock. I ran the blood sample from Brian Castor."

"Does it match the killer's?"

"Yes and no. There are some similar markers, meaning he and the killer are related."

"So the unsub has to be his brother, who was adopted. Not Harlan."

He hung up and relayed the news to Jake, then phoned the lieutenant to see if he could locate Brian Castor.

Jake roared into the street, blue lights pulsing and siren blasting. He raced through traffic, spun to the right, and began to climb the mountain. The switchbacks forced him to slow, tires squealing as he rounded curve after curve, The latest snowfall still glittered on the ridges above, the ground frozen from the sleet and hailstorm, the trees bare, branches bowing with the weight of the weather.

The minutes felt like hours, the world slowing, the fear inside Rafe mounting with each mile. What was the unsub doing to Liz now? Was he going to torture her before he killed her?

Amelia began to rock herself back and forth in the car, her gaze trained outside her window.

"She can't be dead," Amelia whispered. "She can't be. I have to stop him."

"We will," Jake assured her.

Rafe hoped to hell he was right. He didn't know how he'd go on if he lost her.

Dammit. He never should have left her alone.

"There, to the left." Amanda pointed to a turnoff that was hardly visible. It looked more like a man-made path than a road. Jake flipped off the siren and lights, not wanting to alert Six that they were coming.

The car bounced over the rough dirt road as it wound deeper into the woods. Finally they spotted a clearing ahead.

An outbuilding sat to the left of the main house. Rafe spotted a low light burning inside it.

"Have you been out there?" Rafe asked.

Amelia sniffled. "Yes, once. But I only went in the house." She gestured to the outbuilding. "He . . . told me not to go out there."

Jake slowed to a stop and cut off the engine. "Wait here, Amelia," Jake said.

"No, I'm going." She jutted up her chin. "I know him, Jake. Maybe I can talk to him and make him stop what he's doing."

Jake glanced at Rafe, and Rafe shrugged an okay. They emerged from the car, pulling their guns.

"Stay behind us," Jake told Amelia.

She nodded, clasping her hands as she followed them.

Rafe motioned for Jake to search the main house while he checked the outbuilding. He slowly crept up to it, squatting low and staying out of sight.

His breath rattling with fear, he rose just high enough to peer into a window. Sheer terror shot through him.

The man had covered the walls and windows with heavy plastic. Liz was lying on a table in the middle, unmoving.

On a shelf, facing Liz, sat jars holding the Dissector's trophies.

# Chapter Thirty-One

———— o ————

Liz did not want to die. She had to stall.

Her abductor's phone buzzed, and he snatched it up. "Hey, Nine."

*Nine.* They were all connected, communicating, and protecting each other. If that was true, they might be adopting each other's MOs, or parts of MOs, to throw the police off.

Their plan had worked.

Her attacker turned away, lowered his voice, and paced for a moment. When he ended the call, he seemed even more agitated.

"I know you were part of the experiment, and that you were horribly mistreated," Liz said, dragging her gaze away from the jars of body parts on the wall. The eye the Dissector had taken seemed to stare at Liz, condemning her for not saving the woman it had come from.

Her attacker waved the scalpel in front of her face. It was dark, but a dim lamp in the corner gave just enough light for her to see him.

"Six?"

"Yes," he said with a leer.

Only she knew this man. Not Brian Castor or J. R. Truitt.

The director of the Sanitarium.

Anderson Loggins.

*He* was Jeremy Castor.

"You said you came to the sanitarium to clean it up," Liz said.

"I did." A bitter laugh escaped him. "That's what I've been doing. Cleaning away all the dirty ones from the past."

"The people who hurt you?"

"Who hurt me and Amelia. They treated her so badly."

"Then you found out about your brother, Brian?"

A bitter look sharpened his eyes. "Brian. He got all the love. They gave me away."

Liz mentally pieced together the facts. The Castors had adopted the boys, but by then Jeremy was already exhibiting problems.

"I'm so sorry," Liz said. "I understand now why you killed those nurses."

His eyes flickered with a wildness that sent a shiver through Liz. The stench of blood and death permeated the room.

"Nurses are supposed to be angels," Loggins said. "They're supposed to protect and take care of children, not hurt them."

"You're right," Liz said, struggling with the bindings around her wrists.

"And they're not supposed to split up brothers."

Loggins paused, then nodded slowly.

"Why did we only find paperwork for Brian?" Liz continued cautiously.

He returned to his frenetic pacing and waved his hand. "I had to get rid of those adoption papers."

"Why is that?"

He barked a sinister laugh. "I didn't want a paper trail. I had to wipe out any trace that I existed so no one would look for me."

"And you gave us that file so we wouldn't look for any more subjects."

"I had to protect them."

"Tell me who they are and I'll protect them."

Loggins shook his head, his movements jerky. "No. You'll send them back to the nuthouse." He pointed the scalpel at her. "No way that's going to happen."

Panic seized Liz. He looked as if he was going to explode with rage any moment. The rage that made him kill. "Then tell me the names of the others who hurt you, and I'll arrest them and make sure they never hurt anyone else again."

Six paced the room, his agitation mounting. "No, no, they have to die." He lunged back at Liz, waving the scalpel above her face. "And so do you."

---

The Dissector waved the scalpel in front of Liz's face, and Rafe saw red. His gun at the ready, he burst into the room from a back door. "Drop the weapon or I'll shoot."

The Dissector whirled around, his eyes crazed. "No . . . I have to finish."

Rafe aimed the gun at his chest. Loggins. He had insinuated himself into the sanitarium as the new director. That gave him access to files and the staff, where he could destroy records, cover for all the subjects.

"I said put down the weapon, or I'll shoot."

Behind him the floor squeaked, and Amelia and Jake stepped into the doorway, "Please, drop it," Amelia said softly. She inched up beside him. "I don't want them to hurt you."

Indecision clouded his eyes as he glanced back and forth between them. "But they have to die. You know what they did to us."

"Agent Lucas never hurt us," Amelia said, tears in her voice. "She wants to find the people who abused us and make them pay."

"That's true," Liz said softly. "I promise I'll help you."

"She will," Amelia said. "Please don't hurt her, Six. I . . . don't want to lose you."

Six made a low sound in his throat, as if debating what to do.

271

"Please, look at me," Amelia said. "Remember the future we talked about."

"If they take me to jail, we won't have that future," Six cried. He lowered the blade an inch, but Rafe lunged forward and grabbed him around the neck.

Six fought and struggled, but Rafe knocked the scalpel from his hand and sent it flying across the room. Another sharp blow, and he threw Six down to the floor, grabbed his hands, and hand-cuffed them behind his back.

"Her brain . . . I need her brain to finish my collection. The brain controls movement and thoughts and emotions. The cer-ebellum, the medulla, the brain stem . . . it's all important. I have to have her brain."

"Shut up," Rafe growled as he flipped the man over. "Not another word, or I'll shoot you in the damn head. Then we'll collect your brain."

Six grew still, his eyes darting to Amelia. Amelia ran to him and wrapped her arms around him, rocking him and soothing him with low words.

Rafe yanked out his pocketknife and sawed at the straps holding Liz to that fucking table. "Are you all right?"

Liz nodded, but she was trembling as he helped her down. Unable to resist, he pulled her into his arms and held her.

---

"How did you know where I was?" Liz asked in a ragged whisper.

Rafe stroked her back. "Amelia. She heard you scream when she called Six. She saved you, Liz."

Liz wiped at her eyes and pulled away to look at Amelia. Amelia glanced up at her with a tormented look. Six had quieted, but looked almost as if he'd lapsed into a catatonic state.

"I'm sorry," Amelia said, her voice breaking. "I . . . didn't know. I didn't believe it."

Liz offered her a sympathetic look. "It's okay, Amelia. You saved my life. That took courage."

"I need to call Maddison." Rafe gestured toward the bloody plastic on the wall and the jars. "It looks like we can close this case now, too."

Liz tried to pull herself together while the men made the necessary phone calls.

A few minutes later CSI arrived to process the place. Nick and Sadie rushed up shortly afterward, and Nick took Six into custody. Amelia was so upset that Sadie gathered her in her arms to console her, then drove her sister home while Jake accompanied Nick.

Maddison shook his head as they hauled Six out to the squad car. "I can't believe he was right under our noses all the time. I had one of my men pick up Brian Castor. He's taking him to the sheriff's office for questioning."

Liz cleared her throat. "If he knew Loggins was his brother, and realized what he was doing, Brian is an accomplice."

Liz released a shaky breath. *He had wanted to cut out her brain.*

Damn her. She *would* hold herself together until they got home, and she could completely fall apart where no one would see.

Silence stretched inside the car, filled with the horrors of what had happened. And the distance Rafe had put between them after he'd learned about her pregnancy.

When they reached her house, relief made her shoulders sag. A hot bath, a glass of wine, and she'd collapse in bed.

Except she feared the nightmares would come again.

Rafe parked, and they walked up to the door together. She reached for the doorknob, desperate to get inside before she could beg him to spend the night and chase the bad dreams away.

———————————— · ————————————

Rafe's heart was still racing with fear as Liz unlocked the door and stepped inside. She turned to say good-bye, but he couldn't leave her tonight.

*She didn't tell you about the baby.*

He didn't care. She had her reasons. Besides, he'd almost lost her tonight.

"Liz, I'm not leaving you."

Liz licked her lip, drawing his gaze to her mouth. He wanted to kiss her.

"I don't need a bodyguard anymore, Rafe. Harlan is dead, and the Dissector is in custody."

An image of that killing room hit him, and emotions threatened to send Rafe to his knees. "I know, but I still want to come inside."

Liz narrowed her eyes. "Rafe?"

Rafe scraped a hand through his hair and looked down, words tangling on his tongue. But he took a deep breath and spit them out. "I love you, Liz. I . . . God, I went crazy tonight when I saw you tied up in that killing room."

A soft smile curved Liz's mouth. "I love you, too, Rafe."

A heartbeat of silence, then Rafe stepped into Liz's house and her arms.

Seconds later they were tearing off each other's clothes, falling into bed, touching and loving and caressing every inch of each other.

When Rafe rose above her and entered her, he looked into her eyes. "I meant it when I said I love you." He thrust deeper, eliciting a moan. "Marry me, Liz."

Liz remembered their argument about the job, the pain of losing their baby . . .

She pressed a hand to his cheek and kissed him tenderly. They could work all that out later. Tonight they needed to celebrate their love and that they were both alive.

So she whispered yes, then he thrust deeper, in and out, and they built a rhythm with their bodies until they both came together in a blinding sea of pleasure.

# Chapter Thirty-Two

———————— o ————————

Rafe led Liz into the conference room for the wrap-up meeting, anxious to close the case so they could go back to bed together. But work had to come first. The town was waiting for answers.

Lieutenant Maddison, Dr. Bullock, Jake, and Nick joined them, the mood somber.

Rafe took charge. "Ned Harlan is dead. Although he confessed to being Six and the Dissector, we now know that that wasn't the case. The actual perp is the man who called himself Anderson Loggins, real name Jeremy Castor."

Rafe pointed to the photos on the whiteboard. "Jeremy Castor and our original suspect, J. R. Truitt, are fraternal twins. DNA confirms this. Their brother is Brian Castor. The boys were born to Ester Banning's sister. After her sister, along with her sister's husband, died in a car crash, Ester placed Brian and Jeremy up for adoption. At the time, J. R. was in the hospital because he'd been in the car with his parents. Before Ester could place him for adoption, Social Services intervened and gave him to another family, the Truitts.

"Jeremy and J. R. were four at the time. When the Castors sent Jeremy away because of emotional problems, the Commander used him in his experiments. When Jeremy mentioned his twin, the Commander tracked Truitt down to compare them." Rafe turned to Lieutenant Maddison to elaborate. "The question is— did Brian Castor find out about his brothers and help Six?"

Maddison cleared his throat. "Brian denies knowing that Jeremy was his brother. He tried to get information from the social worker who handled the case, Rusty Lintell, but she was murdered before he got answers. He was still trying to locate his brother."

"He didn't know about the twins?" Liz asked.

"No. The Castors had only taken in Jeremy, not J. R., so Brian had no idea he had two brothers."

"You believe him?" Nick asked.

Maddison nodded. "Brian took a polygraph and passed. He has stated that he wants to meet his brothers. Maybe he and Truitt can connect."

"What about Truitt?" Liz asked.

"I questioned him again," Jake said. "Apparently, at the nursing home, he overheard a conversation between his adoptive mother and Ester. That's when he learned he was adopted and had at least one sibling."

"When Ester abused his mother, Truitt grew suspicious," Liz surmised. "He may have had the photograph of Ester because he was trying to learn about his birth family."

Jake nodded.

"With all the hype about the Slaughter Creek cases and the social worker's death, Brian Castor became suspicious as well," Maddison interjected. "He went to the prison to find out if the Commander knew anything about his brother."

Nick spoke up. "Roper admitted that when Ester realized Brian and Truitt were snooping around, she'd tried to make contact with the Commander."

Jake drummed his fingers on the table. "Ironic that Truitt ran the slaughterhouse, but otherwise he's innocent."

Murmurs of agreement rippled through the room.

"Maybe his adoptive parents helped channel his urges through their business," Liz suggested. "And when the father died, he inherited the farm."

More murmurs.

Liz turned to Jake. "What about Amelia?" Liz asked. "Will she be charged as an accomplice?"

Jake shook his head. "No—she didn't know about the murders. When she figured it out, she came to me for help."

"She did save me," Liz said, relieved for Amelia's sake. She'd already suffered too much.

"What about the body on Truitt's farm?" Nick asked.

"DNA proved it was Truitt's adoptive mother," Dr. Bullock said. "It was illegal to bury her on his property, but we have confirmation that it was at his mother's request."

Liz rubbed her forehead. "So we know that Six was Jeremy, and Chet Roper was Ten. What about Eight and Nine?"

"Ned Harlan was Eight, J. R. Truitt Nine," Rafe said. "Roper filled in the blanks."

"Then it really is over," Liz said.

"My family is finally safe," Jake said.

"And so is the rest of Slaughter Creek," Nick added.

The relief in the room was palpable.

"I'm sure Brenda is chomping at the bit for the scoop," Jake said wryly.

Nick gave them a lopsided grin. "Of course she's waiting outside for the go-ahead."

"Good work," Rafe said. "Everyone get some rest."

The group stood and shook hands, relief reverberating in the air as they dispersed.

———————— · ————————

As Liz and Rafe filed from the conference room, Liz's emotions ping-ponged back and forth. Finally she was free from Harlan, and the town was safe.

Rafe's confession of love and his marriage proposal made her giddy with joy.

But they still needed to talk. She couldn't marry Rafe without telling him everything.

He could still change his mind.

Rafe pulled her up against him when they reached his vehicle, giving her a kiss. "Now we can take a day or two off."

Liz's heart fluttered at the passion in his eyes. There was nothing she wanted more than to make love to him again. "We have to talk, Rafe."

He raised a brow, one finger trailing along her shoulder. "Uh-oh. You haven't changed your mind about marrying me, have you?"

"No, but you might change yours."

"Why the hell would I do that?"

Liz blinked back tears. "Because after Harlan's attack, after I lost the baby"—she paused to swallow—"I had internal injuries." She had to spit it out. "The doctor said I might never be able to carry a baby to term."

Rafe's jaw tightened, his eyes darkening for a moment before he dipped his head and looked straight into her eyes. "You think that matters to me?"

Liz held her breath. "I don't know."

He took a step back, making her heart sink. "Come on. I want to take you someplace."

Liz was confused. "Where?"

"Just get in," he said, motioning to the passenger-side door.

They picked up coffee and doughnuts at a drive-through and then drove to a building on the edge of town.

The sign read BOYS' CLUB.

Rafe paused in the entryway, and Liz stared across the room at groups of kids. They varied in ages from preschool to teenagers. Some were making bird feeders, some playing games, some painting. Older kids were playing basketball in an attached gym.

Suddenly a little boy of about four, wearing faded clothes and sporting a bad haircut, raced toward Rafe, calling his name. "Rafe, Rafe . . ."

Rafe scooped up the kid with a laugh and hugged him to his chest. "Hey, Benny. What's up, bud?"

Benny started to babble about making pinecone birdfeeders, and Liz smiled. Rafe was good with children. He needed and deserved to have one of his own.

How could she deny him that?

A teenager with dark hair and a scar on the side of his face approached and shook Rafe's hand. A minute later, he and Benny hurried back to join their group.

Rafe pulled Liz up against him. "If we have a baby, I'd love that. If we don't, I have a family here. I'll share them with you." He gestured toward Benny. "In fact, that's only one of the kids here who needs a home."

Liz's throat closed. She loved Rafe more than she'd ever thought possible.

Smiling through her tears, she threw her arms around his neck and nodded, then kissed him again with all her love.

A few months ago, she'd thought her life was over. That Rafe was gone.

But now she was looking forward to forever.

# Acknowledgments

───── ○ ─────

First, a special thanks to all the fans of the Slaughter Creek series! I'm glad you're enjoying my dark, sinister plots.

Also thanks to my critique partner Stephanie Bond for reading through the rough draft, to fellow writer Jennifer St. Giles for brainstorming lunches, and to fellow writer Debra Webb for her support and for answering questions about law enforcement.

And last but not least, thanks to the amazing team at Amazon for liking my dark side, and for their editorial and marketing support. You guys are awesome!

*Look for the next exciting story in the Slaughter Creek series,* Dying for Love, *coming soon from Amazon Montlake!*

# Prologue

———— o ————

I wish I could leave my body behind. I'd take my mind to another place, somewhere nice and soft and warm. Someplace where rainbows made pretty colors, and I had friends and a mommy who'd sing to me at night.

Then the monsters could do whatever they wanted to me, and I wouldn't feel any pain.

I try so hard to make it happen. To levitate and leave the room. To float to another place far away so I can tell . . .

*Help me. Please help me*, I cry.

But I'm only a kid, and nobody listens. Nobody hears me cry at night. No one comes to chase the bogeyman away.

No one says it'll be okay.

Because they don't lie to little boys where I am. And they don't care if you're afraid.

Death whispers in my ear a thousand times a day. "You can run, and you can hide, Zack. But I'll get you anyway."

No . . . I would escape one day.

I picked up the nail I found under my metal bed and scratched a picture on the concrete wall. A drawing of the monster who kept me locked up. It had hideous features, distorted and bulging. Coppery eyes that shot daggers dripping with blood at my feet.

And sharp fangs that snapped at my skin and tore it off into pieces like rags.

The woman's voice drifted through the eaves of the cold halls. The lullaby she was singing. Only it wasn't a lullaby but a call for the dead. A warning of what was to come.

The room was black. The door bolted. The keys turning in locks down the hall screeching like banshees.

I know what banshees are. They're creatures of the night.

People who are about to be murdered see them.

I hear her mourning call from the woods outside.

She's washing the bloody clothes of someone who just died.

Is she coming for me next?

# Chapter One

———— o ————

Amelia Nettleton jerked from sleep, jumped up from her bed, and went to the window to look out at the morning sunlight, grateful for the beginning of a new day. Last night had been filled with horrible dreams.

Nightmares of Six cutting off body parts and storing them in jars to look at like they were prizes he'd won for being so smart.

The thought sickened her. At least her psychosis hadn't entailed mutilating others.She'd hurt herself with the alters, although Skid had been violent a few times. But only when he'd been protecting her.

When she finally fell back asleep, another dream had seeped into her sleep. A tiny voice, whispering that he needed her.

Images of her holding a baby taunted her. Then images of her in a hospital delivery room.

The dream was so vivid it seemed real. As if she'd been launched back in time.

*"Push, Amelia, push. The baby's coming!"*

*Pain ricocheted through Amelia's abdomen, fear choking her. What if something went wrong?*

*"Come on, you can do it."*

*Hands lifted her shoulders. A voice ordered her to grip her knees and push again. She heaved a breath, fighting through the pain of the contraction and imagining the moment she would hold her newborn in her arms.*

*Finally.*

*She wished Sadie were here. Wished for Papaw and her mother and all the people she'd lost when they'd locked her up.*

*But he was here. The baby's father. The man who was going to save her and take her away. Then the two of them would raise their baby together and have a real home.*

*She reached for his hand, desperate for his touch. She couldn't lose him, like she'd lost everyone else. He was the only one who believed her, who didn't think she was crazy.*

*The only one who knew the truth about what they'd done to her at the sanitarium.*

*But her fingers touched empty air. And suddenly he was gone.*

*The bright lights blinded her, and the room blurred, spinning in circles. White coats with nameless faces floated past, the sound of voices echoing as if they came from a faraway place. As if they were in a tunnel.*

*"She'll never know."*

*"Don't tell her."*

*"She's too crazy to have a baby."*

*"No one can ever find out what we did."*

*She struggled to make out who was talking, but another contraction gripped her, then another. They were right on top of each other.*

*She lost her breath and gulped back a sob. Another push, and a baby's cry echoed through the room.*

*Her baby's cry.*

*Machines beeped. Footsteps pounded. Hushed voices spoke.*

*"It's a boy," someone said through the chaotic haze.*

*Tears blinded Amelia, but she blinked them back, then reached out her arms. "Let me hold him . . ."*

*But another pair of hands shoved her down on the bed. They were tying her down again.*

*Amelia struggled, kicking wildly. "Please, give him to me! Let me hold him!"*

*The lights dimmed. Something sharp stung her arm. The baby's cry grew more distant. Hushed voices drifted in the silence.*

*Then there was another voice . . . one she recognized.*

*The man she hated and feared most was here. The Commander.*

*Then her baby was gone.*

*And the room went black.*

Amelia pressed her hands over her ears, forcing the voices and images away as she paced the room. But the painting she'd done the night before disturbed her.

A man's face. The man from her dreams. The one she'd loved. The father of her child.

She paused and studied his features. He was tall, muscular, broad-shouldered. A soldier's body. Square jaw. Beard stubble.

Dark, stormy, mesmerizing eyes.

She'd been dreaming of him for weeks now. Had sketches of him all over her studio. For some reason she couldn't get him out of her mind.

But he wasn't real . . .

Just like the baby in her dream wasn't real. She'd never given birth.

So why was she having these nightmares? Were they delusions?

Maybe it was some kind of twin jealousy because Sadie was pregnant?

That had to be the reason. She'd always had a connection with Sadie.

Was something wrong with Sadie's baby?

Or was another alter trying to emerge in her own mind?

Her phone trilled, and she raced to answer it. When Sadie's name appeared on the caller ID, her hand began to shake.

"Hello."

"Amelia, it's Jake. Sadie and I are at the hospital. The baby's coming now."

Cold fear swept over Amelia. She had to get to the hospital and make sure Sadie's baby was okay.

─────────── , ───────────

There were too many damn missing kids in the United States.

Special Agent John Strong held his gun at the ready as he crept toward the clapboard house deep in the mountains.

Hell, a lot of the missing persons cases involved parental disputes/kidnappings. There were hundreds of runaway teens. Kidnappings for ransom. Abductions by mentally disturbed individuals desperate for a child of their own.

The reasons went on and on.

Many of the lost children were already dead. Some they'd never find or learn what happened to them. Others were locked somewhere, being abused or tormented.

Worse were the child traffickers. Bunch of sick fucks.

And then there were the pedophiles . . .

Even sicker fucks.

His partner, Special Agent Scott Coulter, gave a quick nod from the opposite side of the house from his vantage point inside the front window, indicating that he had visual confirmation that the man they were looking for was inside.

John prayed the kid was, too. Six-year-old Darby Wesley. He'd been missing less than twenty-four hours.

Every hour that passed decreased the chances of finding the boy alive.

But they'd caught a break when the clerk at a gas station had heard a noise coming from the back of a white utility van.

A noise that sounded like a little boy's scream for help.

The clerk had played it cool, but scribbled down the van's tag number and then called 911 as soon as the driver peeled out of the parking lot and headed into the foothills.

A helicopter search had narrowed down the location.

John inched around to the left, checking the side windows, then the back door. "No visual on the child," he said into his mic.

"Suspect is passed out on the couch," Coulter replied.

"I'm going in the back."

"Copy that. I'll take the front."

John jiggled the doorknob. Unlocked. Either they had the wrong man, or the bastard was so cocky, he thought he'd already gotten away with his crime. That he was so far off the grid that no one would find him.

Then he could rest up before he did whatever heinous thing he had planned with the child.

That wasn't going to happen on John's watch.

Unless he already had hurt the boy . . .

They'd lost the suspect for two hours after that 911 call. He could have killed the child and ditched him someplace in the woods or thrown him off a ridge, and no one would know. It might take days for them to recover his body.

And in that time no telling what the animals might do to him.

Nausea gripped his belly into a knot.

Days that would be torture for his mother and father, who were already crazed with worry and guilt.

Hand clenched around his Sig Sauer, he crept into the kitchen, his gaze sweeping the room. A pizza box on the counter. A fast food bag with a kid's toy.

So the man had had a child with him.

He hoped to hell that he was alive.

John eased through the kitchen, glancing sideways into the bedroom to the left. A rusted metal bed with a quilt thrown over it, a pair of men's work boots, a pair of overalls on the floor. He didn't see Darby.

Dammit.

Coulter was waiting on him, so he moved swiftly into the hall and checked the second room. A twin bed, blue comforter on top.

Shit. A bed for a little boy.

But he didn't see him inside.

What had the bastard done with him?

Heart racing, he crept to the edge of the living room and spotted the big guy on the couch, sprawled and snoring as if he hadn't slept in days. He looked scruffy, a patchy beard growing in, a gut that indicated he liked fried food and beer.

A shotgun sat propped by the couch within a finger's touch.

Coulter acknowledged that he saw John in the doorway, raised his fingers in a one-two-three count, then kicked the door open with a bang.

"TBI!" Coulter shouted, his gun already raised and aimed at the man.

The meathead on the couch jolted upright and reached for his gun.

"I wouldn't do that," John said from behind him.

The suspect jerked his head around, stunned, and John pointed the barrel of the gun at his face. "Where's Darby?"

"Get the hell out of my house," the man muttered.

Coulter took a step closer, closing in. "You have one more chance. Tell us where he is, and I won't put a bullet in your brain."

The bastard was just stupid enough to ignore John's warning and lunge for his shotgun.

John and Coulter shot at the same time. Coulter's bullet hit the man between the eyes, while John's pierced his heart.

They both cursed at the same time as the bastard collapsed, blood and brain matter splattering.

Rage ripped through John. If little Darby wasn't in the house, they might never find him now.

Amelia raced into the hospital, frantic to talk to Sadie.

Ayla, Jake's daughter, and their nanny, Gigi, who was like a grandmother to Ayla, were in the waiting room, looking nervous and excited at the same time. Ayla jumped up and ran toward her. "Aunt Amelia, Sadie's having the baby!" Gigi grinned at her from behind Ayla, as if she couldn't wait to welcome the newest member into their family.

A soul-deep ache seized Amelia. She'd give anything to have the kind of love Sadie and Jake shared. To have a family and a future to look forward to.

Jake suddenly stepped into the hallway, his face glowing like a Christmas tree. "It's a boy!"

Gigi and Ayla rushed toward him, and Ayla threw herself into his arms. "Can I see him, Daddy? Please, please, please . . ."

Jake swung Ayla around. "Of course you can. But remember Sadie's tummy might be a little sore, so we can't jump on her."

"I've got a brother, a brother, a brother," Ayla sang.

"Is Sadie okay?" Amelia asked.

Jake grinned. "She's great. Come on, and you can meet my son." He waved for them to follow him, and Amelia's nerves settled slightly. As they entered Sadie's room, she saw her twin propped against several pillows, a tiny infant cradled in her arms.

Amelia's heart skipped a beat at the sight. Déjà vu hit her again, though, and she saw herself holding her own baby. Then a scream reverberated in her ears as someone took her son away.

Ayla and Gigi raced over to dote over the child, and Jake lifted Ayla onto the bed. Sadie wrapped her arm around Ayla and whispered low to her, smiling as Ayla studied her little brother.

"Congratulations, sis," Amelia said, her earlier worries mounting.

"We're going to name him Ben," Sadie said as she stroked the newborn's head.

After their father. They'd lost him, along with their mother, when they were only two.

Was naming him Ben a good omen or a sign of bad to come?

Amelia backed toward the door. "Jake, can I talk to you for a minute?" Jake gave her a curious look, but nodded and told Sadie they'd be back. As soon as they stepped into the hallway and the door was closed, Amelia clutched Jake's arm.

"Jake, I'm scared."

"What's going on?" Jake asked.

"I've been having these bad dreams, nightmares about having a baby, and then someone takes him away. I think the Commander is there, that he's behind it."

Jake heaved a weary breath. "Amelia, maybe you should talk to your therapist—"

"No, you don't understand. I think the dream is about Sadie. We've always had a connection." Her heart hammered. "I'm afraid the Commander is alive, and he'll come after Ben."

# About the Author

———— o ————

Bestselling author Rita Herron has written over sixty romance novels and loves penning dark romantic suspense tales, especially those set in small Southern towns. She earned a *RT Book Reviews* Career Achievement Award for her work in Series Romantic Suspense, and has received rave reviews for the Slaughter Creek novels *Her Dying Breath* and *Dying to Tell*. A native of Milledgeville, Georgia, and a proud mother and grandmother, she lives just outside of Atlanta.